Changeling Press, LLC
ChangelingPress.com

Xavier/Pain Duet
A Bones MC Romance
Marteeka Karland

Xavier/Pain Duet
A Bones MC Romance
Marteeka Karland

ISBN: 978-1-60521-962-2

Publisher:
Changeling Press LLC
315 N. Centre St.
Martinsburg, WV 25404
ChangelingPress.com

Printed in the U.S.A.

Editor: Jean Cooper
Cover Artist: Marteeka Karland

The individual stories in this anthology have been previously released in E-Book format.

Table of Contents

Xavier (Kiss of Death MC 5)
A Bones MC Romance
Marteeka Karland

Xavier may be an ex-con, but he's strong, protective, and totally sexy. He's my hero.

Tillie -- At the lowest time in my life, I realize I might have gained my very own guardian angel. I never saw Xavier as more than a friend, but then he went to prison for me. I'll never forget his sacrifice. He's the man I've built up in my little fantasy world as being the perfect husband. Only problem is, I forgot he's still a killer. How can I be with a man who's capable of taking a life? I'm torn between my growing feelings for him and my fear of what it means to love a man like Xavier.

Xavier -- Did I have to kill the man who beat Tillie? No. But I was headed to prison anyway, so why not? Tillie defended me to anyone who would listen, but I never expected she'd come to see me every Saturday. I also didn't expect to fall in love with the beautiful, spirited woman. Seeing her smile now is worth the extra time. Unfortunately, my little Tillie's a magnet for trouble. Good thing she has me to protect her, because there's nothing I won't do for Tillie. *Nothing*. If I have to kill for her again, so be it. Anyone who touches her is dead. May God have mercy, because I won't.

Chapter One

Xavier

"Hey, Sugar." The one bright spot in my life was Tillie St. Martin. Ironic, because the night I found her was in the middle of the worst damned storm I'd ever tried to drive through. That was also the night that changed both our lives forever.

I think I had a weird sort of connection with her from the second she looked at me over her shoulder, soaked to the skin in ripped and blood-stained clothing, with an angry-looking bruise forming on her left cheek. She was walking down a two-lane country road at one in the morning. Nothing good happens at one in the morning if you're forced to walk on a deserted road in the middle of a storm.

"I did it, Xave!" She grinned brightly at me through the bulletproof glass. She had the wall phone to her ear and looked so happy my heart was breaking.

Then I frowned. "Wait a minute. You're not moving to San Diego with that creep you were telling me about last month, are you?"

"What?" She jerked back, a scowl on her face. "You honestly think I'm that stupid?"

I had a moment of panic. Clearly, I'd fucked up. I just wasn't sure how. "Of course, you're not stupid!" I rubbed my hand over the back of my neck. "But I'm not sure what I said to make you think I'd think you were stupid?" She raised her eyebrows. "OK, clearly, we need to start over."

She broke out into giggles. "You're so cute when you think I'm irritated at you."

"I kinda thought I'd said something to thoroughly piss you off."

"*Pfft.*" She waved away my words. "I could

never be pissed at you. You're my hero after all."

"Aww, Tillie. You have no idea... Seeing you smile, how much happier you look now... You kind of gave me a whole new outlook on life."

"Oh?" She was still smiling but she looked genuinely curious. Not like she was humoring me. "What's that?"

"Sometimes, the outcome is worth the fuckin' consequence." I grumbled out the words, but it was the fucking truth. Yes, I was in prison. Would I rather be on the outside with my brothers? Sure. But I could pull my weight with the club in prison same as I could out. Given that I had some good connections here in Terre Haute, I figured I'd make the best of a bad situation. Like I said, some things were just worth the cost.

Tillie's face softened and she put her palm against the window. I put mine over hers against the glass. I'd never actually touched her skin, but I could imagine how her hand would entwine with mine. She was twenty-three years old. Way too fucking young for me when compared to my thirty-eight years, but her life experiences made her seem older sometimes.

"You ended my nightmare, Xavier. I will never take that for granted. I'd be dead if it weren't for you."

"Only thing I ever want from you is for you to be happy. You never have to come back here, Tillie. I know this is a scary place sometimes. But if you do come by occasionally, I hope you always have a smile this bright on your face." That got me another beautiful smile, but also a trembling chin and two tears from her pale green eyes. "So. If you're not moving to San Diego with Dipshit, what's got you all smiles, Sugar?"

She gave a watery laugh as she swiped at her tears. "I did it."

"Well, yeah, you said that." I grinned, trying not

to chuckle but failing miserably. "Gonna have to give me an antecedent to go with your pronoun, baby."

That really got an amused laugh from her. "Really? Antecedent?"

"Hey. You're the author between the two of us. You should know those kinds of words, what they mean, and how to avoid making me say them."

"Fine. It refers to buying a house." She bounced in her seat excitedly.

I grinned. "You'll have to show me pictures when you get moved in."

"Oh, I will." Her grin got even wider. "Want to know the best part?"

"What's that, sweetheart?"

"I'm moving to Terre Haute."

OK, this was unexpected. She lived an hour and a half away but had never mentioned she was moving, let alone anywhere close by. "Honey, why would you move to Terre Haute?"

"Two reasons." She straightened, her smile still really wide. "First, Terre Haute has way more affordable housing. I found a house for half the price in Terre Haute than I could find in Indianapolis."

"I could see that." I tried to keep a lighthearted expression on my face, but I could tell something was up. "But why get a place of your own at all? I thought you were happy to stay with your folks."

"Well, that's the second reason." She still smiled and still seemed happy, but also… sad? Scared?

"Tillie…" I gave her a stern look, knowing something was off. Every instinct in my body was now screaming at me. Not because I thought she was in danger. Because, I knew with every fiber of my being, someone had hurt her feelings. And that simply was not acceptable. "What. Happened?"

She gave me a nervous laugh and I noticed her chin trembling again. "So, Mom found out I'm an author." She smiled again, but I could see tears gathering in her eyes to spill over again. "She wasn't really impressed with the kind of books I write." She nodded her head, not meeting my gaze as she tucked a lock of strawberry blonde hair behind her ear. "She didn't understand how I could write about such... uh... graphic things after what happened to me."

I had to take a deep breath. It was paramount to keep calm when expressing negative emotion around Tillie. Anytime in her life someone had been upset with her or raised their voice, she knew she was going to get hurt. Given the way we met, I'm surprised she wasn't terrified of me. Maybe because I was behind bulletproof glass now and she knew I couldn't get to her. I hadn't hurt her, but the situation had still been a violent encounter. If there was anything about that night I regret, it was that Tillie saw how violent I could be. Or, at least, she saw the aftermath.

"You told me several months ago you were thinking about movin' out. Only reason you didn't go then was to take care of your parents since your dad broke his hip. I thought they wanted you to stay with them."

"Yeah." She shrugged, smiling even as she wiped tears from her cheeks with her fingers again. "They indicated they didn't need my help anymore. I might have told them to go take a flying leap. But I plead the fifth."

"Good for you, baby." I smiled with her, surprised at how proud I was of her for taking up for herself. It was something she had trouble doing. Tillie was a pleaser. "So you found a place you could afford?"

She took a breath and continued to compose herself. I could practically see the emotional release as she told me about the little house she'd found on the outskirts. The longer she talked, the more she relaxed, and I could see that, despite being hurt by her parents' rejection of her, she was genuinely happy about this change in her life.

Personally, I wanted to howl with relief. She'd stayed with her parents after her husband had been killed, but they had never been fully on her side. At least that was the way it seemed to me at the sentencing. Their body language was very standoffish and both of them looked at her like they'd just stuck lemons in their mouths. It had seemed to me then they were more upset with her for speaking up than they were because she'd lost her husband.

"Oh!" She shifted around in her seat happily. Thank God she'd shaken off her sadness. I wasn't sure how I'd have managed if she cried anything other than happy tears. "I have a cell phone now. Do you want to write the number down? I mean," she ducked her head, looking both shy and embarrassed, "I know you can't just pick up the phone and call me all willy nilly." She gave a nervous chuckle. "But, you know, in case you can call. Or need me to bring you something."

I smiled. "I'll remember if you want to tell me. I can write it down when I get back to my cell." She rattled off the number, which I committed to memory. Phone numbers were a quirk of mine. I remembered them easily. I had no idea why, but I was fucking grateful for the ability.

"You have five minutes remaining." The automated voice interrupted us, meaning we needed to wrap things up.

"I guess that's all for this time." She gave me that

soft look she always gave me when the time came for her to leave. "I'm so sorry you got involved in my mess, Xave. You don't deserve to be here, and I feel like it's my fault."

"Look, honey." I put my hand back up on the window between us. "I want you to listen to me and really hear what I'm telling you." She put her hand against the glass over mine once more and nodded. She looked so lost and riddled with guilt I wanted to see her husband dead all over again. "I *chose* to stop that night when I saw you on the road. I *chose* to offer you a ride. I *chose* to ask you to take me to the bastard who'd beaten and terrorized you. Then I *chose* to kill the son of a bitch. *Me*. You didn't ask me. You didn't force me. And I didn't ask you if you wanted me to kill him. I'd never seen you before in my life that night I picked you up. But I never pick up hitchhikers. I'm also never in a car or a pickup because I'm always on my bike. Even in the rain. So me driving that old Ford Ranger the night I found you and actually stopping to pick you up? The whole thing should never have happened. That means things happened the way they were supposed to. Seeing you here when you come to see me with that big smile on your face, seeing you truly happy, is worth any amount of time I have to do in here, honey." I grinned. "Besides, the food's hot and mostly decent. I pulled a few strings to get my own cell. This ain't the Hilton, but it's a hell of a lot better than where I sent that bastard." I shrugged, trying to lighten the mood. "No pun intended."

She teared up again but giggled. "I don't know when you'll be out, but when you are I'll help you any way I can, Xavier. A place to stay, money, a job... I'll share everything I have with you."

"Don't worry about me, darlin'. I'm not alone.

Even in here, my brothers are looking out for me."

Her eyes widened. "They are?"

I grinned. "Yeah. Do you have a pen and paper?"

"Yeah." She shifted in her seat and pulled out a small notebook from her back pocket. "One of the perks of being a writer. I've always got something to write with and on." She held up a... crayon? At my confused look she grinned. "I'm not allowed to bring sharp objects in here. I have to wait sometimes, so I brought something to write with. Just in case."

I just chuckled. She was too sweet for words. "I'm going to give you a phone number. Keep it with you. If you ever need anything, call that number. Tell whoever answers you're a friend of Xavier's." I gave her the number. She jotted it down, then repeated the number back to me. "Good. When I say anything, Tillie, I mean if you're short on gas money or need groceries, if you don't feel safe for any reason, anything at all you need, you call that number. They will come to you, no questions asked."

"Why?" She glanced at the clock frantically, using every minute she could. "Why would you do all this, sacrifice a big part of your life? Give me a number if I need help? For me?"

I didn't flinch. "Why *not* you? Could have been anyone on that street, but it was you. It was me. You needed something I could help with, so I provided."

"Xavier, I swear, no matter what happens to either of us in the future, I will never forget what you did for me. I'll pay it forward as best I can and I'll make your sacrifice count. And I will never, *ever* not come to see you. I owe you my life! The least I can do is come visit."

It should have sounded like a cheesy movie, but the sincerity in her voice and her tears were heart-melting. "You just keep writin' your stories. Live your dream."

"Your time is up. Please exit to your right." The automated voice cut us off, but Tillie sat there, her hand still against mine with the glass between us. She hung up the phone and kept her gaze on me for long moments.

She turned her head and nodded at someone, then looked back at me. "Thank you." I couldn't hear her, but I read her lips easily enough. I nodded at her and hung up my phone.

Tillie never left the cubby before I left the room. I imagined she wanted every possible second with me. I touched the glass under her palm once more then turned and left.

It was Saturday afternoon. Tillie always came on Saturdays. Every week since I'd gone to prison, without fail. I always told her not to come. Since the first time she showed up, I tried to get her to stay away for her own good. But she kept showing up. And I soaked up each visit like a sponge to water.

As I approached the guard, I looked back over my shoulder one last time at Tillie. I had to top off my fix of looking at her. It could be the last time I ever saw her. One day, she would take my advice to heart. I just wasn't sure what I was going to do when she did.

Chapter Two

Tillie

I wished with all my heart I could have met Xavier in another life. Or, at least before I'd met Paul St. Martin. Paul had been charismatic, handsome, and way out of my league. But we'd met at church and my parents had loved him. Mostly because he had money and owned a local meat processing plant. My father thought Paul was his path to easy street. My mother thought her standing with the church women would rise.

I let them push me toward him, never seeing the monster hiding under his charming exterior. The worst part was that no one believed me when I told them he'd hurt me. At least, I'd thought it was the worst part. I found out how wrong I was when word got back to him of my accusations.

I shook the memory. The very last person I wanted to think about today was Paul. Saturdays were my happy days. I got to spend an hour talking with Xavier. There was always the glass between us, but it still felt personal. He'd sacrificed everything to free me from hell. Me. A stranger he'd come across on the road during a raging storm. The least I could do was come visit him once a week.

As I got in my car, I pulled my notebook and crayon out of my back pocket and set them down. Then I started the engine and adjusted the air conditioning before taking my phone out and putting the number Xavier had given me into my contacts. I doubted I'd ever use it, but the contact was one more tie I had with Xavier and, right or wrong, I wanted every tie to the man I could get. He was everything Paul was not, and everything I never knew I wanted.

My new home was only twenty minutes away from the prison property. I hadn't done it on purpose, but when I found this small but wonderful farmhouse with thirteen acres of land at such a reasonable price, it had seemed like fate. This was where I was supposed to be. And really, I could write anywhere in the world I wanted to. Sure, electricity and the Internet would be a huge help but weren't strictly necessary. The fact my place was off by itself where no one would bother me guaranteed I'd spend many days and evenings on the front porch with my laptop.

* * *

It had been two weeks since I'd told Xavier about my house. I'd printed out pictures to show him last week. I'd hoped to print out a few more before I went to see him tomorrow.

I'd taken actual possession of the property yesterday morning. I hadn't brought much with me because I didn't have much. My clothes, laptop, office chair, a makeshift desk, and my car. That was all. My mother and father had sold off anything I got from Paul's estate as payment for me living with them after Paul's death so while I had a bit of cash and a decent vehicle, I had very little else. Thank God for that money, too, because I'd been living in a hotel for two months before I found and bought this place. The cash payment I'd offered was the only way I'd managed the purchase. The owner came down on what I thought was an already pretty good price and let me have the keys a week later once the paperwork had all been filed.

I sighed happily as I pulled onto the long drive to the house and into the attached garage. This was my new home. I was proud I'd been able to buy the place by myself. If the money I'd used to make the purchase had come from my dead husband, I'd still count it as buying the house with my blood and so much pain. Besides, I might not make much money as an author, but I made enough for payments on this house even if I'd taken out a mortgage. I counted that as proof I was a success. Small-time, maybe, but a success nonetheless.

Saturdays were devoted to Xavier, but Sunday through Thursday brought me back to the real world. Figuratively speaking. Because my world was pure fantasy. Literally. I could make up any world I wanted and that was my reality for the next six days. The only time I had to poke my head out into the *real* real world was to go to the grocery on Friday mornings. Technically I also went out on Saturdays to see Xavier, but then I didn't think about anything other than my time with him. It was important to me to make every minute count. For both of us.

* * *

It was now Friday afternoon, over a month since Xavier had given me a way to contact him. I hadn't needed to use the phone number, obviously, but I liked having that connection in my hand. I often stared at the number I'd labeled "Xavier's Friends." It made me feel less alone.

I always allowed myself Friday afternoon to do whatever I wanted. I'd read or binge-watch a TV show or bake something. I'd just come from doing my weekly shopping and was going to make my favorite recipe of egg noodles, cheese, ground beef, and tomatoes. It was my comfort food.

Tomorrow was my hour with Xavier. It wasn't as long a day as before I moved to Terre Haute, but I liked to have a dinner I could heat up quickly at home. Not often, but occasionally, they extended visiting for an additional hour or two. Sometimes, that additional time wasn't in the same block. So I might have to wait a couple hours between them. Having leftovers made one less thing for me to have to do when I got home. Without fail, I was always emotionally exhausted. Because, the fact was, I couldn't imagine my life without our visits.

Before I entered the house with my groceries, a chill went up my spine. I froze, key in the lock, looking around the area. The garage door was off the kitchen with a covered walkway between the two. I stood in the walkway and set my bags on the concrete.

"Who's there?" I called out, not sure what I expected to happen but really hoping I was being paranoid. Sometimes, going to the prison was more than a little scary, so it was certainly possible I was imagining things. "Hello?"

Just as I was about to relax, a large figure stepped part way out of the shadows, enough for me to see the imposing figure in dark jeans, a dark, long-sleeved shirt, and black leather gloves. I couldn't see his face or any identifying marks, but surely there couldn't be many men as large as this guy.

"You're not to go past the fuckin' fence in the backyard. If you do, you won't fuckin' live to get back inside the fuckin' fence." When I said nothing, he shifted his weight and I shied away instinctively. "Understand, girl?" I nodded, but he clenched his fists in anger. "Bitch, say you understand," he snarled.

"I-I under-understand."

"Don't leave this fuckin' house until Monday. Go inside and don't leave. Don't get your fuckin' mail. Don't answer your door if anyone comes the fuck over. Understand?"

I nodded again before finding my voice. "Yes. I

understand."

Then he stepped into the shadows and disappeared.

For several long seconds I stood frozen in place, unable to make myself move. My heart pounded so hard I could feel my throat throb as well. Was I hallucinating? Had I imagined the entire encounter?

But the faint scent of sweat and stale cigarette smoke lingering on the soft breeze confirmed I hadn't dreamed the encounter. Someone had been waiting for me outside my house. Warning me not to go past the fence. I wasn't sure what to do. I didn't want to stay here, but it sounded like it might be safer to do what he said. One thing was for *damn* sure, I wasn't going past the fucking fence. I had no one to help me, and after my experience with the police when I was with Paul, I couldn't make myself call 9-1-1 for help. At least I'd had cuts and bruises to prove Paul had been hitting me. How was I going to prove someone had been outside my house threatening me?

When I finally spurred myself into action, I unlocked the door with trembling hands and nearly tripped over my grocery sack I'd set next to the door. Thank God, it was only one large sack. I was able to loop it over my arm while I stumbled inside and shut the door, pushed the deadbolt closed, and turned the lock on the knob.

I dropped the sack before rushing through my house and turning on every light in the place. I checked in every closet and cabinet, every hidden nook and cranny I knew about.

I hurried to check the front and back doors. Both remained deadbolted and the knob locks were engaged. There were no broken windows or anything indicating someone had been in my house, but I was still officially freaked the fuck out. I wasn't sure how safe I felt here but, unless I called the cops, I was stuck for now.

Pulling out my phone, I pulled up the app controlling my lights. If the guy had someone watching the house, the last thing I wanted was for them to know which room I was in. So I shut them all out at once and crouched in the corner by the stove, a cast-iron skillet in my white-knuckled grip.

The kitchen floor was cold against my bare legs as I huddled there, trembling. Part of me wanted to crawl into a closet, but I couldn't make myself move from my spot. Every creak of the house settling sent fresh waves of panic through me.

I'd survived Paul. I'd started building a new life. And now this?

My phone glowed in the darkness as I stared at it. The screen dimmed, then went black. I tapped the screen awake again and pulled up my contact list. My mother. My father. Right. No help there.

Xavier.

No. No way. Not again. The man had literally sacrificed his freedom to help me once. I couldn't ask him -- or his friends -- to do anything more for me. Especially since this could really get someone hurt. I'd hurt Xavier enough. I didn't need to destroy his family as well as his life.

My stomach clenched painfully. I needed a different option, but who could I call? My only friend in town was a barista I'd talked to three times. Even if I had a friend nearby, I didn't know *anyone* who would know what to do in a situation like this.

The number Xavier had given me burned in my memory. He'd been insistent. "Anything at all you need." Could I really call? Wouldn't that mean I was using him yet again?

Outside, a branch scraped against the window. I nearly dropped the skillet as I jerked toward the sound. My heart hammered wildly in my chest, and I could feel sweat erupt over my skin as I fought to catch my breath.

I couldn't take it anymore. Maybe I was the most horrible person imaginable to take advantage of someone's kindness, or to take a chance on getting Xavier's friends hurt, but I knew I was going to make the call. With shaking fingers, I pulled up "Xavier's Friends" in my contacts and hit "Call." The phone rang three times before a deep, gruff voice answered.

"Yeah?"

My voice caught in my throat. What was I supposed to say?

"Hello? Who's this?" The man's tone sharpened.

"I -- I'm Tillie," I managed. "A friend of Xavier's."

There was a beat of silence, then the man's entire demeanor changed. "Shit. You all right?"

"I-I don't kn-know." The relief coursing through me made me lightheaded. I could also feel myself start to lose any control I had.

"Where are you? What's the address?"

I gave it to him. "Be careful. I came home to find a stranger waiting for me. He told me not to leave the house, and he didn't seem like the type of person to ask questions before he started shooting."

"Understood. Are you armed?"

"O-only with a cast-iron skillet."

The guy on the other end coughed a couple of times. "Good, honey." He cleared his throat again. "That's good. Is your phone charged?"

"Yes."

"OK. I've got some guys in Terre Haute I'm sending your way. Don't hit one of 'em with that fuckin' skillet." He sounded amused, though I wasn't sure why.

"I'll try not to."

"Just keep the phone with you and stay where you are, honey. They'll be there in less than fifteen minutes."

"Thank you." My voice cracked on the words. "I'm sorry to --"

"Don't apologize, Tillie. Xavier would have our heads if we didn't help you, and rightly so. You're family now. We protect our own."

I sobbed out a muffled relieved cry, putting my hand over my mouth. I didn't want to make any noise if I could help it. I kept my voice as soft as I could.

The line was silent for a moment before he spoke again, his voice gentler. "Stay on the line with me until they get there, all right?"

"OK." I clutched the phone like a lifeline, still gripping the skillet with my other hand.

"Name's Knight, by the way."

"I'm Tillie."

"Yeah, honey. I got that. I'll get word to Xavier we're going after you. He's gonna want you to come back with my guy. Will you do that?"

"G-go with a s-strange man?" My voice got higher as fear bit me hard.

"Hey, hey. It's all right. Would it help if Xavier told you himself what he wanted you to do?"

"Xavier? But... but he's..."

"I know, honey. I can get a phone to him. Tiny was on the way to Xavier, anyway. They can both come to you."

"What?" I thought my heart would stop. "What

does that mean?"

"Honey, he wanted to surprise you when you visited him tomorrow. The truth is, we knew there was trouble headed your way, so a guy we know moved up Xavier's release. Him and Tiny are headed your way now. Fifteen minutes tops."

I couldn't help it. I let out a sob of relief. "Xavier."

"Yeah. I've got him on the line now. He wants to talk to you."

"Yes! Xavier!" I was officially losing it. I was going to dissolve into hysterics, and there wasn't a Goddamned thing I could do about it.

"Tillie? Baby, it's me." Xavier's deep voice washed over me, steadying me like nothing else could.

"Xavier, oh God, I'm so scared! There was a man. He threatened me. Told me not to leave the house until Monday." The words tumbled out between hiccuping sobs.

"Listen to me, baby." His voice had that deadly calm I remembered from the night we met. "I need you to stay exactly where you are. Don't move, don't make noise. As long as you don't move or try to leave the house, you'll be OK. Tiny and I are almost there."

"You're really coming?" I whispered.

"Yeah, baby. I'm really comin'. I'll be there before you know it." Xavier's voice held a fierce promise that warmed me despite my terror. "Stay put and keep that skillet handy, just in case."

I nodded before realizing he couldn't see me, then I whispered, "OK."

Minutes stretched like hours until I heard the faint crunch of tires on gravel. My breath caught. The instinct to run out the door to Xavier was so strong, I nearly managed to get to my feet before falling back on my ass.

"Xavier? Is that you?"

"Yeah. It's me. Stay where you are. I'm coming to you."

I pulled my knees to my chest. I still clutched the skillet. From a seated position, there wasn't much I could do, but it seemed better than nothing.

The front door opened. I heard the click of the locks as they slid out of place, then the soft *thud* as the door was shut again. There was a soft murmur of male voices, then I heard footsteps going through the house.

"Clear."

"Clear here too, Xavier. Let's get your girl and get the fuck outta here."

"Tillie? Come on out, honey."

I stood, the skillet falling to the floor. Later, I was sure I'd be embarrassed at how I acted, but I threw myself at Xavier, wrapping my arms and legs around him, and sobbed into his neck.

Chapter Three

Xavier

I'd never been so glad to have Tiny as my backup as I was now. Standing in the little farmhouse with Tillie wrapped around me, clinging to me like I was her whole world, felt like nothing I'd ever imagined existed. I could savor the moment, and Tiny would watch over us. I glanced at the big guy and he nodded before going outside to give us a moment.

For a hot minute, my mind drifted to possibilities I knew better than to dwell on. Sure, I was out of prison now. Had no plans on that changing. But this girl... This fucking girl... She deserved everything in life I could never give her. Like this fucking house.

What were the odds Tillie had been the one to buy this property? No one had made it past talking to the real estate agent in years. Sure, the owner desperately wanted rid of it, but there was an old maintenance road along the southern edge of the property he didn't own the right of way for.

That road was like the fucking *Autobahn* for smugglers from Mobile to Indianapolis as a way to be off the radar. The interstate was the preferred route, but the more experienced mules used that small road to bypass the interstate in and around Nashville.

Because the road was no longer necessary after the coal mines were closed, the road wasn't on modern maps. A cartel presence in the area maintained the road, but as long as no one got in their way they didn't hinder anyone else.

Eventually word got around and the locals stopped trying to buy the property. Those who either didn't know or were too stubborn to believe the stories soon got the same warning Tillie just got.

* * *

"Thank fuck we got here when we did." Tiny spoke softly as he took a hard left, weaving in and out of traffic. "Sorry as shit we didn't get there sooner, man."

"We got here before she was hurt. That's the main thing. It's my fault someone wasn't already here waiting to get her to safety. I should have realized when she told me the house she'd bought was in Terre Haute."

"Did I do something wrong, Xavier?" Tillie and I were in the back seat of the big F-150 Tiny brought for the trip here. Tillie was still plastered against me, chest to chest, with her arms wrapped tightly around my neck, straddling me. Her voice was barely above a whisper. She sounded so Goddamned fragile it was breaking my heart.

"No, honey. There's no way you could have known about that property. I'll explain all that later. For now. I want you to stay right where you are until you feel like moving."

"Shouldn't I sit in the seat and buckle up?"

"Only when you're ready. Tiny's our road captain for a reason. He'll keep us safe."

"Once we get on the interstate I'll ease up," Tiny said. "They won't follow us even if they were watching, but I'm not taking chances."

"You leave a calling card?" I met Tiny's gaze in the rearview mirror.

"Yep. They ain't comin' after us." Tiny adjusted his grip on the steering wheel. "Even they know better."

I expected Tillie to question us or at least ask where we were going, but she seemed content to stay silent and where she was. The slight tremor of her body told me she was probably in shock and still terrified. I reached for the blanket I'd put in the seat beside us. It was one she'd brought me, and I got the impression she'd liked it herself. I draped the throw over her, so she was covered from the neck down. The large blanket even draped over her feet and legs.

I held her securely, rubbing my hand up and down her back, needing to soothe her as much as I could.

"It's all right now, baby. You're safe with me," I murmured into her hair, inhaling her scent. Vanilla, and something uniquely Tillie. It was intoxicating.

She nuzzled closer, her breath warm against my neck. "I was so scared, Xave. I thought… I thought he might…"

"Shh. I know. But he didn't. And no one's gonna hurt you now." My arms tightened around her instinctively. The thought of someone threatening her made my blood boil, but I kept my voice steady. I felt like this was at least partly my fault. I should have had Knight keep closer tabs on her. If I had, I'd have known she was headed toward trouble and kept her away.

"Knuckles is sendin' an escort in our direction." Tiny spoke softly, respectful of Tillie's fragile state. "Said Venus and Piston will be joining us shortly, and will have our six until Chains and Oktober meet us and bring us home."

I snorted. "They escorting us to safety or just out of their territory?"

Tiny shrugged. "Does it matter? Even if they're makin' sure we're just passin' through, they'd be good to have at our back in a fight."

"Fair point."

"Wh-where are we going?" Tillie still shook, but

the soft rhythm of mine and Tiny's conversation seemed to have settled her somewhat.

"Nashville, honey." I tried to soothe her as best I could when this kind of care wasn't in my nature. She seemed to need the gentle caresses, and I didn't blame her.

When she didn't say anything more, I thought maybe she'd settled enough to drift off. Sleeping off adrenaline drop was the easiest way to feel human again.

I was wrong, though. After a couple of minutes, she spoke again. "That was my home. I don't have anywhere to go." She sounded so forlorn it tore at my heart. If we were right and the Menendez family had sent a goon to scare her, I was going to make someone bleed.

"Yeah, you do, honey. You're stayin' with me. You trust me. Right?"

She lifted her head to look straight into my eyes. The pain, fear, and absolute devastation was so stark in her expression I wanted to kill someone. "I think you're the only person in my life I *do* trust, Xave."

Christ, this girl! "Good. Then stay right where you are. Let me hold you as long as you need to feel more like yourself. We've got a four-hour drive. Take all the time you need. When Tiny thinks it's safe enough to stop, we'll find a fast-food place and grab a bite and take a piss." As I hoped, that got a small giggle from her. "There's my girl." I gave her a light, reassuring squeeze before resuming my steady rubbing up and down her back. "Talk it out if you need to, honey. Or sleep. Or whatever you need. I'm here. Ain't lettin' anyone hurt you."

She was silent for a long time. I actually thought she'd gone to sleep. "I just wanted a place that felt like a home should." She spoke so softly I barely heard her. "I've never had a place I felt like I belonged. Mom and Dad basically used me as a transaction, and Paul..."

"I get it," I said, not able to stand her bringing up that fucking monster. Any man who could hurt a woman as sweet, giving, and caring as Tillie deserved to die fucking hard. I'd shot the bastard, but if I had it to do over, I'd draw out the process and no one would ever have found the body. But there was more to that story than I ever wanted Tillie to know. "You figured if you weren't born with a proper home, hadn't been able to find a proper home after you got hitched, you'd make your own fuckin' proper home." I growled out my interpretation with a bit more anger in my voice than I wanted, but Tillie either didn't notice or didn't take my tone to mean I was upset with her.

"Yes!" She sat back a little so she could study me closer. Her eyes were wide and a pale silvery-green that'd mesmerized me from the day I'd met her. "That's it exactly! I was going to make my own home. A place I always felt safe and like I was in charge of my life because I could do anything I wanted. Go to bed when I wanted. Eat junk food all day in front of the television if I wanted. If I didn't want to get dressed, I could wear my pajamas all day and no one could say one Goddamned thing!" By the end, tears were streaming down her cheeks and those gorgeous eyes of hers were swimming in a luminous pool of tears. The headlights from a passing car made her eyes shimmer almost like glitter.

I couldn't stop myself from brushing one tear away with my thumb as it rolled down her cheek. "You'll have all of that and more, baby. I swear on my Goddamned life." Why the absolute fuck had I said that out loud?

Didn't make the statement any less true, but I'd have preferred we were alone when I told her I was claiming her. Now, with Tiny here, giving me a look in the rearview mirror, I knew I'd fucked up. Not necessarily in a bad way, but in a way that would get me picked on mercilessly if Tillie didn't want me to claim her.

Her eyes widened in shock. "What?"

"Don't worry about all that right now." I tried to steer the conversation to something else, needing some time to really think about this because, honestly, I'd never considered I'd be in a position to actually make Tillie mine. If not for the threat to her, I'd still be in prison. The second I realized there might be a problem, Knuckles started working on getting me out. The man had some serious pull in and out of the system. Someone who had enough power to get me an unscheduled release in hours rather than days, weeks or even months.

"Why wait?" Tiny gave me a shit-eating grin in the rearview mirror. Bastard. "Got hours before we get home."

Tillie narrowed her eyes, giving a wary look. "I just told you you're the one person in my life I completely trust. Did I misjudge you?"

"No, honey. You didn't misjudge me." I tugged her back to lie against my chest. She resisted at first, but then melted against me, burrowing her face in my neck once more. I wanted to leave it at that. Let her rest. Fuck that bastard, Tiny, anyway. But my mouth had other plans. "You're the woman who's haunted my dreams since that fuckin' day I met you. I'm a son of a bitch on the best of days, but I'm your son of a bitch. Leave it at that. For now."

She trembled in my arms, but she didn't pull

back. Instead, her fists bunched in my shirt. She heaved in a shuddering breath before letting it out. "You swear?"

Christ.

"Yeah, baby. I fuckin' promise. On my fuckin' life."

Chapter Four

Tillie

I should be scared.

No. Scratch that.

I should be fucking *terrified* right now.

Maybe?

To my parents' way of thinking, this man -- who'd killed my husband -- and his club -- my parents would associate any sentence with "club" at the end with "gang" -- were all terrible people. The problem with believing my parents were right and that I shouldn't trust Xavier was the fact they'd shoved me into an unwanted marriage for their own financial benefit. They would not believe me when I told them Paul had been the one to break my arm and bust my lip. Xavier not only believed me, he'd taken care of the problem. No questions asked. Irony was the pink elephant in the room. So to speak.

Instead of being terrified, I felt safer than I had in years, wrapped in Xavier's arms and surrounded by his scent. He was older than me by a good fifteen years and had this air of calm about him I'd never felt from anyone else in my life. A man my parents would call a criminal, a man who'd spent time in prison for killing my abuser, felt like my safest harbor. What did that say about the people in my life?

"What does that mean?" I asked, my voice barely above a whisper. "You being my son of a bitch?" I felt his chest expand with a deep breath. His hand never stopped its soothing motion on my back.

"It means I protect what's mine. You're mine, same as I'm yours. It means no one touches you. No one threatens you. You're gonna be safe and fuckin' disgustingly happy." He sounded disgruntled, but also so sincere I felt my lips tugging into a smile. I had talked to the man every week for more than a year. I knew when he was uncomfortable with his feelings.

"You don't sound too happy about this, Xave."

"Ain't." He glanced down, meeting my gaze briefly. "Don't change nothin'. You're still mine."

His words were both soothing yet painful. They felt like an electric blanket on high when the house was cool in winter. Not strictly necessary, but *so good*! They were more freeing than I wanted to admit. I should have been offended at being claimed like property, but there was something in his tone that made me feel like this was about protection rather than possession. Besides, he'd told me about his club. At least the finer points of belonging to a brotherhood of found family. I knew what being claimed was and I knew what an old lady was. What hurt was the fact Xavier didn't seem to want me like I wanted him. Not for the long term, anyway.

"Why aren't you happy?" I asked, keeping my voice low even though I knew Tiny could certainly hear us.

Xavier sighed, his chest rising and falling beneath me. "Because you deserve better than a fuckin' ex-con with more enemies than friends. But that don't change what is." His hand continued its steady path up and down my spine. It was soothing. Lulling. "I swear to you, I'll make you happy, Tillie. Give me a chance. Yeah?"

"Yes," I whispered, not hesitating. Maybe I should have. Maybe I should have asked for time to think about it. But honestly, what was there to think about? I'd spent a year visiting this man every week, pouring out my heart to him, learning about his life, sharing mine. I'd never felt as wanted, understood, or safe as I did with Xavier.

"You sure, baby? This ain't somethin' I'll let you take back later."

I shifted in his lap so I could see his face better. His dark eyes were intense, searching mine for any sign of doubt. I found none within myself. "I'm sure," I said, my voice stronger now. "You saved me, Xavier. I have no idea how much of an inconvenience it was for you either time -- other than the prison sentence obviously -- but you came for me when I needed you most. Not once, but twice. I've never been more sure of anything in my life."

The corner of his mouth ticked up. "Good." He pressed a gentle kiss to my forehead before pulling me back against him, and I felt the comforting warmth of his body spread through my body. Safety. Security. Xavier was a man who absolutely would keep me safe. I didn't want to lose his friendship for anything in this world. I needed him in my life desperately! While I wasn't entirely sure about a sexual encounter, I knew Xavier would let me have the time I needed. Why? Because he knew exactly what I'd gone through with Paul.

From the front seat, Tiny cleared his throat. "Hate to break up this touching moment, but we've got company."

Xavier's body tensed beneath me, his arms tightening protectively. "How many?"

"Two bikes, about a quarter mile back. Been following us since we hit the highway."

"Venus and Piston?"

There was a pause before Tiny answered. "Unless there's another pink monstrosity claiming to be a Harley, yeah. It's Venus and Piston."

I felt Xavier's deep chuckle where my front was

plastered against his chest. "I'm tellin' her you said that."

"I'll deny it." Tiny didn't sound angry or annoyed, in fact, they both sounded amused.

I heard the loud rumble and moved my head to look out the window. Sure enough, a bright pink motorcycle eased beside us. The rider was the most remarkable woman I'd ever seen. She was slight of build but with finely muscled arms left bare by the vest she was wearing. It matched the color of her bike. As did her leather pants, and her motorcycle boots. And her hair. The woman gave us a two-finger salute before easing back to join another bike behind us.

I couldn't help but stare as the pink-haired warrior woman fell back behind us. Her companion was almost her opposite. He was big, with wide shoulders and heavily muscled arms. He wore a short-sleeved black shirt under his vest while his bike was black and chrome that gleamed even in the dim highway lights.

"That's Venus," Xavier explained, his breath warm against my ear. "Don't let the pink fool you. She's the deadliest fighter in her club. I've heard she was once an assassin, but I can't confirm the rumor."

"And she likes pink," I murmured, still watching the rearview mirror where I could occasionally catch glimpses of them. It seemed like an inane thing to say, but that's what came out when I opened my mouth.

Xavier laughed, a deep rumble that vibrated through me. "Yeah, baby. She likes pink."

"Actually," Tiny interrupted. "I heard the coloring had something to do with some kind of spy tech in the form of contact lenses or some shit. Apparently, they don't come in anything but pink, and she was trying to blend in."

That got a startled laugh from me. Xavier joined me with a warm chuckle. "I don't even know why that was funny. She reminds me of an anime heroine or something."

"The guy with her is Piston," Tiny added from the front seat. "Ain't exactly sure what he does, but he protects Venus like a rabid guard dog."

"I thought she was an assassin." I turned and saw Tiny's mischievous grin in the rearview mirror.

"Oh, she is. Piston's just overprotective. Doesn't mind her gettin' in fights. In fact, sometimes Venus is the one to pick the fight. Piston just wants everyone to know he has her back. That way, they'll think twice about trying to ambush her."

I turned to Xavier. His smile was soft, and he stroked my cheek lightly with his thumb. "Is she part of your club?"

"No." Xavier took up the explanation. "But she and Piston represent a coalition of motorcycle clubs. They all operate independently but help each other out if necessary. We aren't part of them, but our former president used to be vice president of a club in their coalition."

I nodded, taking it all in. These people, these dangerous, capable people, were here because of me? Because Xavier had asked them to be? The realization was both humbling and overwhelming.

"You okay?" Xavier asked softly, his fingers gently kneading my tight muscles.

"Just processing," I admitted. "It's a lot."

"I know." He pressed a kiss to the top of my head. "Just know you're safe. Everything else will take care of itself."

"I'll take your word for it," I whispered with a smile, laying my head against his chest.

The steady rhythm of his heartbeat was comforting, proof I wasn't alone anymore, that someone was in my corner. Outside the window, the night scenery blurred by, lights from passing cars occasionally illuminating the interior. My muscles were now the consistency of goo in the warmth of Xavier's embrace. This was where I wanted to stay.

It was strange how quickly my life had changed. This morning I'd been grocery shopping, planning another quiet weekend with my Saturday visit to Xavier. Now I was speeding down a highway with him, flanked by motorcycles, running from threats I didn't understand.

"You should try to get some sleep," Xavier murmured against my hair. "We've got a long drive ahead. You want to lay your head on the seat? You can put your feet in my lap."

"I don't want to move. Feels too good." My eyelids felt impossibly heavy. The adrenaline crash was hitting me hard.

"How about you just close your eyes for a bit," he coaxed. "I'll wake you if anything happens."

I wanted to protest, to stay alert, but the rhythmic motion of the truck and Xavier's steady heartbeat were lulling me into a drowsy, contented lethargy.

"Xavier?"

"Yeah, baby."

"Am I dumb to trust you like this?"

He didn't answer right away. Instead, he paused in his rubbing of my back for a couple of seconds before he started up again. "What do you think?"

"You're the only person who's ever supported and protected me. You're everything my parents would hate, but you're the one person who's been there during the scariest moments of my life, doing what needed to be done."

"I think that should tell you what you need to know."

"Yeah." I lay my head on his chest. This time, Xavier put his other hand on the back of my head to hold me to him.

"I've got you, Tillie Girl. I've got you."

Those were the last words I heard before I surrendered to sleep, Xavier's steady heartbeat coaxing me to drift…

Until sleep took me.

Chapter Five

Xavier

A couple hours into the drive, four more bikes pulled up beside us. I was surprised that Venus and Piston didn't veer off and leave the escort to us, Kiss of Death, but Oktober moved alongside Piston; the two fist-bumped in greeting. The whole convoy continued on like nothing was amiss. I had to smile. Prison had been hard. Fuckin' hard. But the connections and family I'd made there were the closest and most supportive I'd had.

"Two escorts," Tiny chuckled softly. "Right. Bet they had to make the rest of the guys stay home."

I was grateful Tiny was considerate of Tillie and kept his voice down. She was sound asleep in my arms. Once she'd finally settled against my chest, she didn't move except for her steady breathing. If she let out a small, delicate snore now and then, I'd never tell her.

"Fuckin' missed the guys. And home."

"You had a job to do. And you know you could have come home once you finished. Why the fuck did you stay in that hellhole so long anyway?"

"You really have to ask me that?" I glared at him over Tillie's head.

"Yeah. You coulda been home instead in some cell like a fuckin' animal." Tiny frowned at me through the mirror. "Her?" I knew what he meant.

"Yeah."

We were silent for a while before Tiny spoke again. "Worth it." It wasn't a question. Tiny could see me. He'd always seen me, even when no one else could. We'd been in the same foster home as kids and had stuck together. Even when sticking together meant we both got in trouble with the law.

"Was."

Yeah. We were guys. Why waste breath on a full sentence when a couple words would do?

We stopped an hour outside of Nashville when Tillie stirred. "Where are we?" She didn't lift her head, just shifted her position slightly and snuggled in deeper. I grinned, rubbing her back again.

"Just pulled into a truck stop," Tiny supplied cheerfully. "You ready for some chow?"

Then Tillie stiffened, her eyes flew open. "Ohmigod!" She pushed up but I held her still, not wanting her to bump her head on the roof of the truck.

"Easy, honey. What's wrong?"

"How long have I been asleep? And straddling your lap?" She sounded so mortified I couldn't help but laugh.

"You were sleeping so peacefully, there was no way I was waking you." I helped her sit up slowly. "Besides, I liked knowing you were secure where you were." I smiled at her as I brushed a lock of hair off her cheek.

She gave me an adorably confused look. "But I was sitting in your lap."

"Exactly."

Her eyes got wide and she snort-laughed before covering her mouth with her hand. Tiny chuckled and I knew my grin got wider.

She scowled and wagged her finger to scold me. "It's not nice to laugh at someone when they accidentally snort."

That tickled even me and I chuckled, pulling her to me so I could drop a kiss on her temple. "Come on, Little Piggy. Let's get you some chow."

Tillie sighed, shaking her head. "That's not going

away anytime soon, is it?"

"Honey." Tiny turned to look at us from the front seat as he spoke. "You're about to enter a place where every single man in the area is going to look at you and see a little sister. We are gonna bug the shit outta you. We're also going to protect you with our lives and run off any potential boyfriends on general principle. It's what big brothers do."

Tillie looked from Tiny to me and back. "I don't have siblings."

"You're fixin' to, baby." I gave her ass a light swat through the blanket still draped around her. "Go on, then. Up you get."

Tiny opened his door and hopped down to fuel us up, leaving us in the truck to untangle and get out at our leisure. Tillie slid off my lap. As she did, she rubbed over my cock for a brief moment when she shifted her weight. She sucked in a breath and stiffened when I hissed in surprise.

"I'm sorry!" She looked panicked, holding her weight on her knees, still on either side of my hips. "I didn't mean --"

"Shh, baby. It's fine. Normal reaction to a beautiful woman." I rested my hands on her hips lightly. "I'm not gonna jump you or hit on you or do anything else to make you uncomfortable. OK? I just want you safe and comfortable. You were so sound asleep, I hated to wake you to make you move."

Her breath came in deep, rapid breaths for a couple seconds, then she nodded her head. I could visibly see the second she saw the sincerity in my expression. "I'm sorry. It's not that I think you'll hurt me, Xavier. Of all the people in the world, you've earned my trust. I guess I just wasn't expecting you to..." Her face grew red and she waved her hand in the air. "You know." Then she gave a nervous, embarrassed smile. "I suppose a woman straddling you and plastering herself against your body, any man would have the same reaction, huh?"

"Don't kid yourself, honey. I most definitely want you. Just because I ain't acting on it don't mean I don't want to. But you need a friend right now. Not a horny biker trying to get into your panties." I leveled my gaze on hers and held it, needing her to see my sincerity. "If you decide you want me too, you make the move. Know upfront that I will not reject you, Tillie. But I ain't bringin' you home to fuck you. I'm bringing you to my club so you're safe and protected until I can get this other shit sorted out. After that, you can stay with me, or I'll help you find a place you like where you feel safe." I brushed my thumb across her cheek and smiled at her. "Now let's get you some food. You must be starving."

She climbed off my lap with a shy smile, carefully folding the blanket and setting it aside. Her movements were measured, deliberate, like she was trying to regain her equilibrium after our conversation.

When we stepped out of the truck, Venus and Piston were already lounging against their bikes. Oktober, Chains, Noose, and Griffin formed a loose perimeter around the truck and the gas pumps next to us.

Tillie's eyes widened as she took in the gathering. "Are they all here for us?"

"For you," I corrected, placing my hand at the small of her back. The gesture was both protective and possessive.

Venus pushed away from her bike and sauntered over, her pink hair gleaming under the harsh truck stoplights. "So this is famous Tillie." Her voice was surprisingly soft for someone with such a deadly reputation, her Russian accent evident but not so thick I couldn't understand. The smile she gave Tillie was warm and inviting, despite the freaky-as-shit pink eyes. "This one" -- she nodded at me -- "called Knuckles S.O.S., demanding we send someone to your new house double time, to get him out of prison, and get him ride straight to you."

Tillie started, her eyes widening as she swung her gaze from Venus to me. "What?"

"I know it sounds creepy, but I wasn't about to let you get hurt if I could help it, Tillie." I wasn't sure of how she'd take this part, but that wasn't really what had me worried. I knew I'd have to tell her, but I had thought I'd have time to figure out how to word my explanation. Then I figured out what property Tillie had "purchased" and had to have Knuckles pull a miracle out of his ass. Which he did. And, honest to God, there was never any doubt on my end. I knew Knuckles would take care of everything I couldn't. "I called my president, and he took care of the rest."

"But how could he get you out of prison?" She looked at me with hesitation but not fear. Just like a child might look at a doctor after he promises not to give the child a shot if he'll cooperate. She trusted me but was suspicious.

"I'll explain it all once we get back in the truck. Tiny is certain we won't be followed, but I don't like being stopped too long just in case."

She nodded. "You're right. And I trust you. Even if this is kind of sounding a little creepy. Sounds like you could have gotten out of prison any time you wanted. I never kept my life secret. You knew where I lived. Where I worked. You knew it all. If you meant me harm, you'd have done something long before now."

Venus gripped her shoulder in a gentle squeeze. "You keep believing in him, little sister. He is good man, if unorthodox."

Tillie gave Venus a solemn look. "I know he's a good man. He's the only person in my whole life who's ever taken up for me or cared if I was happy. He never let me leave our visits any way other than with a smile on my face."

"These men at Kiss of Death make up their minds on spot. Expect Xavier to follow you around like puppy dog from here on out." She winked at Tillie before sauntering back to Piston and looping her arm through his as they walked into the store.

I leaned in to kiss Tillie's temple. "Come on, Miss Piggy."

"Nope." She shook her head almost violently. "Not happening."

God, she was fun! "We'll have to put it to a vote. You know. After I get someone to make you giggle-snort."

"That's diabolical."

"Never said I played fair."

"I'd be concerned if you tried to convince me otherwise." Any suspicion or wariness she might have had earlier melted away and she gave me the brightest, most beautiful smile I'd ever seen.

God, I'd never wanted to kiss a woman more in my life! I could almost taste her sweet lips, feel their softness against my own lips. I even thought I could trust myself to keep things light, but I was not about to break my word two seconds after I made it. Instead, I took her hand and tugged her toward the convenience store area of the truck stop.

They had an array of gas station rolly food --

taquitos, tornados, and various sausages -- as well as hot sandwiches, salads, and cup desserts. I snagged us a bunch of everything and some drinks while Tillie and Venus went to the restroom. The guys would want to take five minutes in the parking lot to wolf something down, but Venus and Tillie might not want to inhale their food.

I unloaded my cache of goodies onto the counter to pay when Tiny came up behind me. "Do you even have money to pay for all that?"

"Nope. Knew you were on the way. Figured by the time the young lady finished ringin' everything up, you'd be here to foot the bill."

Tiny stared hard at me while we stood there as the girl totaled everything. "This is payback for me laughing at you earlier. Isn't it?"

"Ain't sayin' it is, and ain't sayin' it isn't. But I will say I feel a whole lot less bad about makin' you pay."

Tiny barked out a laugh even as he pulled out his wallet and handed the clerk some bills. She sacked everything up, and me and Tiny waited for the women. Piston stood at the door keeping an eye on the parking lot.

As we approached the older man, Tiny shifted his sacks to one hand. "What is it, Piston?"

"Not sure. Just a feelin'."

"While you were taking care of Tillie," Tiny said, "I captured one of the guards and tied him to the tree stand they were using to keep an eye on the road and the farmhouse. I made sure he understood Tillie was under our protection and they were to back off. Menendez's men know better than to tangle with us because of our relationship with the Miles family."

Piston grunted. "Menendez has been getting

cocky. Don't count him out yet."

"The cartel doesn't care if people stay away from the place." I shook my head. I wasn't going to borrow trouble. "Menendez just doesn't want anyone messing with that road. With Tillie gone, that's a win for him."

Piston took in a deep breath and held it before letting it out slowly. "Yeah. Maybe."

Now I looked at the shadows in front of the parking areas with suspicion, seeing threats where there were none. "Maybe we shouldn't linger."

Tiny nodded. "Yeah."

Venus and Tillie emerged from the bathroom. Venus quartered the area as they walked the length of the store toward us. Venus's gaze landed on Piston's, then mine. Her face hardened and her eyes grew even more focused than usual. Tillie seemed oblivious to the undercurrents surrounding her.

We all exited the store, headed to the truck and bikes. Then, the glass storefront of the truck stop exploded, raining shards across the sidewalk, and the sudden crack of gunfire shattered the night air.

"Down!" I shoved Tillie to the concrete, covering her body with mine as bullets peppered the ground around us. The gas pump next to Tiny's truck burst into a shower of sparks. There must have been an emergency shut off tripped somewhere, or we were just lucky, because the place didn't erupt in an explosion that would have leveled a whole fucking city block.

A black SUV with tinted windows roared past, muzzle flashes illuminating the dark interior as the shooters unloaded in our direction. Venus hit the pavement and rolled, coming up on one knee with a pistol already drawn. She squeezed off three shots at the retreating vehicle.

"Fuck!" Chains bellowed, blood streaming from his upper arm as he ducked behind a concrete barrier. "Menendez cartel!"

The SUV screeched around the perimeter of the truck stop and came back for another pass. Oktober and Griffin were already moving, weapons drawn, taking positions behind parked semis.

"Stay down!" I pressed Tillie harder against the ground as another volley of bullets ricocheted off the metal fuel pump above us. Her body trembled beneath mine, but she remained silent, her arms going up to cover her head instinctively.

"Xavier," Tillie whispered, her voice barely audible over the chaos. "What's happening?"

"Not sure, honey." I kept my body covering hers, my eyes scanning for an opportunity to move. The SUV was coming around for another pass. "When I say go, we're making a run for Tiny's truck. You stay low and do exactly what I say, understand?"

She nodded against my chest, and I could feel her heart hammering wildly. The rhythmic thud of boots on pavement told me our backup was repositioning.

"Piston! Left flank!" Venus's voice rang out, clear and commanding despite the mayhem.

The SUV's engine roared as it accelerated toward us again. I moved Tillie to the wall at the corner of the building and pinned her between the hard brick and my body, covering her as completely as I could.

Several gunshots rang out in the night as all around us, people screamed and ran for cover. Piston waited until the vehicle was clear of the pumps and any bystanders before he fired off a shot at the same time Venus did. Each of them got one back tire and the SUV skidded as it made the turn out of the parking lot and onto the interstate ramp.

"They won't get far," Piston growled as he holstered his weapon.

"Come on, Tillie." I snagged her hand and tugged her along with me. I heard Tiny giving Knuckles the rundown on the phone as I lifted Tillie into the truck and followed her. "Are you hurt, honey?" I tried to keep my voice calm to reassure her. The woman was going to be scarred for life after this.

"No. I didn't get hurt. I promise." Her eyes were wide, but she didn't seem like she was on the verge of panic. "I thought I heard someone yell during the... commotion."

"I think Chains got hit, but it looked more like the bullet grazed his arm." Tiny said as he ended his call. "All in all, we got out unscathed."

"What about all these people?" Now Tillie looked concerned. "Won't they tell the police?"

"Likely. But don't worry. Knuckles will take care of everything." I smiled down at her. "Buckle up. Tiny's gonna speed things up just a hair. I don't want to take any unnecessary chances. OK?" She nodded and did as I told her.

Once we were peeled out of the parking lot, we came across the same SUV on the side of the road. "Fuck," Tiny swore softly. "Wanted to take the state road because it's less likely to be watched, but I ain't takin' chances with these fuckers still out there."

"At this point I think speed over stealth is the better option."

"Yep," Tiny agreed. "I think you're right."

Chapter Six

Tillie

I'd always heard it didn't matter if you were speeding down the interstate, you could only go so fast. The likelihood of you making it to your destination more than a couple minutes faster than anticipated by speeding is slim to none. Math is involved, and I could never be bothered to work it out. It was obvious Tiny had never heard of this rule.

"Who's he talking to?" I was afraid to speak too loudly. The last thing I wanted to do was break Tiny's concentration. I sat in the seat behind Tiny while Xavier sat next to me. I gripped his hand.

"Likely Knight. Knight will have eyes on us and can keep the police away from us. Don't ask me how, because I have no idea. But he'll let Tiny know which way to go if he needs to take an alternate route." Xavier squeezed my hand and met my gaze. "Everything's going to be fine."

I nodded and squeezed his hand back. I wasn't sure I had the correct words to tell him what he meant to me and how grateful I was for his help and protection. "I owe you so much, Xave."

"Not another word, Tillie." There was fire in his eyes. "You owe me nothing." I could tell he was serious, but I didn't agree with him. There was nothing he could ever say to convince me our scales were even. Then he pulled my hand to him and kissed my fingers.

That simple gesture sent a rush of warmth through me despite our dire circumstances. I could feel my cheeks flush as his lips lingered on my skin. When he lowered my hand, I didn't pull it away. He didn't either.

The highway stretched before us like a black

ribbon, illuminated only by our headlights and the occasional passing car. Venus and Piston had fallen back slightly, keeping a protective distance behind us while the others had moved into position at various points in front of and behind us, keeping us in the middle and other traffic away from us.

"That's twice now someone's either threatened or tried to kill me," I murmured, the reality of the situation finally sinking in. "And I still don't understand why."

Xavier's jaw tightened. "It's not you they're after, exactly. It's that property."

"A farmhouse? Why would anyone care about my little farmhouse?"

Xavier exchanged a glance with Tiny through the rearview mirror before facing me again. "That maintenance road at the back of your property isn't on any maps, but it's a main smuggling route for the Menendez cartel. They've been using it for years."

"A drug cartel?" My voice rose an octave. "In my backyard?"

He winced. "Yeah. And it actually is as bad as it sounds."

"But I was leaving! Why would they have followed me all this way?" Now that we were on the road, I expected a letdown like before, but I was fucking wired.

Xavier scrubbed a hand over his face. "Because you left. We took you away from there."

"I thought that would have been the goal."

"Yeah, but they also told you to not leave the house. My guess is they were moving a shipment and didn't want you to see them."

"Why not kill me?" I winced. "Never mind. I'm grateful they didn't, so who really cares why?"

He gave me a slight smile. "I know. They don't kill people first. They have a loose agreement to warn people instead of killing them. They've been pretty good at sticking to the agreement, but they only give one chance."

"Fuckin' scum shoulda left her alone after we let them know she was under our protection. Knuckles ain't gonna be happy about that."

"Tiny." Xavier glared at the other man where their gazes met in the rearview mirror. We were all silent for a long time after that. Tiny spoke occasionally to whomever was giving him instructions, but otherwise we were all silent.

About two hours later, we rolled through the gate to a motorcycle club. I was sure there was a way my parents would expect me to feel, but their feelings and mine weren't even on the same planet. The second we were through the gate, I relaxed at the same time I felt the tension leave Xavier's grip on my hand.

I turned my head to see his expression. His look said everything I needed to know about my surroundings. I'd been going to see Xavier every week for almost a year and a half. I'd memorized every expression, every crease on his brow and around his eyes and what they meant. This was the first time I'd seen him truly relaxed.

"You have complete faith we're safe here. Don't you, Xave?" I kept my voice down, mainly because the guys had been silent the entire second half of the trip and I didn't feel right about breaking the silence too much.

"It's home," he said simply, his voice low. "And these men are my brothers. We protect each other."

As Tiny parked the truck, I could see a group of men emerging from the clubhouse. It seemed this place grew them one size, and that was fucking *big*. All of them wore leather vests similar to Xavier's. Their expressions were a mix of concern and what looked like relief.

"Come on," Xavier said, releasing my hand to open his door. "Let's go inside. We'll find a place to get you settled."

That alarmed me. "What?"

"There's plenty of room. Each building has apartments on the top floors. Most of us prefer the single-room apartments but there are larger ones in several of the buildings."

"Oh." The punch of hurt hit me out of nowhere when I had no business being hurt by what I perceived as rejection.

"What's wrong, Tillie?" He'd been about to open his door, but he stopped and turned to face me more fully.

"Nothing! Everything's fine! Thank you for making sure I have a place to stay." The last thing I wanted was for him to think I wasn't grateful for everything he'd done for me.

"Are you sure? I want you to have your own space, but I'm not going to be far away."

"Yes." I let out a breath, needing to take a moment. As much as I really didn't want Xavier out of my sight, I knew this was for the best. I needed to take time to process what had happened over the past few hours, as well as really think about this fantasy I had where Xavier was the perfect suburban husband, catering to my every whim. Even considering what he'd done for me, Xavier didn't seem the domesticated type. "I'm sure. Thank you." I squeezed his hand reassuringly. Time to put on my big girl panties.

If I'd expected some kind of male bonding

reunion or something, I'd have been disappointed. Instead, the guys put me and Xavier between them and hurried us inside and didn't stop until we were on the second floor in the middle of the big, open room. Then everyone started talking at once.

"Holy shit, man!"

"Talk about a welcome home."

"'Bout time you got your ass home, Xavier."

Several of the guys clapped Xavier on the back. A couple of them gave me respectful nods and introduced themselves. Then four women pushed their way through the gang of men catching up with Xavier.

"Don't mind them." A slender woman with light brown curls smiled and held out her hand. "I'm Hannah. Knuckles is my husband. These are Pippa, Carrie, and Violet."

"Welcome to the jungle, honey." Violet gave me a quick hug. "We put a care package together until you can get anything you're missing. We all know about life on the run or making a quick exit."

"I'm so sorry. I didn't want to put anyone else in danger, especially not people I'd never met."

"Don't you dare be sorry," Pippa said, a fierce, almost pained expression on her face. "These guys are a tight bunch. You mean something to Xavier, so they have a driving need to help Xavier protect you."

"Sounds like something out of a fairy tale." I could feel tears pricking the back of my eyes. All my life I'd been weak. I let my parents push me around. I stayed with Paul after he hit me more than once and didn't try to leave until the night Xavier found me. I absolutely would not show weakness in front of these women by crying now. But, Goddamnit! What Pippa described sounded like my most fervent dreams!

"Takes some getting used to," Violet said with a

soft smile. "I'm still learning."

I ducked my head. "Thank you for coming to meet me here. All the testosterone is a bit overwhelming."

Carrie laughed, her smile bright and beautiful. "I had about the same reaction. Though, to be fair, I freaked them out more than they freaked me out. Long story, but I watched the movie *Carrie* the other night with Riot like everyone kept telling me to, and I finally understood why poor Chains is afraid of me."

A thought occurred to me. "I don't wish ill will on anyone, but please tell me you at least looked like you had blood all over you."

Carrie laughed gleefully. "I totally did! When Chains found out my mother's name was Margaret, he started sprinkling holy water over mine and Riot's door."

OK, there was no way to contain my laughter. "That's a story I've got to hear soon."

"Once you get settled in and get some rest, we'll take you to Oasis Number Two, drink too many margaritas, and we'll tell you about it." Hannah handed me a phone as she spoke. "This is yours while you're here. The guys want us to use clean phones when calling or texting inside the compound. Everyone here has been to prison. Knuckles knows every single one of them personally, or they don't get in."

Hannah continued with the explanation. "Knuckles has extreme pull with local law enforcement. He prefers not to leave any openings if he can help it."

"All our numbers are programmed in" -- Pippa handed me the phone -- "as well as Xavier's new number. You can reach out to any of us if you need anything at all, or if you're uncomfortable with anything. Especially the guys. They absolutely will not do anything you don't want, but that's not to say they won't flirt their asses off. If someone won't back off, you call one of us or Xavier. We'll shut them down for you."

All I could do was move my gaze from woman to woman, trying to see if they were playing me. The only thing I saw was complete sincerity. They meant every word. "Is this place even real?"

"Oh, honey." Violet gave me a sympathetic smile. "I know exactly what you mean. My advice is to just roll with it. I promise you this is the real deal. I can honestly say they've been the best role models for my son. Way better than his own father." A shadow crossed her face, but she smiled, pushing through whatever memory had dampened her mood.

"Xavier saved me." I whispered. "My husband would have killed me, but Xavier made sure he never hurt me again. Just like he promised that night when he…" I took a breath before letting it out and slumping while I smiled up at Carrie, needing to change the subject before I said too much. Or, worse, cried. "What and where is Oasis Number Two?"

"Oasis Number Two is where we've started going since they had to give Oasis Number One a thorough cleaning. Long story, but trust me when I tell you the son of a bitch deserved it."

I should probably be horrified at all there was to unpack in her statement, but I found myself nodding with a grin on my face. "I can wholeheartedly agree with that statement."

Violet looped her arm through mine. "I'm going to give you some advice and I hope you'll take it because this place will change your life, if you're like I was."

"I don't understand." I frowned at the other woman, but the warm, comforting smile on Violet's face never faltered.

"You've been betrayed in the worst ways by people you trusted." Violet didn't phrase it as a question. She spoke like a person who'd been in the same boat I was.

"Can't deny that," I muttered. "Xavier is the only person in my life ever to have sacrificed for me. And what he did for me I can never repay."

"Riot told me Xavier killed your abuser." Violet didn't look judgmental or like she was fishing for information. "Riot protected me and my son, Caleb. He would have gladly killed my husband if he could have." She put her shoulders back and her chin up. "I beat him to it."

I gasped, reaching out to take Violet's hand. "Oh, no! I'm so sorry! That had to have been horrible."

"Only thing I hated about it was that Caleb was there and that he'd nearly killed Doug himself. Doug Harrington was a bastard who needed to die."

"I'm glad you found your escape, Violet."

"I am too. That's why I want to tell you to take this club at face value. Don't judge them, though I seriously doubt you have that problem given how you met Xavier."

Hannah handed me a bottle of water. "We've got food on the way up, but I'm sure you're thirsty."

"Thanks." I unscrewed the bottle and took a pull.

"Anyway, Knuckles knows every single guy here," Hanna continued. "He said Xavier wanted you to be his, but you need to know you always have a choice. These guys are the super protective and possessive types, but they're some of the best people I've ever met. If they have one flaw, I'd have to say it's the tolerance they show the club girls."

"Hannah!" Pippa put her hands on her cheeks like she couldn't believe Hannah had said such a thing. "They're not going to be mean to the women."

"No. And I don't want them to be." Hannah huffed out a breath. "But the next girl who touches Knuckles is gonna leave missing a paw."

I nearly snorted water out of my nose as I laughed. "I'm so sorry!" I was equal parts horrified and resigned. Because, really. There was no recovering from water out the nose.

"Don't be." Hannah handed me a napkin. "Just get used to it. You stay around here long enough and you'll discover we've all got a really morbid sense of humor."

"I guess sometimes it's either laugh or cry."

"Exactly." Hannah gave me a crisp nod, her smile wide and mischievous before sobering again. "The point is, these are good men. I know you probably feel like you've followed the White Rabbit down the hole, but these men are the real deal, Tillie. They're socially awkward, and most of them are stone-cold killers, but they have a strong moral code and they are all protective of women and children in general." She glanced at Pippa. "Which is why they let the club girls get away with way more than they should."

Pippa shook her head but still grinned. "I can't deny they're becoming a problem. I had to cut one woman's hair the other day." Pippa's eyes were wide and solemn, like she felt sorry for the other woman. Then she shrugged. "It was only hair. Right?"

"Um, how short did you cut it?" I knew before I asked the question what her answer would be.

"I shaved it." She grinned. "Well, OK, so I

partially shaved it. I caught the club girl in question asleep and shaved a strip of hair from the top of her forehead to the back of her head before she got away from me."

I couldn't help but laugh. These women were outrageous, and I could tell I was going to love them.

"Tillie!" Xavier's voice had me turning to find him several feet away, pushing through his brothers with warm smiles and claps on the back as he did. When he got to me, he held out his hand. "Let's go get you settled."

"I've got a couple choices for you." Hannah held up two sets of keys. "This one," she shook one set, "is a single bedroom across the hall from Xavier's room. You can be near him without him being underfoot. You'll have your own space, but privacy too."

"What's the other one?" Xavier snagged my hand in his warm hand, and I laced my fingers with his before I realized I had.

"The other set is to a two-bedroom apartment in the same building with the rest of us. It's not one of the top-floor apartments, but if you decide you want to take one of those let me know. We're still finishing up those rooms. No one wanted them so they weren't a priority."

"Why would I need a two-bedroom?" I looked from Hannah to Xavier and back.

Hannah shrugged. "In case you wanted Xavier to stay with you, you've still got your own bedroom."

I sucked in a breath, because that sounded fucking perfect. But Xavier had his own room, and I was sure he wanted to get back to what he probably considered his home. He wouldn't have any desire to sleep anywhere other than his own bed, and I wouldn't blame him.

"We'll take the two-bedroom," Xavier said, reaching out to take the keys from Hannah.

"What?" My gaze shot to his, but he merely smiled down at me.

"I saw your reaction, pretty girl. You like the idea of us being close."

"I can't lie worth a damn, Xave, so I'm not going to try and pretend you're wrong. But I'll be fine on my own. You don't have to sacrifice staying in your own place after being away so long. I'm sure you --"

Xavier rolled his eyes as he placed his fingers over my lips. "Woman. Staying with you is no fuckin' sacrifice. I don't want you across the hall. Separate bedrooms is far enough away from you."

And just like that, I lost the last piece of my heart. I sobbed out a small laugh. "OK. I'm not going to try to talk you out of staying with me when you're right. I want you close too."

"Awesome!" Hannah clapped her hands as she smiled. "Come on. I'll take you to your apartment. Then you guys can get some rest. I've got everything all set up for you." She talked as she led us outside to a side-by-side ATV. We waved to the other women.

Knuckles followed us outside and dropped a kiss on his wife's cheek. "I take it I owe you that ten bucks, baby?"

"I'll be taking Xavier and Tillie to the apartment next to Hawk and Carrie. And to answer your question, you do owe me ten bucks. I knew when I first saw them together Tillie would want Xavier to have her back until she got acquainted with her new surroundings."

"Good." Knuckles glanced from me to Xavier before sticking his hand out to Xavier who took it in a firm grip. "Let me or Gunnar know when she's ready to wear your property cut. We'll have the girls arrange everything."

I couldn't help myself. I turned into Xavier's embrace and buried my face in his chest, my emotions getting the better of me. As I knew he would, Xavier wrapped his arms around me without hesitation. He and Knuckles spoke for a couple minutes. I soaked up Xavier's support while he let me compose myself and I loved him all the more for it.

"You ready to go see your new home, Tillie Girl?"

I looked up at Xavier, the man who had gone to prison for killing my abusive husband, the man who had come to my rescue when I'd been threatened and was terrified out of my mind, the man who brought me to the place he knew would be safest and circled the wagons with his brothers to protect me. "I think I've been ready my entire life."

Xavier smiled down at me. "Ditto, baby. Ditto."

Chapter Seven

Xavier

Much as I wanted to hunt down the Goddamned sons of bitches who'd attacked us, I couldn't bring myself to leave the apartment I now shared with Tillie. She had lain down on her bed without undressing and covered herself with the soft blanket and curled up into a ball.

"You OK, Miss Piggy?" The corner of her lip rose slightly but she didn't move or speak. "Overload?" She nodded. "Do you want me to leave you alone?" She shook her head and slid one hand out from under the blanket, reaching for me.

I sat on the edge of her bed and took her hand in mine. Tears slid from her eyes as she tightened her fingers around my hand. Fuck. She was breaking my fucking heart.

"Tell me what you need, Tillie. Tell me and it's yours."

That seemed to startle her. She blinked several times looking up at me. "You can't promise that. What If I wanted a million dollars?"

"Then I'll get you a million dollars."

"What about a small island where I can rule my subjects with an iron fist?"

I raised an eyebrow. "You want it in the South Pacific or Mediterranean? I can probably swing the Caribbean as long as we don't go near the Bermuda Triangle. I'm superstitious." I was only half joking. And only about the superstitious part. I happened to know a couple guys with the means who owed me more than one favor. Might be a stretch, but I could make it work.

She didn't change expression but seemed to be

searching my face for something. Maybe to see if I was lying?

After a while she opened her mouth, but nothing came out. Another tear slid from the corner of her eye. Tillie cleared her throat, but instead of trying to voice her request again, she simply scooted over slowly. So there was room for me to lie on the bed beside her?

"Baby, you're gonna have to say what you want. I can't read minds and if you're wanting me to lie down with you, you're gonna have to say so. That ain't somethin' I'm willin' to assume you mean. I gotta have something concrete."

She nodded her head, then croaked out. "Will you please hold me like you did in the truck?"

"Baby." Yep. I was done. This was it. The day I lost my man card. The shit of it was, I wasn't broken up about it. If it meant I was the one to hold this woman together? Well. I was beginning to believe to the depths of my soul, holding this brave, sweet woman together might have been the fucking reason God put me on this earth.

Slowly, letting her have as much time as she needed to change her mind, I lay down next to her. It wasn't necessary, though. The second I lay back, Tillie moved close to me, clinging to my shirt like it was her fucking lifeline.

I wrapped my arms around her, pulling her close. I felt her trembling against me, small tremors that rippled through her body. This woman had been through hell more than once and still found the strength to keep going. I admired her resilience more than she could ever know.

"I'm so tired," she whispered against my chest. "Not just physically. I'm tired of being afraid, of running, of never feeling safe."

That gave me pause. "Tillie, were you hurt while I was in prison? Is there something you've not told me?" If someone else had hurt this woman, I'd be killing again. Only this time, I wouldn't be making any noble fucking sacrifices.

"No. I never expected everything in my life would be all peaches and cream, but I really didn't expect my mom and dad to…" She stopped speaking, her fingers now against her trembling lips. I wanted to press her but wasn't sure what the right move was.

"Did they hurt you?"

"No. Not physically. They just… took *everything*. They sold everything I got from Paul's estate, even the house, because they said I could just live with them. You know. Until they found another man with money who wanted me." She trembled in my arms, clinging harder, which I hadn't thought possible. Her knuckles were white where her fist still bunched in my shirt. She sucked in a ragged breath and held it several seconds before letting the breath out in a slow, deliberate release. "It was never the money, you understand. Not for me. Mom and Dad, though. I think money motivated them to do everything they did with me. They were older when they had me because they were never supposed to need another child."

Something about the way she phrased her statement had my hackles rising. "I don't understand. What do you mean 'need another child'?"

"My brother was supposed to be their ticket to the good life. He was the smart one. The one who touched something, and it turned to gold. Mom was in her late forties when she had me, and only because my brother went to prison for something to do with money laundering and doing something bad with the stock market. They never talked about it, and I only found out about it when they shoved me into Paul's life."

"OK." I took a breath and stroked her arm while I thought over what she'd said. "There's a lot there, honey. This isn't something you've ever mentioned before."

"No. My time with you on Saturdays was my escape. I took as much time as I could to forget everything when I was with you. You gave me so much and the last thing I wanted to do then -- or now -- is for you to think I'm looking for more. The reason I only now bought a place and moved away from my parents was they kept putting me off with the estate sale and settlement. I found out later it was because they'd taken it all. I managed to keep my car and enough to buy" -- she shuddered -- "that little farm, and put back enough to keep me going for a few months if I couldn't write or things got slow for the holidays or something."

I had to concentrate on keeping my breathing slow and even. The last thing she needed was my anger on her behalf spilling over to her right now. "We'll worry about all that later, OK? You're safe now," I promised, stroking her hair. "No one's getting to you here."

She nodded slightly, her breath warm against my neck. "I know. That's what scares me."

I frowned. "What do you mean, baby?"

"What if I get used to feeling safe with you, and then..." She trailed off, but I understood what she couldn't say.

"And then I leave?" I finished for her. "Not happening, Tillie. Not by choice."

She pulled back just enough to look up at me, her silvery-green eyes swimming with emotions I couldn't fully decipher. "But that's just it. Sometimes we don't get a choice. Like with Paul. I didn't choose for him to become a monster. I didn't choose for you to kill him and throw your life into chaos when you could have been happily on your way." The tears really started falling now. She wiped her nose with the back of her wrist, then swiped at her eyes with her fingers.

"My whole life has been one clusterfuck after another, Xave. Since I met you, you've been the only bright spot in my life. I knew things wouldn't be easy just because Paul was gone and I didn't have to be afraid of him anymore. I was fully prepared to work hard to make my own life. It just seems like one thing after another kept dragging me backward, trying to suck me back down into a deep, dark hole I could never escape from!"

I pulled her closer, tucking her head under my chin. "Listen to me, Tillie. You're not going back into any fucking hole. Not while I'm breathing. Metaphorically speaking or not." I stroked her hair, feeling her tears dampening my shirt. "I've spent a year and a half thinking about you every Goddamn day. Planning what I'd do when I got out. How I'd find you, make sure you were good."

"You planned to find me?" Her voice was small against my chest.

"Baby, you only think you know what I'd go through for you." It was the Goddamned truth. "Yeah. I killed for you. But that was just my excuse to go to prison. True, I hadn't planned on killin' anyone, but then you turned up and some people just need killin'."

When her gaze met mine, her eyes were wide with shock and not a small amount of confusion. "What? What are you saying, Xavier?"

"I needed to be in Terre Haute for about six months. That's how long I thought it would take me to do my job. Knuckles made all the arrangements and six months was all I needed."

"Oh no," she gasped, distress on her lovely face.

"Hey. Stop. Let me finish." I gave her a level look, firm but not harsh as I held her gaze. When she settled and nodded her head, I dropped a kiss on top of her head and continued. "We had it all planned out. Me and Knuckles. He was still in prison, but the man has connections I don't want to know about. I helped him prepare this, so I knew I'd be getting out as soon as I could finish the job." She shifted, but I held her where she was. I wasn't sure I could look at her just yet because the woman had rocked me to my core the night I killed her husband.

"I was gonna go in for some trumped-up drug charges or something. Didn't really care as long as I could get out when I wanted. I was supposed to get an eighteen-month sentence, but Knuckles said the Miles family lawyer would get me out in six months tops if I was ready. I was going in to, uh, settle some disputes and stuff." I knew she was about to ask so I cut her off. "It doesn't really matter why right now, only that I had the choice to get out once I'd completed my tasks, which I got done in the six months I'd been allotted. I *chose* to stay because you… kept coming." She sucked in a breath, her eyes going wide with shock and something I wasn't quite sure of.

"Why would you do that?" Her voice was barely above a whisper.

I shrugged and repeated, "You kept coming."

"You said that. Why not ask to meet up when you got out? Or ask for my phone number?"

"Because I'm a big guy. You already know I can be violent when I need to be. I wanted you to be ready for me. I wanted you to have a chance to heal inside and out. But most of all, I wanted you to know me, so you'd know without a shadow of a doubt, I'd never hurt you. Ever, Tillie. Not ever."

"I know you wouldn't. You saved me."

"I'm also the guy who murdered your husband."

"Because he beat me up!" She pushed herself up and braced her forearms on my chest. "Xavier, I never thought you'd hurt me. Not even that night when you went in with the Judge you pulled out from under your seat."

I winced. "Christ. I was hopin' you hadn't actually seen me get my gun."

"It wasn't like I didn't know what you did."

"Yeah, but I didn't want any more violence to touch you. When I killed that bastard, the only thing I cared about was makin' sure you never had violence touch you again."

"I waited in the truck like you said, but I didn't want to. It was so hard watching the police take you away in handcuffs." She shuddered, laying her head back on my chest and snuggling closer. She clutched my shirt tightly once again. "You saved me. When everyone else in my life was blinded by the wealth and privilege Paul's lifestyle afforded them, you were the one who came to my rescue. You didn't question if I was lying or if there had been a good reason for me being beat all to shit." She sat up then, crossing her legs, tailor fashion. "I've replayed that night over and over in my mind, Xave. You knew. From the second I became aware of you, when I first looked into your eyes, I didn't have to tell you what had happened. You just assumed."

"Honey, I knew. Anyone with half a brain could tell what happened to you wasn't an accident. Especially with the way you shied away from me when

I stopped."

"God, the rain was coming down so hard." She gazed away from me, looking off in the distance, staring into the past. "The storm was probably the only reason I got away from the bastard that night."

"Prissy fucker didn't like gettin' wet?"

"He was a coward," she snapped. "Fucking terrified of storms." Then Tillie winced and sighed. "That's not fair. Lots of people are afraid of rough weather. But it's the only reason I got out of the driveway."

"I killed that son of a bitch too fuckin' quick." I hadn't meant to mutter that out loud, but when Tillie gave me a faint smile, I decided maybe I hadn't said something to scare her.

"When you stopped that night, I think I'd resigned myself to whatever happened. I didn't want to be raped or beaten or anything. I just wanted it all to be over."

"Christ, baby." I reached for her then, pulling her on top of me so she straddled my hips. Wrapping my arms around her, I held her so tight I was afraid she wouldn't be able to breathe, but when I loosened my hold, she whimpered.

"More."

"Don't let me hurt you, honey. I don't ever want to hurt you."

She shifted and moved higher in my arms so we were face-to-face. "And you never will, Xave. It's just the kind of man you are."

Then, to my complete and utter surprise, Tillie met my lips with hers.

Chapter Eight

Tillie

I don't know why I kissed Xavier. One second I was lost in the nightmare of my past, the next I knew I'd die if I didn't taste him. His lips were warm and firm against mine, a stark contrast to my hesitant touch. For a moment he froze, then his hand came up to cradle the back of my head, his fingers tangling in my hair as he returned the kiss with gentle restraint.

I could feel him holding back, careful not to frighten me, and that tenderness made something break loose inside me. I pressed closer, deepening the kiss, desperate to feel more of him. His other arm tightened around my waist, and he groaned softly against my mouth.

When we finally broke apart, it was Xavier who ended the kiss. We were both breathing heavily and I'm sure the desire in Xavier's eyes mirrored my own. Still, because he was the man he was, Xavier had to make sure this was what I really wanted.

"Tillie," he whispered, his voice rough. "You don't have to do this. Not for me. Not because you think you owe me something."

I shook my head, cupping his face between my palms. "I'm not. I want this. I want you."

His expression was a mixture of hope and disbelief. "You've been through hell today. I don't want you to do something you'll regret when you're thinking clearer."

I couldn't help but be amused. "I can't tell you how many nights I lay in my bed by myself and dreamed you'd come to me. I'd wake up just as you were sliding your cock inside me and want to cry in frustration." That made him suck in a breath, his eyes going wide. "Yeah, Xave. Do you want to know why I'm absolutely sure this is what I want?"

He swallowed, nervous. "I want to point out that bikers and convicts have a certain… reputation." He looked and sounded like he was giving me a lecture, and I nearly smiled. "While I most certainly have the necessary equipment at or above the average size, I haven't had sex since a month and three days before I went to prison." I knew better than to smile, but it was getting harder and harder. "Do not take this first time to mean I'm gonna be a wham-bam-thank-you-ma'am kind of fuck. I might come before you the first time, but I swear by God Almighty you *will* come. Several times."

That was all I could take. I burst into giggles while leaning in to kiss him again. He sighed, then let out a disgruntled grumble against my lips. "Don't see anything so Goddamned funny." But there was no heat in his voice.

"This is one of many reasons I know I'm absolutely making the right decision. There was never any doubt in my mind you'd make sex good for me. But now I'm worried I might be rushing things." As soon as the words left my mouth, I wished them back. So, I put a finger in his face and gave him what I hoped was a stern look. "But you absolutely will not go find another woman to fuck. You want to fuck, I'm all over that shit. But it will be me. Not someone else, so forget I said I was rushing things. Seems like I've not moved fast enough."

Now it was his turn to laugh. "Little bloodthirsty, baby?"

I shrugged. "Maybe. I just want things clear from the start. You said you'd never reject me for sex, and I'm OK for it to be just sex." I winced, shaking my head. "OK, that's not true. I won't be OK with it, but I'll still accept it. I want you that much, Xave. I'll take what you're willing to give."

"Good," he grunted before snaking his arms back around me. The feeling of security was immediate. Being held tightly in this man's arms was like nothing I'd ever experienced. I wanted to stay with him forever, but if this was all I ever got, I'd hold it in my heart forever and smile every time I thought about it. "Because, baby, you ain't gettin' just sex from me." His voice was low and rough, his dark eyes intense as they searched mine. "What you're gettin' is everything I got to give. All of me, for as long as you'll have me."

My breath caught in my throat. "Xavier..."

"Shh." He brushed his thumb across my bottom lip. "Let me show you what you mean to me, Tillie Girl."

This time when our lips met, there was no hesitation from either of us. The kiss was deeper, hungrier, filled with all the longing that had built up between us over countless Saturday visits separated by bulletproof glass. His hands roamed across my back, pulling me impossibly closer as I melted against him.

When he rolled us over so I was beneath him, he braced himself on his forearms, careful not to crush me with his weight. "You tell me if you need me to stop, yeah? Anytime, for any reason."

I nodded, running my hands up his muscled arms. "I will. But I won't need to."

He studied my face for a long moment, then slowly began kissing his way over my chin and down my neck to the swell of my breast. His lips traced a path of fire across my skin, and I arched into his touch, desperate for more. Every careful caress erased another memory of pain, replacing it with pleasure so intense I could barely breathe.

"Xavier," I gasped as his hand slipped under my shirt, his calloused fingers skimming along my ribs with surprising gentleness.

"I got you, baby," he murmured against my collarbone. "Let me take care of you."

My breath hitched as his lips slid up and down my neck, his beard creating a delicious friction against my sensitive skin. Each touch was reverent, almost worshipful, so different from anything I'd experienced before.

"Can I take this off?" Xavier murmured against my collarbone, his fingers playing with the hem of my shirt.

"Yes," I whispered, lifting my arms to help him. "Please." The cool air hit my skin as he pulled the fabric over my head, but any chill was immediately replaced by the heat of his gaze.

"Beautiful," he breathed, taking in the sight of me in my simple cotton bra. His calloused fingers traced the edge of the fabric, sending shivers down my spine. "So fucking beautiful."

I reached for his shirt, suddenly desperate to feel his skin against mine. "Need you, Xave."

With a crooked smile, Xavier sat back on his heels and pulled his shirt off in one fluid motion. I couldn't help but stare at the expanse of tattooed muscle revealed to me. My fingers itched to trace every line, every scar, every inch of him. He was heavily muscled but not overly large. Just perfect for me.

"Like what you see?" There was a hint of vulnerability beneath his teasing grin.

"Pretty sure you know exactly how yummy you look."

"Make no mistake about it, sweetheart. I *am*

yummy." His cocky, boyish grin made me laugh. Especially when he flexed. Xavier always had the power to make me laugh, even when I'd been sad, afraid, or felt defeated. Of course, he'd make me comfortable during intimacy. Xavier would settle for nothing less than our first time together being absolutely perfect.

I should have felt self-conscious. I wasn't wearing anything fancy, and my body bore the faint marks of old scars Paul had left. The way Xavier looked at me, though, made me feel like the most desirable woman on earth.

When he unhooked my bra and slid it off, I didn't try to cover myself. Instead, I watched his face as he gazed at my breasts, the naked hunger in his expression giving me much needed courage.

Xavier lowered his head to press a reverent kiss to the slope of one breast. "Been dreaming about this for too fuckin' long."

His mouth closed over my nipple and I gasped, arching into the wet heat of his tongue. I tangled my fingers in his hair, holding him to me as waves of pleasure radiated through my body. Every gentle suck, every swirl of his tongue sent jolts of electricity straight to my core. I couldn't hold in my moans and whimpers and didn't bother trying.

When he shifted his attention to my other breast, his hand slid down my stomach to the waistband of my jeans. He paused there, his eyes finding mine in silent question.

"Yes," I whispered, lifting my hips. "Please, Xavier."

He made quick work of the button and zipper, then eased my jeans down my legs with agonizing slowness, his fingertips trailing fire along my skin.

When he tossed them aside and looked at me lying there in just my panties, the raw hunger in his expression made me tremble.

"God, Tillie," he breathed, running his palm up my thigh. "You have no idea how fuckin' perfect you are."

"I'm far from perfect," I whispered, suddenly aware of every flaw, every scar that marred my skin.

"No," Xavier said firmly, his hand stilling on my thigh as his eyes met mine. "Don't you dare. Don't you fucking dare diminish yourself." His voice was fierce, protective. "Every mark on your body tells the story of how strong you are. How you survived. You're perfect to me, Tillie Girl. Every Goddamn inch of you."

Tears pricked my eyes at the raw honesty in his voice. No one had ever spoken to me like that before. Like I was precious. Like I mattered.

"Xavier," I breathed, reaching for him. "What did I ever do to deserve your care and protection?"

He shook his head. "You ain't the lucky one, honey. You're the woman who has to put up with a caveman followin' you around like a fuckin' puppy dog."

Holding back my smile was impossible. "I mean" -- I shrugged -- "puppies *are* cute. I'm not really seeing the issue."

His chuckle filled me like warm honey, heating me from the inside out. He kissed me then, deep and claiming, pouring all his emotion into the press of our lips and slick glide of his tongue against mine.

When he pulled back, his breathing was ragged. "I need to touch you," he said, his voice strained. "Need to make you feel good. Will you let me?"

Instead of answering with words, I hooked my thumbs in the waistband of my panties and pushed them down. Xavier's eyes went dark as he helped me slide them off completely, leaving me bare beneath his heated gaze.

"Christ," he whispered reverently, his hands skimming up my calves to my thighs. "You're gonna be the death of me, woman."

His touch was featherlight as he slid his hands over my hips and up to my breasts. When his thumb brushed over my nipple, I gasped and arched into his hand. The next thing I knew, Xavier had latched onto my other nipple and was sucking at the sensitive peak with steady pulls before licking the swollen nub with the flat of his tongue.

We both groaned. I threaded my fingers through his hair and held him to me, afraid he'd change his mind and leave me like this. But Xavier's big body trembled against mine, his skin growing slick with sweat.

"I've never tasted anything so fuckin' good in my fuckin' life." Xavier sounded almost in awe. Like he was in the middle of the most wonderful experience he'd ever imagined and was afraid to break the spell woven around him. "Need more."

"Yes!" I nodded my head furiously. "Definitely need more."

Xavier slid down my body, pressing open-mouthed kisses along my stomach, my hip bones, the tops of my thighs. Each touch left me trembling, anticipation building as he settled between my legs. His broad shoulders pushed my thighs wider, and I felt completely exposed before him.

"Xavier," I whispered, suddenly nervous.

He looked up at me from between my legs, his dark eyes intense. "I've got you, baby. Let me play for a bit." As he looked up my body at me, sweat dotted my own skin. I was sure there had never been a more erotic moment in my entire life than Xavier with his mouth hovering above my pussy.

Then his mouth was on me, and coherent thought fled. The first slow stroke of his tongue had me arching off the bed with a startled cry. He chuckled against my sensitive flesh, the vibration adding to the pleasure coursing through me.

"That's it," he murmured, his breath hot against me. "Let me hear how good it feels."

I couldn't have held back if I tried. Each swirl of his tongue, each gentle suck at my clit sent waves of pleasure rippling through my body. I clutched the sheets, then his hair, then the sheets again as I writhed beneath his skilled mouth. The sensations he created within me were so intense it bordered on pain and, silly as it sounds, I didn't know what to do with my hands.

When he slipped one thick finger inside me, I cried out. It felt like I was spiraling out of control, like my body wasn't my own. Only Xavier held the key to pleasure like this and I was greedy for more. But only with Xavier. I knew in my heart and soul I'd never be able to give my body willingly to another man as long as I lived. For good or ill, I was all in with this man.

"So fucking wet for me," he murmured, his fingers exploring my folds with gentle expertise. "Tell me what you like, baby. Tell me how to make you feel good."

I couldn't form coherent words as his thumb found my clit, circling it with just the right pressure. "That," I gasped, my hips rising to meet his touch. "Oh, God! Just like that!"

Xavier watched my face intently as he slipped one thick finger inside me, then another, stretching me gently as his thumb continued its maddening circles. The dual sensation had me writhing beneath him, my hands clutching at his shoulders.

"Xavier," I moaned, feeling the tension building inside me. "Please, I need --"

Before I could finish my plea, Xavier covered my pussy with his mouth...

And it. Was. *On*.

Chapter Nine

Xavier

I recognized I was in serious trouble when Tillie came the second I touched her pussy with my mouth. Not only was I fighting out of my weight class with this woman, Tillie embraced my attention and welcomed my touch. In fact, she reveled in the way I ate her pussy and held none of her cries and screams back as she came on a hard, wet rush. Because, you know, no pressure or anything.

The taste of her flooded my mouth, sweet and musky, and I groaned against her sensitive flesh. Her thighs trembled around my head as she rode out her orgasm, her hips undulating over my mouth, her fingers tangled in my hair, holding me right where she wanted me. I kept my tongue moving, gentler now, easing her through the aftershocks. I would give this woman anything she wanted. Do anything she wanted. If it gave her this much pleasure, there was nothing I'd deny her. I'd eat her pussy until she either passed out or made me fuck her. Maybe if I gave her all the pleasure she could stand before I actually fucked her, she wouldn't be disappointed if I didn't last past the first couple strokes.

"Oh my God," she gasped, her chest heaving. "Oh, my God!" Tillie screamed and screamed, her cries growing more and more hoarse.

"That's it, baby," I growled next to her clit, before flicking it a couple times with my tongue. "You come nice and hard for me. I want to drink you up."

"Xavier!"

With a final scream, Tillie orgasmed again. Her pussy clenched around my fingers, wetting my hand and chin. Her sweet, slightly musky scent was like a homecoming. My reward for the extra months I'd stayed in prison. Knuckles was the only person who knew why I'd remained behind bars, and he'd thought I'd lost my Goddamned mind. And maybe he was right. I could have gotten out of prison and approached Tillie on the outside, but that hadn't felt right at the time. My only regret was that I hadn't gotten to her before she'd purchased the exact wrong piece of property. Because I knew in my soul Tillie had needed the time and separation as she got to know me. She needed to feel safe and in control. I was right, too. Tillie now knew there was nothing I wouldn't do for her. I was hers. I just hoped like hell I could make her mine too.

I looked up at her from between her legs, unable to hold back my satisfied smile. Her face was flushed, her hair a wild tangle around her head, her eyes half-lidded with pleasure.

"Just when I thought you couldn't get more beautiful. Post-orgasm is a really good look for you." I kissed the inside of her thigh.

Tillie reached for me, tugging at my shoulders. "Come here. Need to feel you."

I crawled up her body, my jeans uncomfortably tight against my straining cock. When our mouths met, she moaned at the taste of herself on my lips, and the sound nearly undid me.

"You're still wearing too many clothes," she complained, her hands fumbling with my belt.

I chuckled against her neck. "Couldn't agree more, baby." I kissed her before finding her breast again, sucking the nipple and grazing the puckered flesh with my teeth. I was rewarded with her sharp cry.

I sat on my heels and worked at my belt with

shaking hands. Tillie watched me with heavy-lidded eyes, her gaze following my every movement as I slid from the bed and stripped out of my jeans and boxers. Before dropping everything on the floor, I fished out one of the two condoms in my back pocket. When I was finally naked, her eyes widened slightly as she took in the sight of my hard cock.

She sat up slightly, resting on one arm as she reached out to me. With reverent fingers, she stroked my length before taking my cock in her hand and stroking a couple of times. Her eyes were glazed and dreamy, like she was mesmerized. Which wasn't a small boost to my ego.

"Fuck, baby. Been too Goddamned long since anyone but me touched my cock."

Her hand moved slowly, exploring, and I had to grit my teeth to maintain control. When she swiped her thumb over the head, collecting the bead of moisture there, I nearly lost my mind.

"Come back," she said, a wicked gleam in her eye as she pulled gently at my cock to bring me to the bed.

"I'm in so much fuckin' trouble," I muttered as I covered her body with mine.

Her skin was like silk. Once I took care of a couple things I was going to keep her naked and in bed until I'd tasted every single inch of her at least three times. And her smile... was simply to God breathtaking.

"Only the best kind, I hope."

"Oh yeah. The very best."

I ripped open the condom and rolled it over my cock, stopping to grip the base and regain some semblance of control.

"I should probably at least raise an eyebrow that

you're prepared for this, but the truth is I'm just grateful because, yet again, you're looking out for me when I didn't look out for myself."

"I ain't had sex since I went to prison and I didn't do drugs on the inside. I was careful, but there were a lot of fights and blood. I'd rather get tested to be sure before I take you bare."

"How the fuck are you even real, Xave?" She looked equal parts amused, annoyed, and so fucking happy. "I'd say you're too good to be true, but I know that's wrong. You're exactly what you appear and I'm not sure I would have ever believed any of this if I hadn't come to see you every Saturday."

I rested my weight on top of her, my arms on either side of her head. One curl lay over her forehead, threatening to fall into her eye so I reached up to gently brush it away. "Understand me, Tillie. There's nothing I wouldn't do for you. To keep you safe, happy, and livin' your fuckin' best life. But that's for you. I'm a killer."

"Fully aware of that, Xave. I was there."

"That bastard was a clean kill because I let my temper get the better of me. I'm fully willing and capable of carrying out the grisliest torture and death you can imagine, then coming home to you and sleeping like a baby. I'm a monster. But I'm your monster."

She reached up and stroked my beard, threading her fingers through the crisp strands. "It feels good to have the monster on my side for once."

Yep. I was done. With a defeated groan, I kissed her again. I guided my cock to her entrance before covering her fully and sinking in one slow inch at a time.

Tillie gasped beneath me, her eyes fluttering

closed and her nails digging into my shoulders as I filled her completely. She was so tight, so perfect around me I had to pause, breathing hard against her neck to keep from losing control entirely. I stilled, giving her time to adjust, my forehead pressed against hers as we both breathed heavily.

"You okay?" I managed to rasp out, though speaking was nearly impossible with how good she felt wrapped around my cock.

Her legs came up to my waist, pulling me deeper. "More than okay," she whispered. "You feel… God, Xavier! You feel incredible."

I started to move then, slow and careful at first, watching her face for any sign of discomfort. But there was only pleasure there, her lips parted as soft moans escaped with each thrust. Her nails dug into my shoulders with sharp little stings, and I knew I was going to wear those marks like badges of honor.

"Faster," she pleaded, her hips rising to meet mine. "Please, I need more."

I obliged, picking up the pace, driving into her with steady strokes that had her crying out. The sound of my name on her lips was better than any drug, and I found myself chasing that high, wanting to hear it again and again.

"So Goddamned fuckin' perfect." I breathed my words against her neck before latching on and sucking gently, leaving my mark on her for all to see.

I growled low in my throat as she tightened around me, her inner walls gripping my cock like a silken vise. My rhythm faltered as I fought for control, determined to make this last.

"That's it," I encouraged as her body arched beneath mine. "Take what you need, baby. Do it now!"

She moved with me now, finding our rhythm,

her hips rising to meet each thrust, clutching at my back and shoulders.

"Xavier," she gasped, her voice breaking.

I slipped a hand between us, finding her clit with my thumb. The moment I touched her there, she cried out, her body going rigid beneath me.

"Look at me," I commanded softly. "Want to see your eyes when you come."

Her gaze locked with mine, vulnerable and trusting in a way that made my chest ache. As I circled her clit, her eyes widened, and I watched as pleasure overtook her. Her pupils dilated, her lips parted on a silent scream, and then she was convulsing around me, her pussy clenching around me and I knew that was it. I came as Tillie's pussy squeezed and milked my cock, demanding I put my cum inside her despite the condom.

Tillie didn't look away from me. She kept her gaze focused on mine just like I'd told her. The connection between us was electric, raw and primal, yet somehow more intimate than anything I'd ever experienced. And it wasn't just this one time. In my heart, I'd known the night I killed her husband she was the woman for me. Sex with her only reinforced the notion.

For several long moments, we lay tangled together, our breathing gradually slowing, our bodies still connected. I pressed soft kisses to her neck, her cheek, her forehead, unable to stop touching her now that I finally could.

"I can't believe you stayed in prison for me," Tillie whispered, her fingers tracing patterns on my chest.

I carefully rolled to my side, taking her with me so we remained face to face. "Best decision I ever made. Got to know you. The real you."

"But all those months..." Her voice trailed off, and I could see her struggling to comprehend the sacrifice.

"Worth every second," I said firmly. "I'd do it again if it meant it got me to where I'm at right now." When she opened her mouth, I leaned in to kiss her before continuing. "I don't mean sex either, baby. Though..." I grinned down at her as I brushed a strand of hair clinging to her cheek. "I'm definitely glad I got there too. But I mean where we are in our relationship with each other. I think, even without the sex, we built a good foundation, becoming friends first."

Tillie's eyes filled with tears, but they were different from before. These were the kind that came from something good, something overwhelming in the best possible way.

I couldn't help kissing away the offending moisture before finding her mouth with mine for another lingering kiss. There was nothing I wanted more than to lie here and hold her until she came down softly, but I had to get cleaned up. "I should probably get rid of this," I said, gesturing to the condom. "Be right back." I stood but stopped and turned back to her. "Don't go anywhere. Understand?" I tried to put a stern note in my voice, but Tillie grinned at me.

"Afraid I'll leave without saying goodbye?"

"Yes." I gave her a solemn look, then frowned. "I don't like that thought." Absently, I rubbed the center of my chest before turning back to the bathroom.

As I shut the door, I heard Tillie speak to me softly. "As long as you want me, Xavier, I'll never leave you. Especially without saying goodbye."

I grinned at her, but I was disturbed at the

instant relief. Yeah. This whole finding my woman thing had more twists and turns than I ever expected. Especially where my emotions were concerned. The need to keep her close, to protect her from everything, was overriding everything in my life.

Knuckles knew how much she meant to me. It was why he'd moved heaven and earth to give me what I wanted when I insisted on staying in prison, and when I needed to get the fuck out. I had no idea how he did it, but I called him in a fucking panic and he made it happen. I figured the Miles family had something to do with it. Knuckles had allied us with that family for them to use us as paid muscle. Normally, that kind of move would have been a hard pass for me, but I knew the kind of man Knuckles was. I trusted him with my life. More importantly, I trusted him with Tillie's life. If he took the job, then he was satisfied the Miles' weren't going to have them hurt innocents. Now, if they needed me to bust a bunch of drug dealers' balls, I was down with that.

I cleaned up, then looked at myself in the mirror. There was no denying Tillie was too good for me. I accepted I was fighting out of my weight class with this woman. She was definitely too good to be with an ex-con. But, as I studied myself, I made a vow. Tillie was going to be happy. She was going to be and feel safe. She was going to have the best life I could possibly give her. Anyone who went against that plan was going to meet my wrath.

Chapter Ten

Tillie
Two Weeks Later...

I kept waiting for the other shoe to drop, so to speak. Life was as idyllic as I'd always wanted. Xavier spent almost every waking moment with me. If he was busy with something club-related, he would turn up at random wherever I was and stand around like a schoolboy with a crush. He never intruded and remained in the background unless I invited him over. Like I'd ever leave him standing off to the side by himself. I always welcomed him with open arms and a big, wet, sloppy kiss, which he got the biggest kick out of.

There were only two things making my life less than perfect inside the Kiss of Death MC compound, and I found the irony amusing as fuck. First, I knew Xavier was meeting with Knuckles and several other members of the club to get the rundown on how they were dealing with what Xavier termed "the cartel problem." I had a suspicion their pest removal involved some permanent solutions, but Xavier didn't tell me and I didn't ask. Fuckers deserved what they got. As for my house that I barely got to live in, apparently everyone in the area knew about the problems with drug runners. It was why I not only got a bargain price when I purchased it, but why they settled for a lower amount when I said I was paying cash. The guy was just happy to get rid of the place and recoup some of his losses. Xavier told me to let him deal with it. He'd make sure I got my money back and then some. I honestly didn't care as long as I never had to see that house again.

Secondly, my parents had started blowing up my

phone. I hadn't answered and let my voicemail catch it, but I hadn't listened to any of the messages yet. I'd barely skimmed the first couple of transcripts of their voicemails, but honestly, they'd been the ones to turn their backs on me. The gist of the whole thing was, one of my parents heard from a friend who heard from a friend and so on, that I was famous or something and wanted to know what their friend had meant. No doubt they were seeing dollar signs. I hated jumping to negative conclusions about my parents, but I knew them too well to think anything else. I hadn't told Xavier about them calling because I had learned my man well enough to know that he'd go scorched earth if he found out they'd upset me. Which -- I couldn't lie -- I found sexy as fuck.

I'd kept to myself for the most part. A social butterfly I was not. But Xavier had brought me a new laptop, saying Knight had an extra one he wasn't using. I had my doubts, but the computer meant I could put my notes into some kind of loose outline for my next book. It had been at the house, and I still hadn't been back. There was really nothing I wanted there other than the laptop. I was big on saving everything to one cloud service or another in case I needed to work from somewhere other than my own computer, so it was easy to get set up and running. Once I'd gotten started, the words flowed better than they ever had.

Writing days like I'd had the last couple of weeks were the reason I'd wanted to write in the first place. I loved telling stories, but more than anything, I liked having control over my world. Sure, there were times the characters tried to bully me, but I'd simply put them aside and work with another set of characters. I might be a pushover in real life, but I was in control...

Right. So, maybe control was an illusion. Or maybe I was just that fucking crazy.

As I looked with satisfaction at my work today, I realized how at ease I was while I was writing. Had I ever truly been comfortable in my own home? The short answer was, not like this.

From my first full day in the compound, I'd been treated like a little sister by the men. The women all seemed really close. Well, the women who were old ladies. The club girls, or club whores, were a different story altogether. I could already tell they were going to test me, and I'd expected it. Kind of like the biker version of *Mean Girls*.

During our Saturdays together, Xavier had told me all about club life, including the territorial nature of club whores. He'd also assured me the men in Kiss of Death pampered their women, whether they were old ladies or not. He'd said they'd created monsters. Now the club girls were pushing back against the old ladies, demanding attention. He said the guys never let it go too far, and they always took the side of their old ladies, but they all kind of enjoyed the cat fights as long as no one got hurt. Pudding or Jell-O never hurt either.

But just as Xavier had promised, as long as I stayed in our apartment, the club girls left me alone. The only time anyone disturbed me was at lunch and when Xavier came home from whatever club business he was tasked with. At lunch, Hannah, Pippa, Violet, and Carrie brought me food. Sometimes a simple sandwich and chips, other times they'd bring burgers or hot dogs. Or pizza. They made me eat and talk with them for an hour, then let me get back to work. Violet said I needed the break and good, friendly human interaction. Always, the women were unfailingly kind.

All of them read my books and eagerly talked about what they'd read during our lunches. I loved every single one of them.

I'd just finished a chapter when the door opened and Xavier stepped inside. "Honey, I'm home!" It was his favorite thing to say when he stepped through the door. Without fail, he had a huge smile on his face. If I wasn't at my desk working or in the kitchen baking something, Xavier searched me out until he found me. If I'd pulled an all nighter and he found me in bed? Well. Those times had been great fun.

I stood and ran to Xavier. As always, he opened his arms and I jumped into them, wrapping my legs around his waist while I giggled and kissed him.

"Damn, baby." Xavier chuckled against my lips, his eyes alight with humor and more than a little desire. "Gonna have to insist you welcome me home like this every day."

"Maybe I should stop greeting you like this," I teased, nipping at his bottom lip. "You're getting spoiled."

"Don't you dare." He carried me to the couch and sat down with me still in his lap before leaning in and blowing a raspberry against my neck, making me squeal. Then he gave me a lingering kiss before sighing and sitting back against the couch. "How's the writing going?"

I beamed at him. "Really good. I finished another chapter today."

"That's my girl." He tucked a strand of hair behind my ear, his touch gentle despite his rough hands. "Knuckles wants to see us tonight."

I tensed slightly. "Both of us? Why?"

"Nothing bad," he assured me quickly. "He's got some news about your house situation, and he wants to talk about making you official."

"Official?"

Xavier's eyes grew serious. "My old lady. Wearing my patch. If you want that."

My heart skipped. "You mean like getting a property patch?"

"Yeah." His thumb traced my cheekbone. "But only if you're ready for that. No pressure."

Was I? I thought I might be. Xavier had proven to be telling the truth about club life and everything he'd told me about Kiss of Death. He also continued to show me care and positive attention. And the man was a sex god.

A slow smile spread across my lips as I considered his offer. "Yeah. I'm ready. You are the same man out of prison I got to know in prison. And I've been in love with you for quite some time, Xavier. I'm not even going to try to deny it." Xavier sucked in a sharp breath, but I continued before he could say anything. "You've shown me what it feels like to be loved. You may not be ready to admit it yet, but I know you love me. In whatever way. Platonically. Romantically. You love me. And I love you."

Xavier's eyes went dark and intense, his hands tightening on my waist. "Tillie," he said, his voice rough with emotion. "Baby, there ain't nothing platonic about what I feel for you." He cupped my face in his hands, his thumbs brushing across my cheeks. "I've been in love with you since that first Saturday you walked into that visiting room," he continued, his forehead resting against mine. "Scared the shit out of me because I knew I was gonna have to let you go at the end of every visit. But I couldn't tell you to stay away."

Tears pricked my eyes as his words washed over

me. "Xavier…"

"I love you, Tillie Girl. More than I ever thought I could love anything. You're everything good in this world and somehow you chose me." His voice cracked slightly. "I don't deserve you, but I'll spend every day trying to be worthy of you."

I kissed him then, pouring all my love into it, trying to show him what he meant to me. When we broke apart, we were both breathing hard.

"So that's a yes to the property patch?" he asked with a crooked grin.

"It's a yes to everything with you," I whispered against his lips. "Property patch, your old lady, whatever label you want to give me. I'm yours."

Xavier growled low in his throat. His hands slid down to grip my thighs where they straddled him. In one fluid motion, he stood, lifting me with him. I squealed and wrapped my arms tighter around his neck as he carried me toward the bedroom.

"Need you," he murmured, his beard tickling my neck as he pressed hot, open-mouthed kisses along my throat. "Right fucking now."

"Yes," I breathed, already tugging at his shirt, desperate to feel his skin against mine. "Please."

He kicked the bedroom door shut behind us and laid me down on the mattress with surprising gentleness for a man so clearly consumed with desire. His eyes burned into mine as he pulled his shirt over his head, revealing the tattooed expanse of his chest and abs that I still couldn't get enough of.

I reached for him, but he caught my wrists, pinning them gently above my head with one large hand. "My turn to play," he said, his voice a rough caress.

With my wrists pinned above my head, I felt a

delicious vulnerability wash over me. Xavier's weight pressed me into the mattress, his hard body a stark contrast to mine. The hunger in his eyes made my breath catch.

"Xavier," I whispered, arching up against him.

"Need to fuck you hard, baby," he growled, his free hand shoving my shirt over my breasts. I hadn't expected anyone after lunch, so I was in a simple T-shirt and panties with no bra. "Need to mark you, claim you. Need everyone in the Goddamned compound to know you belong to me."

Maybe it made me a freak or something, but I loved this caveman side of Xavier. Probably because I knew Xavier was solidly the caveman who would protect me with his life.

With increasingly quick and jerky movements, Xavier rid me of my panties and shirt before shoving his own jeans down his hips. "Tell me if it's too much," he commanded against my skin, his lips grazing the skin from my inner thigh up to my pussy.

"Oh, God! Do it, Xavier!" My plea was a breathy moan. "Eat my pussy!"

With a husky growl, Xavier shoved away from me, straightening as he finished removing his clothes. Then he gripped my hips and flipped me onto my belly with surprising strength, pulling my hips so I was on my knees before him.

"Gonna fuck you hard, Tillie. You promise me you'll stop me if I get too rough."

"I promise," I wailed. "I promise if you don't fuck me right now, I may castrate you in your fucking sleep!"

Xavier's dark chuckle sent shivers down my spine. "Such a dirty mouth on my sweet girl," he murmured, his hands skimming down my back.

"Gonna have to do something about that."

He positioned himself behind me, and I felt the blunt head of his cock pressing against my entrance. "Pain said my test came back clean, so I'm takin' you bare. You don't want that, say so now because I ain't pullin' out."

That was all I could take. Instead of answering, I lowered my chest to the bed and reached back to grip Xavier's buttocks and pulled me to him as I shoved myself backward onto his cock.

"Mother fuck!" Xavier bellowed as he tightened his grip on my hips until I was sure I'd have bruises. I loved every fucking second of it.

He held still for several seconds before he started to ride me hard, setting a punishing rhythm. "So tight, so perfect. So... *mine.*"

"Yes!" I gasped, pushing back against him, meeting each thrust. "Yours, Xavier. Only yours. Always!"

The sound of skin slapping against skin filled the room, punctuated by our moans and cries and screams. Xavier's pace was relentless, and I reveled in the raw possession of it all.

"That's it, baby," he panted, one hand sliding up my spine to tangle in my hair. "Take everything I give you."

I could feel myself spiraling toward the edge, every nerve ending on fire. When his hand snaked around to find my clit, I screamed his name, my body convulsing around him as I came harder than I ever had before. Xavier followed me over the edge with a roar of his own. His cum was hot inside me. Some of the warm, sticky fluid trickled down my inner thigh as I overflowed. Still, Xavier held himself as deep inside me as he could before falling forward on top of me, pinning me to the bed beneath him.

I welcomed his heavy weight. His cock still throbbed inside me, not showing signs of going to sleep any time soon. Sweat coated us both.

With a groan, Xavier shifted so his body was no longer on top of mine. Instead, he wrapped his arms around me and held me close to him, my back to his chest. The occasional jump of his dick made little zings of pleasure flutter through me.

"Holy shit," he breathed out. "Holy. Shit." He was as winded as I was. I had to smile.

I couldn't help the giggle that escaped me as I felt Xavier's warm breath against my neck.

"What's so funny?" he murmured, nuzzling against my hair. He didn't sound put out, merely curious. If I knew Xave, he wanted to share in the merriment. He played as hard as he worked. And I loved playing with my gruff biker.

"Nothing. Just happy." I sighed contentedly, pressing back against him. "I never thought I'd have this."

His arms tightened around me. "This?"

"Safety. Happiness." I twisted in his arms to face him. "Love."

Xavier's eyes softened as he traced my cheek with his thumb. "You've got all of that and more, baby. Forever."

We lay there in comfortable silence, our breathing synchronizing as we basked in the afterglow. Eventually, Xavier pressed a kiss to my forehead.

"We should probably get cleaned up. Meeting with Knuckles is in an hour."

I groaned, reluctant to leave our cocoon. "Do we have to?"

"Afraid so. Man doesn't like to be kept waiting."

He grinned, dropping a quick kiss on my lips before sliding out of bed. "Come on. We can shower together."

I grinned. "Sounds perfect."

Knuckles would just have to get over it, because I had the feeling we were going to be late to that meeting.

Chapter Eleven
Xavier

"Good thing I'm a patient man." Knuckles lounged behind his desk, one booted foot propped on the edge. "I told you an hour and a half ago the meeting was in an hour. There a good Goddamned reason you kept me here half an hour before you decided to show up?"

I grinned. "Yep."

Knuckles grunted, nodding at Tillie, who held firmly to my hand as we walked into the other man's office. "Probably has something to do with that sweet girl you corrupted after you went to prison, so I guess I can't really fault you." Knuckles pointed at Tillie. "Family first, honey. He tries to put the club first, you come talk to me. I'll kick his ass."

Tillie sniffed before clearing her throat. "I swear to God, Knuckles, if you make me cry I will put hair remover in your beard oil."

My president sat up straight, a look of horror on his face. "Now, look here, little miss. No messin' with the beard. That's a step too far."

Tillie laughed so hard she was crying, and Knuckles gave me a wary look. "Don't you let her mess with my beard oil, Xavier. I didn't make her cry. That's all on her."

I chuckled, pulling Tillie closer to my side. "Can't make any promises, boss. Woman's got a mind of her own."

"That's what I'm afraid of," Knuckles muttered, but his eyes were warm with affection when he winked at Tillie and grinned. "All right, let's get down to business. First things first. Your property situation."

He pulled out a thick manila folder and dropped

it on his desk. "Got some good news and some better news. Which you want first?"

Tillie squeezed my hand. "Good news?"

"Menendez cartel won't be bothering you anymore. Ever." Knuckles' expression turned cold and deadly. "Let's just say they got the message loud and clear that you're under our protection. And they know we are the muscle for the Miles family."

I felt Tillie tense beside me, but she didn't ask for details. Smart woman. Knuckles seemed to be studying her reaction but said nothing.

"And the better news?" I prompted.

Knuckles didn't take his gaze from Tillie's. Instead, he started a line of questioning I wasn't really comfortable with.

"Tillie, do you know the Miles family?"

"Not personally." Tillie looked extremely uncomfortable, but not like she was going to balk.

"Wouldn't expect you to know them personally, honey. You know who the Miles family is, though. Right?"

She took a deep breath, then met Knuckles' gaze with a direct one of her own. "I know they have mafia ties. Other than that, not much. They've been in the news some."

"Yeah. They try to keep a low profile, but it's hard not to get noticed." He took a breath and let it out slowly, waiting patiently. I knew he wanted Tillie to ask questions, but she looked like she was at a loss.

"Knuckles. Just say what you need to." I wasn't going to let my president make Tillie uncomfortable when there wasn't a reason. "She's not gonna faint if you tell her the truth."

Tillie surprised me by addressing Knuckles. "Look. I don't have a problem with what you do. If all of you are like Xavier, I know you're not shaking down mom-and-pop shops for protection money or some shit. That's not who Xavier is. He wouldn't stand for anyone else doing it." Knuckles' lips twitched but he held his expression blank. "Having said that, I know you're not always on the right side of the law. And I know you kill when you have to."

Knuckles shrugged. "Or when someone needs it."

"Exactly!" Tillie's smile was genuine as she continued. "I'm sure every single one of you has a mean streak in you, but you're not the kind of men who'd beat up on people weaker than you are."

"I like this girl, Xavier. Wasn't sure about her at first. Seemed a little too gentle for this place, but she's got fire." The big oaf grinned. At my woman.

"You got your own old lady, asshole. Don't grin at mine."

"Wouldn't think of it. And you're a jealous prick for thinkin' I would."

"Damn straight I'm a jealous prick!" I draped an arm around Tillie and pulled her closer. "Mine."

"Why not just pee on her and be done with it?" The voice wasn't one I recognized. Instinctively I turned, sweeping Tillie behind me to keep myself between her and danger. "Knuckles." He addressed our president instead of me, which was just as good.

"Antonio." Knuckles stood and took the hand Antonio offered. "Thank you for coming on short notice."

"Kiss of Death has made my life easier since our collaboration began. And, to be honest, if we work something out here it's going to benefit me much more than her."

"What does that mean?" I could feel my hackles

rising. "Who are you talking about?"

Antonio turned his attention to me. "Antonio Miles." He held out his hand. I didn't immediately take it, but Antonio didn't drop his hand yet. "Xavier, I presume?"

"That's my name."

"I'm here to help Ms. St. Martin with a piece of property, which includes a house she might wish to liquidate." Antonio didn't seem impatient and still stood there with his hand out, like he knew he had to let me have time to make up my mind.

I thought about telling the bastard to fuck himself, but that was the green-eyed monster inside me I hadn't realized existed. I took his hand in a firm grip. "Sorry. I'm a bit rough around the edges."

"No apology necessary. Might I speak to your woman?" The bastard had to be all polite and shit. Didn't change my answer.

"Not alone. You want to talk to her, you do it here." My tolerance only went so far.

Antonio grinned. "Of course. Ms. Matilda St. Martin?"

"Tillie," she said.

"Tillie, then. Please call me Tonio."

"Why would you want to speak to me?" I felt Tillie curl her fingers into the waist of my pants.

"Because you have a house I'm fairly certain you'd like to never see again. I'm willing to pay you a fair price for that little farm."

"You realize that place isn't safe. Right?"

Antonio smiled at her. "Of course, you'd warn me. But yes. I'm fully aware of everything going on there. So, my question to you is, would you be willing to sell the property to me?"

"Not that I'm not grateful or anything, but why

would you want that place? I don't know you, but you seem nice. I don't want anyone getting hurt."

I had to bite back a growl when Antonio Miles grinned at my woman. "Sweetheart, the very last person you need to worry about is me. I promise you I am fully aware of everything and will take all necessary precautions."

Tillie seemed to consider Antonio for a long moment. I expected she'd ask why he wanted her land but when she spoke, that's not what she said. "I paid cash for the place, so the guy who sold it to me came down on the price so I could afford it. I don't think it's right for me to ask for the market value when I didn't pay that for it. I mean, you're doing me a favor. Not the other way around."

"There's where you're wrong." Antonio sat in a chair on the other side of Knuckles' desk and spoke to Tillie. He wasn't mean. In fact, he seemed amused. Not in an obnoxious way or anything, but like he found it cute Tillie was concerned she was ripping him off. "I can't get into specifics, but by purchasing your farm from you without an agent, and since I'd have control over your end of the paperwork as well as my own, I have a unique opportunity to obtain a property with the most prolific narcotic highway in the country. The one maintained road that's not on a map. I can control the paper trail and everything official in the sale, then I'll be in a better position to control the flow of narcotics from Mexico all the way to the Great Lakes."

Tillie groaned. "Why did you tell me that? Now I know!"

"You do?" Antonio's amusement was really grating on my nerves. I hated the guy on principle because he was rich, good-looking, and could give Tillie everything I couldn't. I never thought I was insecure, but it seemed like I was finding out more about myself than I ever cared to know. "What exactly do you know?"

"I don't know! Just…" Tillie took a deep breath and closed her eyes before exhaling and flashing Antonio a bright smile. "Nothing. Nothing at all."

"Relax, Tillie. I'm a hardass and I'm not a good person, but I don't threaten or intimidate women for any reason. You're here with Xavier and Knuckles." He indicated our joined hands and the property cut Knuckles had tossed to me while Antonio spoke to Tillie. "You're Xavier's woman, so you know no one here is completely legit and they do things sometimes not accepted in polite society."

"Don't we all." God, Tillie's musical laughter warmed my soul in ways I never thought possible. "Honestly, I don't care. But I don't want you mad at me if something goes wrong."

"Absolutely not!"

"No fuckin' way."

"Ms. St. Martin, I can assure you something like that will never happen." Antonio looked genuinely incensed. "I never do anything without all the information available and, honestly, I'd suspect just about anyone here before I'd suspect you."

"What? You don't know me. How can you say that?"

"Honey, I'm the one who got Xavier out of prison on a moment's notice. Knuckles and his club work for me. I take care of my own. So when I got the call, I looked into you. You wouldn't betray me. It's just not who you are."

"You got Xavier out of prison?"

"Yes. He went in because of me in the first place. I don't send my people in someplace without making sure I can get them out quickly. Sure, it still took a few hours, but I put the extraction plan in motion the second I got off the phone with Knuckles."

"Then, acceptable risk and a backup?"

"See? You understand. I'm a predator, Tillie. Make no mistake. But I don't hurt my family for my own gain. I expect their loyalty, but I give them mine in return."

"You know what? Who am I to judge? My life looked ideal, but it was a nightmare. Every single person in my life failed me in more ways than I thought possible. Xavier was the only person to help me. Whatever you guys do, I don't care. I'm pretty sure you're better people than anyone else I know."

"Thank you, Tillie." Antonio sat back in his chair. "In my research, I also found the amount you paid for your property. I'm telling you that so you'll know I am fully aware of what you have in the place. I'll have my lawyer draw up the necessary paperwork for you to sign in a few days, along with a check. I'm giving you double the amount you paid for it, plus a little extra."

"What? No! You shouldn't to do that."

"I never do anything I don't want to do, honey. Trust me. I could pay you three times that amount and still have the better deal." He shrugged. "Might do that anyway." He winked at Tillie. "Just 'cause you're too cute." He chuckled. "Worried I didn't know the place was dangerous. That was adorable."

Tillie leaned into me, clutching my arm. "Something's wrong with him. I don't think he's all right," she whispered. "You know. Upstairs."

"He's fine." I tried hard to scowl at Antonio, the bastard, but it was hard because honestly, it *was* kind of cute. My little Tillie was worried about the man who was probably the biggest crime lord in the region not understanding the place was dangerous. It really was a funny notion.

"Are you sure you want to buy that place?"

"Yes, Tillie. I promise."

"I can't say I'm not relieved. I didn't really care about the money, but I'm glad I'm not going to lose it."

"I'll be in touch with Knuckles. We'll set up a time for you to sign the paperwork."

Antonio stood, and everyone but Knuckles followed suit. Antonio held out his hand to Tillie, who took it without hesitation. "Thank you, Tillie." As he walked to the door, Antonio turned back. "Oh. You might want to expect a call from your parents."

"Crap. That was your fault?" Tillie put her hands on her hips and glared at Antonio.

"Wait, what?" I looked from Tillie to Antonio. "What do you mean his fault?"

"They've been blowing up my phone, Xavier. I haven't talked to them. I'm not really sure I want to." She wrinkled her nose delicately. "What did you tell them anyway? They've been going on about me being famous or something. I'm not famous."

"Apparently one of your mother's friends is a fan. I only know because I hacked into your mom's phone's cloud service and found all sorts of things she probably didn't want me to know. Your dad too."

"See? I told you he wasn't all right, Xavier. I think he's crazy."

"Like a fox." Antonio grinned before walking out the door.

"Why didn't you tell me your parents had been harassing you?"

"Out of everything he just said, that's your takeaway?"

"Tillie."

"I can deal with my parents. I let them push me around for a long time, but now that I know what a real family is supposed to be like, they don't intimidate me anymore. I also find it difficult to believe they ever loved me. Or my brother."

"Doesn't matter," Knuckles said, sticking his chin out stubbornly. "You've got all of us now. We'll look out for you."

"I really am grateful to you guys. For everything."

"That's what family does." Knuckles' expression grew serious then. "When Antonio mentioned your parents, you looked like you swallowed a lemon. They gonna be a problem for you?"

"No. They just want to see if they can get more money out of me."

"Right," I muttered. "Ain't happenin'."

"I don't want to talk about them right now." Where before Tillie had been almost carefree, this meeting had seriously dampened her mood. I could see it in the set of her mouth. She was stressing, and I didn't like it.

"Come on." I took her hand and headed out of Knuckles' office. "We'll catch up with you later, Prez." I threw my hand up at Knuckles as I led Tillie out of the room.

"Where we going?"

I didn't look at her as I guided her through the building to the outside. "To put a smile back on your face."

A couple hours and several orgasms later, I'd definitely put the smile back on my precious Tillie's face.

Chapter Twelve

Tillie

"Not again."

My phone rang practically nonstop for the next several days. I'd debated blocking their number, but couldn't quite make myself do it.

"If this doesn't stop, I'm going to deal with it." Xavier was as easygoing as they came. Until someone fucked with me. While I had no desire for my parents to be hurt or anything, it was sexy as fuck to know this man had my back in everything.

"Honestly, it's as much my fault as it is theirs. If I'd talk to them, they'd stop calling."

"Want me to talk to them? Because I'd love to."

If we both lived to be a hundred, I'd never tire of this man's unwavering loyalty. "I appreciate the offer more than you could ever know, but I'll handle them." My phone started ringing again. "Just not right now."

I powered down my phone with a grimace and tossed it onto the couch. "Maybe tomorrow."

Xavier's expression darkened as he watched me. "You don't owe them a damn thing, Tillie. Not your time, not an explanation. Nothing."

"I know." I sighed, running a hand through my hair. "But they're still my parents. As awful as they are, there's this stupid part of me that keeps hoping they'll change. Or that they'd at least accept me for who I am. Not what I can do for them."

Xavier crossed the room and pulled me against his chest, his arms a fortress around me. "That ain't stupid, baby. That's just you being who you are. You're someone who's been through hell and back and still made a new life for herself."

"I never could have done it without you, you

know," I confessed softly, smiling up at him. "Best therapy ever." I melted into his embrace, drawing strength from his solid presence. "When did you get so wise?"

"Prison gives a man time to think." His chuckle rumbled through his chest against my cheek. "That, and watching you every Saturday, learning who you are."

I smiled against his chest, breathing in his familiar scent of leather, soap, and something uniquely Xavier. "I'm not sure I'll ever get used to that."

"To what?" His fingers traced lazy patterns along my spine.

"That you chose to stay in prison longer just to get to know me better." I pulled back to look at his face. "It's the most romantic, terrifying thing anyone's ever done for me."

"Romantic, huh?" His eyes crinkled at the corners. "That's what the kids are calling it these days?"

I swatted his arm playfully. "You know what I mean."

"Yeah." I love the rasp of his words in that lazy drawl he had going on sometimes. "I know. Just don't use the R word in front of my brothers, OK? They'll get all pissy if I outdo them."

I let it go another week before I decided on a course of action. There was no way around talking to them, so I was going to have to bite the bullet and get it over with. But, dammit, it was so fucking hard!

"Honey, I'm home!" Christ, that man! Xavier could put a smile on my face under the worst of circumstances.

Like I knew he loved, I ran to him and jumped into his arms. "I missed you!"

"Missed you too, honey. You busy this afternoon?"

"Not really. I think I'm actually done for the day."

"Good. I've got to go talk to someone and thought you might like to come with me." He winked at me. "We'll take the bike. Chicks dig the bike."

I couldn't help but laugh. "Yeah, I can't argue with that. You know I always jump at the chance to go riding with you."

"Good. Grab your helmet and come on."

Ten minutes later we were rolling down the interstate. Two of the guys from the club rode in front of us, two in back, putting us safely in the middle. I had no idea where we were going and didn't particularly care. The only things that mattered were the bike, the guys surrounding us in a bubble of protection, and the man I had my arms wrapped around.

I wasn't sure how far we went. Not far enough as far as I was concerned. I was too busy looking at the scenery to worry about our destination. We pulled off the interstate and into an older section of Nashville to a strip mall with a nightclub and a couple of restaurants in a huge parking lot. The place looked like it had been abandoned for several years. The windows in every building other than the nightclub were dusty and grungy. A couple had the windows broken. The nightclub looked as seedy as they came.

There seemed to be only one other car in the lot, and we were driving toward it. The closer we got, the more sickeningly familiar the vehicle became.

We rolled to a stop in front of the Cadillac SUV. Dad always had to have a new vehicle every year, so he leased. The guys revved the engines a couple times before everyone shut down.

Xavier helped me off his bike and turned me to face him. Putting his hands on my shoulders he gave me an encouraging look. "I'm sorry, but I didn't want you stressing over this. I'm here to support you while you do this. So are the rest of the guys."

"I should be mad at you, but I can't be." I smiled up at him and Xavier leaned in to kiss me.

"You got this, baby. I'll be with you the whole time."

"I'm not afraid of them, Xavier. They're not going to hurt me."

"Lots of ways of hurtin' someone. Words are sometimes as bad as blows."

"Matilda!" I winced as my mother called out to me from their vehicle. "Matilda, come here, please."

I took a breath, popping my neck before putting my shoulders back. "I got this." My muttered pep talk wasn't much, but I wasn't as nervous as I thought I would be. Like, maybe I'd built this up to be worse than it had to be.

As I walked between Oktober and Chains to my waiting parents, Xavier took my hand and squeezed. When I looked up at him, he winked at me and I smiled. I was so in love with this man it wasn't even funny.

Mom's face was a carefully composed mask of polite concern, but I could see the flicker of disgust in her eyes as she took in my companions. Dad stood ramrod straight beside the Cadillac, his fingers drumming impatiently against the door.

"What on earth are you wearing?" Mom hissed as I approached, eyeing my leather vest.

"Oh, you haven't gotten to the good part of my outfit yet." I smiled and turned around where Xavier's property patch was prominently displayed. When I faced her again, I kept my smile firmly in place as I made introductions. "This is Xavier. These are my parents, Richard and Eleanor Dyson."

Xavier nodded once, his hand still firmly clasped in mine. "Ma'am. Sir."

Dad's gaze swept over Xavier, taking in his tattooed neck, his cut, his entire presence, before dismissing him entirely. "We've been trying to reach you for weeks, Matilda. You shouldn't worry your mother."

"Wait a minute." My mother's eyes had grown wide, and her mouth was now open in a silent "O" of shock. "Oh. My. God! That's the man who killed poor Paul! Richard! Push the OnStar button! Call 911!" My mother was actually fanning herself. I'd have felt sorry for her except I knew she wasn't outraged on my behalf. She was angry at Xavier for taking away her ticket to a life of luxury. That's all my parents ever cared about in life. Money.

"We weren't notified you were out of prison." My father was still behind the driver's-side door. I had no doubt he'd already called the police, and I had the urge to leave. No one had done anything, but a group of ex-cons intimidating an older rich couple wouldn't work out well for anyone in my party.

"Why would you be?" I asked, trying to get control of the situation before it spiraled. "You weren't related to him or Paul."

"Paul was like a son to us." My mother dabbed at her eyes. "And this... this... *animal* took him away from us!"

"This animal picked me up on the side of the road in the middle of the worst storm I'd ever seen. I was covered from head to toe in bruises, my clothes ripped and bloodstained. He didn't ask questions, he simply offered me a ride. When he finally coaxed me into confiding in him, he made it so Paul would never hurt me again." Memories swamped me. Reliving my nightmare was almost more painful than going through it the first time. I had a visceral reaction to the trauma, breaking out in a sweat. I had to fight to keep my knees from buckling, but I stayed on my feet. "You scoffed at me. Told me to quit being a drama queen."

"Matilda, really," Mom huffed, crossing her arms. "Paul was under a lot of stress with his company merger. You were always so sensitive, needing all his attention."

Xavier's hand tightened around mine, but he remained silent, letting me fight my own battle. I appreciated that more than he could know.

"I called you from the emergency room with three broken ribs and a fractured cheekbone," I said, my voice flat. "You hung up on me and told Dad I was causing trouble and that if I didn't stop, Paul was sure to divorce me and that would mean you'd be cut off from the monthly allowance he gave you."

My father cleared his throat, glancing around the parking lot as if searching for witnesses. "We should discuss this in private, Matilda. Not in front of... these people."

"These people," I said, gesturing to the bikers surrounding us, "are my family. The only real family I've ever had."

"This is outrageous," my father muttered. "Get in the car, Matilda. We'll talk about everything when we get home."

I decided to change tactics because I was so done with this. "So, you've been trying to get hold of me for weeks." I held my arms out to the side. "Well? Here I am. What's going on?"

"When we get home, Matilda." My mother's face was a mask of disapproval I'd grown very familiar with over my lifetime.

I shrugged. "Suit yourself." I turned to go, knowing Xavier would follow me.

"Wait!" Mother called out to me, actually grabbing my arm to prevent me from leaving. "Come home with us."

"Sorry. Not where I want to be. Either talk or I'm leaving. It's that simple."

"Fine," my mother bit out between clenched teeth, her anger showing when I'd bet everything I owned she didn't intend to wear her emotions so close to the surface. "I heard you're a famous writer. I wanted to congratulate you."

"I'm not famous." Much as I wanted my parents to acknowledge my abilities and talents, I also didn't want to hear the next phase of the conversation. Because this was the part where they asked me for money.

"That's not what Beulah told me. She said you won an award or something."

"No awards."

"She said you wrote a bestseller." My mother actually smiled at me and made a little effort to look impressed -- when I knew how she felt about my chosen genre!

"I've had some luck."

"You must do well for yourself. I heard you bought a place, though I thought it was in Indiana."

"It is." This was painful in more ways than one. I wasn't leading them into what they were truly getting at, and my mother was trying every way in the world to force me into asking her what she wanted. Nope. I might not have been in control of my life all the time, but I was in control now.

When the silence stretched on, my father was the one to finally break character. "Oh, for heaven's sake," he snapped. "We need the rest of the money you got from Paul's estate. Since you're a huge success, you don't need that money."

"I'm sorry, but you guys got everything. All I had was some cash I'd managed to get out of my bank accounts before you had them all frozen. Including my personal account." I wanted to be mad, but really what was the point? They weren't going to change. I couldn't live with them any longer.

"That was payment for you living with us after Paul was murdered. That way you didn't have to work while you were dealing with the murder and then the trial." She glanced at Xavier and shuddered in disgust. "I'll never understand why you took this beast's side over a good man like Paul St. Martin."

I hit my limit. "Mother. Father. I'm really sorry you made this trip for nothing, but I can't help you. Please be careful on your way home. Do not call me again."

Maybe I should feel ashamed to have been mean to my parents. I wasn't a fan of speaking to my elders like I had, but I'd toned it down considerably from what I wanted to say. Instead, I snagged my helmet where I'd set it down and shoved it on my head. I didn't wait for Xavier, simply climbed on the bike and waited for him to follow.

My parents called out to me several times, but I ignored them. When our little convoy started back down the interstate, I felt like I was leaving a huge albatross behind me in our wake.

I knew life wouldn't automatically be perfect,

though I thought it was pretty damned perfect at the moment, but I now had people who cared about me. Their love was genuine and not dependent on something I could do for them. And the most amazing love of the bunch was the love I got from Xavier. Time would tell how strong our connection was, but I knew what we had was real. Because I'd experienced fake. What we had together was the real thing. And it shone brightly.

When we got home, Xavier snagged my hand and hurried with me to our apartment. The second the door was shut he was kissing me. I sighed and surrendered to him.

His hands moved urgently across my body as he stripped away my clothes with practiced ease. My fingers fumbled with his belt, desperate to feel his skin against mine. We stumbled toward the bedroom, leaving a trail of discarded clothing in our wake.

"You were amazing today," Xavier murmured against my neck, his beard creating delicious friction against my sensitive skin. "So fucking proud of you."

I gasped as he lifted me, my legs automatically wrapping around his waist. "I couldn't have done it without you there."

"Yes, you could've," he growled, pressing me against the wall. "You might not have been able to when I first met you. That Tillie was beaten down, but she was still in the fight. Then you healed. Inside and out." He kissed me hard then, swept his tongue inside my mouth in a show of dominance. "You're strong and resilient, but none of that matters now because I'm with you now. I'll always protect you."

His mouth captured mine again in a hungry kiss that left me breathless. His cock was hard against my belly, ready and wanting. When he tucked his cock against my entrance, I tensed, the anticipation sweet even though I was impatient. He entered me with one powerful thrust and I cried out, my head falling back against the wall.

"Fuck, Tillie," he groaned, his hands gripping my thighs as he held me in place. "Need you so much. Never fuckin' get enough."

Every thrust drove me higher, the intensity of his possession matching the emotional high of finally standing up to my parents. I clutched at his shoulders, my nails digging into his skin as pleasure built inside me in a delicious rush.

"Xave!" His name escaped my lips as a desperate cry, my body trembling on the edge of release. Every thrust pushed me higher, the pressure building until I could barely breathe.

"That's it, baby," he growled, his rhythm never faltering. "Come for me. Let me feel you squeezin' my cock."

My clit found the friction I needed against his abdomen, the perfect amount of pressure, and I shattered. My orgasm crashed through me in waves of pleasure so intense I saw stars. I clung to him, my pussy convulsing around his cock as I screamed his name.

Xavier's thrusts became more urgent, his breathing ragged against my neck. "Fuck, Tillie… fuck… mine," he panted, his hands gripping my ass hard enough to bruise as he drove into me.

With a final, powerful thrust, he buried himself deep and came with a guttural roar that reverberated through his chest. I felt the hot pulse of him inside me, claiming me in the most primal way.

For several long moments, we stayed locked together against the wall, our breathing slowly returning to normal. Xavier's forehead rested against mine, his eyes closed as we savored the moment together.

"You are so beautiful," he whispered, gently carrying me to our bed. He laid me down with surprising tenderness for a man who had just taken me so thoroughly against the wall.

As we curled together, my head on his chest, I felt a peace I'd only ever found in this man's arms. The steady rhythm of his heartbeat beneath my ear was the most comforting sound in the world.

"I love you, Xavier," I murmured, tracing one of his tattoos with my fingertip.

"Love you more, Tillie Girl." His hand stroked my hair, his touch gentle and possessive at the same time. "Always love you."

We lay in comfortable silence for several minutes, our bodies cooling as the afternoon breeze wafted through the open windows. Outside, I could hear the distant rumble of motorcycles, the occasional burst of laughter from the compound. Sounds that had become home to me.

"You know what's funny?" I said, propping myself up on one elbow to look at him.

"What's that?" His eyes were soft as they met mine, his expression unguarded in a way I only ever saw when we were alone.

"A year ago, if someone had told me I'd be here in this place with you, and that it would be the happiest I'd ever been in my life, I'd have called them a Goddamned liar."

Xavier's laugh rumbled through his chest. "And I'd have agreed with you. But sometimes the best stories have the most unexpected endings."

I traced the tattoo over his heart -- the one he'd

gotten last week with my name intertwined with his in an intricate design. "Not an ending," I corrected him. "A beginning."

A beginning. I had a feeling this time I'd get the life I'd always wanted. Hell, I had it already.

Pain (Kiss of Death MC 6)
A Bones MC Romance
Marteeka Karland

Redemption doesn't come free. And sometimes, the price is paid in blood.

Pain -- When I walked out of Terre Haute Prison, I wasn't the same man who went in. I've got blood on my hands, but I'm determined to pay my debt and take back what's left of my life. Once I'm home, inside the walls of the motorcycle club that welcomed me when I had no one, I have more hope than I dared to have the whole time I was incarcerated. Problem is, the past doesn't stay buried. When I recognized Nadine, a young woman from my past, and got to know the woman she'd become, I'd convinced myself there's no way to be worthy of a woman like her. Until she's put squarely in the crosshairs of a situation she knows nothing about. That's when it's time to earn my road name and bring her enemies a world of hurt.

Nadine -- I know better than to fall for an ex-con. I've seen the worst of humanity from inside prison walls where I work as a nurse. But something about Dr. Raven, or Pain, as they call him, gets under my skin. There was a time when he was my hero, the person I wanted to be most like. I admit I might have a huge case of hero worship and the tiniest little crush on him. I don't know the rules in his world outside the prison, but I know I need to learn fast. Especially since corrupt cops seem to be hell-bent on cutting in on the Kiss of Death territory. It sometimes feels like

I'm fighting just to breathe. But the scariest part? It's not the blood, the bullets, or the bodies. It's that I might actually be falling in love with Ford "Pain" Raven.

A gritty, steamy romance featuring a protective alpha, a fierce heroine who refuses to break, and the family you choose when the world tries to tear you apart.

Chapter One

Nadine
One Year Ago...

There were days when I seriously had to wonder what the fuck I was thinking taking a nursing job in a maximum security prison. The routine for getting in and out was about what I expected. Tight. Every door had a card swipe and a keypad to enter a code. The guards were armed and plentiful, and in some cases, just as bad as the men they kept incarcerated. I wasn't naive enough to think anyone in this place deserved anything less than what they got from both the government and the guards, but it was the whole power trip thing that left me with a bad taste in my mouth.

As I entered the infirmary, the heavy metal door clanged shut behind me, sealing off the outside world. I took a deep breath, inhaling the familiar scent of disinfectant and despair that permeated the air. My footsteps echoed throughout the mostly empty ward. Nodding at the guards assigned in my area today, I gave them bright smiles.

"Morning, Nadine." Officer Grayson, his bulky frame filling the doorway, gave me the creeps. He had since the first day I'd met him. He hadn't done or said anything overt, it was just a vibe I got. Needless to say, I tried to keep to myself as much as possible.

"Morning," I replied, slipping past him. The fluorescent lights flicked a couple of times before settling into their typical, harsh, unforgiving aura. Just another day at the office.

I set my backpack underneath my desk and got

to work. I wasn't the provider in this little clinic, but as the on-duty nurse, the ward was my responsibility. The night shift had either been relatively light or else someone got froggy and stocked and cleaned. I grinned. Had to be Lisa. She was always doing the little extras to make everyone's life easier.

"Ready for battle?" Dr. Martinez breezed in. Of all the doctors I worked with here, she was by far my favorite. The petite Latina was in her early forties and a force to be reckoned with when she had to be. I couldn't say the men she treated in here on occasion actually respected her, but they were well aware she held the keys to the medicine cabinet and the only way they had of getting anything from the clinic was to make nice with Dr Martinez.

I flashed a wry smile. "As I'll ever be."

Today was supposed to be mostly physical exams and initial assessments of new inmates. I hated new inmate days because these were men I wasn't familiar with. Granted, there was always an inmate I didn't know -- there were thousands of men here -- but I didn't have to be up close and personal with most of them. There were always multiple guards to make sure nothing got out of control.

The day shift medical staff usually tried to come in a couple hours early to prepare. I liked the solitude in the mornings before I started my day. New inmate days were the exception. Everyone was here early in an effort to make sure everything went as quickly and smoothly as possible.

One thing I'd learned since I started working here was that nothing was what it seemed. Every inmate had a story, and they were never pretty. The sweetest little papaw ever had most likely killed, and done it without remorse.

Kind of like the older man sitting on the exam table in front of me.

"How's the arthritis today, Mr. North?" I gave the elderly crime lord what I hoped was a kind yet professional smile. According to his file, Mr. Nicholas 'The Judge' North was head of a West Coast crime syndicate. He had killed more than the three people he'd been convicted of killing, some of them after he'd been put in prison. So yes. Always be nice to the elderly crime lord.

"Same as always, ma'am. Like someone's taking a sledgehammer to my back." Mr. North winced and shifted so he braced a hand on his lower back, like he was working the kinks out. That was something else. Every inmate without exception always addressed me as ma'am. It wasn't because there was any real professional relationship. Not in the least. Every prisoner here knew they were more likely to get what they wanted if they were simply nice about it. If they weren't belligerent, and kept their hands and bodily fluids to themselves, the staff was more cooperative to their wants. Also, every single one of them, without exception, would stab you in the kidney if they thought it would benefit them or in any way make life on the inside more comfortable.

I nodded sympathetically, making a note in his chart. "I'll mention your pain to Dr. Martinez. They had you on some pretty powerful painkillers at your last facility."

He shrugged. "Guess so. They barely touch the pain most days." He waved off my concern, tuning me out now that he knew for certain I wasn't the one who could get his dose increased. Or guarantee Dr. Martinez would keep him on the same medicine at all.

That's pretty much how the rest of the morning

went. I tried to always be respectful of the prisoners, addressing them by their last names, being courteous without being friendly. No matter how sweet the little old men were, or how charming some of the younger men were, they were predators. Every one of them. They weren't my friends and didn't want to be, except where it benefited them. There was a reason the inmates were never allowed outside their cells or general population areas without a minimum of two guards. Some of them, depending on how far they were being moved, required four guards. I'd seen more than one staff member let their guard down at the wrong moment and it never ended well.

It didn't take the day long to get busy. My height made some inmates think they could intimidate me, but I'd learned to ignore their remarks and never get in their personal space unless they were restrained. My only goal was to make it out of this place in one piece. Every. Single. Day.

I'd thought about quitting more than once, but despite the obvious issues I actually loved my job. Corny as it sounded, I became a nurse to make a difference in people's lives. I wished I could say I chose the population I thought was the most underserved or that no one wanted to serve, but the fact was, I had student loan debt and a federal job paid damned good, and the benefits were top of the line. While I doubted I'd make it the twenty years I'd need to retire, the job had grown on me.

I leaned against a counter, stretching my tight muscles in an effort to work out the stiffness. There was a mountain of work left yet, but it was time for a break.

"You okay?" Dr. Martinez asked, concern etching her features.

I nodded, straightening. "Just tired. Nothing a cup of coffee and a hot lunch won't fix."

"I hear you there." She squeezed my shoulder as she passed. "Want me to bring you a burger from the café?"

"God, yes." I laughed as I pulled out a couple of bills from my name badge holder.

Dr. Martinez stayed my hand. "Nope. I've got it. You paid last time and I'm not a freeloader." We shared a laugh as she walked out the door and I went to my desk to work on my charting.

My computer dinged with a new email. As expected, it was the new transfer list. One thing I could say about management here was they ran the place like a well-oiled machine. Considering the innate chaos of the place, I thought it was commendable and likely the result of sheer stubbornness.

I liked to look over the files before we saw the new inmates so I knew what kinds of unique medical issues to expect. There were always the usual things -- congestive heart failure, diabetes, hypertension -- but occasionally I'd run into something like sickle cell anemia or different types of cancer.

"Anything interesting?" I turned as Dr. Martinez entered with our meal. She nodded at my computer. "It's time for the incoming inmate list. Right?"

"Yes." I grinned as I stood, taking my food from her and handing her a drink from the mini fridge on my desk. "I just pulled it up. Haven't had a chance to look yet. Thought I'd try to catch up while I ate."

"Good idea. Give me the rundown when you're done, if you don't mind. I'm not sure I'm up to studying today."

"You still having a rough time of it?"

Dr. Martinez rubbed her slightly protruding

belly. The baby bump had become more prominent the last couple of months. "It's not so bad. I'm forty-two years old. I didn't expect having my first child at this age was going to be easy."

"Go sit in your office for a while. I'll get you if you're needed. Take a long lunch."

"I really want to tell you I appreciate the offer, but I'll be fine. Instead, I'm simply going to say a grateful thank-you, and really hope your offer wasn't just lip service."

I reached for the other woman and gave her a quick hug. "Not lip service. Go take care of little Didi."

"I'm not calling my kid Didi, Nadine."

I shrugged. "I mean, you could just call her Nadine. I can keep it simple."

Dr. Martinez snorted with laughter. "Yeah. Just for that, I might take two lunches." She closed the door to her office and I went back to work still smiling. Fine. Time to get this over with.

I opened the first one, skimming over the actual case file but doing a more thorough examination of the medical file. There were six files in this batch and nothing interesting. Until I came to the last file.

"Ford Raven?" No way. He belonged to an MC called Kiss of Death and he had the nickname of Pain, according to the summary heading. But, honestly, how many Ford Ravens could there be? I backed away from my computer, needing to read on but not wanting to. Dr. Ford Raven had been the reason I'd gone into nursing. He even knew *my* name and I was just a volunteer. There was no way this could be right. My eyes had to be playing tricks on me.

I moved back to my computer, closing my eyes and taking a deep breath. When I opened my eyes, nothing had changed. After reading the first page, I confirmed it was, indeed, Dr. Ford Raven. I couldn't bring myself to read his conviction record. I honestly didn't want to know. So I tried to concentrate on his medical profile. Thankfully, it was clean. Even though this was my job, it still felt wrong. One of the things any hospital drills into employees was that patient confidentiality is a big deal. Which was why I'd known of more than one person who'd been terminated for looking into a colleague or friend's medical record when they were an actual patient. Looking at Dr. Raven's medical file felt like that. Like I was looking at something I shouldn't be.

"You okay?" Dr. Martinez asked. I hadn't noticed she'd left her office, so I was startled when she spoke. "You look like you've seen a ghost." In a way, I suppose I had.

"I'm fine," I managed, my voice steadier than I felt. "Just recognized a name is all."

I took a deep breath, forcing myself back into professional mode. Whatever happened, whatever he did, it didn't change my job. I was here to provide medical care, nothing more. And, by God, I would be as professional as he would be. Even though I felt sick at the thought of whatever had happened to lead Dr. Raven to this place, he was still my secret hero. My schoolgirl crush on a famous celebrity.

"You sure you're okay?"

I nodded, forcing a smile. "Yeah."

"You know, there's every possibility the name you saw isn't the person you know. Right?"

"Doc, his name is Ford Raven. You know a lot of those?" I tried to joke when I was more shaken than I should be. How many times had I heard him say one patient wasn't more important than another? That everyone deserved his very best, no matter if they were the CEO of the hospital or the homeless man by the dumpster. He'd never said it to me directly, but I'd heard him repeating the mantra to his colleagues and other hospital staff on multiple occasions.

Dr. Martinez winced. "Ford Raven. Yeah, can't say I've ever heard of that name anywhere else." She gave me a sympathetic, knowing look. "Is it going to be an issue? There are other nurses who can assist with his initial exam."

"No. I'll be fine. It's just that he's such a caring person. He was always the first person to come to someone's aid."

"Must have been a violent crime for him to end up here. You look at his case summary?"

"No. I can't make myself."

"You know you're going to have to review it at some point before they get here."

"Yeah, but it feels wrong. Whatever happened was probably the worst day of his life. It feels too personal."

"Only you would feel that way." Dr. Martinez squeezed my shoulder. "If I ever have a secret I need taken to the grave, I'm calling you. Just don't get too comfortable around him. You're the most conscientious person I've ever met, Nadine. You pay attention to people and are careful about what you say and how you say it. Did you have a personal relationship with this guy? I mean, like, were you friends?"

I shook my head. "No. Nothing like that. He was a doctor at the hospital I worked at before I came here. I was never actually introduced to him, but he knew my first name and always spoke when he passed me in the hall." I shrugged. "He was soft-spoken and reserved, but always kind. To staff and patients alike."

"Hmm…" Dr. Martinez pursed her lips. "Doesn't sound like the typical person to end up here. What did he do?"

"Beats me. Maybe he didn't get a long sentence and they kept him close to home."

"Maybe." She grabbed her lab coat and headed to the exam area. "When are they transferring in?"

"Any minute now. No one coming in has special needs so they're not giving us our usual supply shipping time. At least, that's what the email said."

Dr. Martinez frowned. "I don't like things out of routine."

"Well, you've been here longer than me, but the change in routine surprised the shit outta me. No one here likes anything out of the ordinary."

"Makes life safer for everyone."

"I hear that."

"Which is why you'll read that damned file." She pointed a stern finger at me. "Knowledge is power. You might not want to know what happened, but you need to know. This isn't the place for you to find out someone you once admired is willing and capable of killing you simply for looking at him funny."

"I know, but it's so hard! I don't want to know the person who inspired me to get into the medical profession intentionally did something horrific to someone else. It would be watching my hero fall. No one wants that."

"Nope. No one wants to be shanked in the back either. You do your best not to judge people. I see it in everything you do here. But you need to consider that not judging people goes both ways. Don't judge him safe when you have concrete evidence he isn't a safe person *now*. Being careful isn't being judgmental."

Chapter Two

Pain

The minute I stepped foot in the infirmary, the smell of antiseptic hit me like a damn freight train. It was the same scent that used to greet me every morning when I started my day as a surgical intern five years earlier. That scent had been soothing to me then, proof of how clean and organized my environment was. But now it's a black stench, tainted with the putridity of this godforsaken place. You'd think after months of being in prison I would have been immune to the smell, but I guess some things just stuck with you. Besides, every hospital -- or infirmary -- had a unique scent underneath all the bleach and other chemical cleaners. This infirmary was no different.

I was escorted by a guard who probably ate doughnuts for every meal and kicked puppies for fun, but hey, I'm not judging or anything. He shoved me into a chair, cuffed me to the table, and disappeared, probably off to shake down an old lady or something. I seriously doubted he was capable of anything more strenuous.

"See ya around, Brutus." I lifted my chin at the rotund man. He frowned at me, but I just grinned. I liked to pick one guard at a place and harass him until he broke. I was a surgeon and, if I was honest, I didn't think I saw psychiatrists as "real" doctors. I'm ashamed to admit it now for multiple reasons. Mostly because I've been in places in the prison system where there is more true mental illness than I ever thought could possibly be concentrated in a single building, but also because I've learned a new appreciation for how a good psychiatrist could get into someone's head. It was a powerful feeling. I had no desire to fuck with someone's head -- much -- but teasing them a little was too fun to resist. The guards, anyway. Occasionally I'd fuck with other staff members or the occasional prisoner if he was a pain in my ass, but mostly it was the guards.

As I sat there, I caught a glimpse of a nurse. She looked like a tiny, curvy angel in this sea of steel and misery. Honey-colored hair pulled up in a messy bun, and those gray eyes that seem to see right through me. For some reason, I didn't associate those eyes with a woman. I knew I'd seen them before, but for the life of me, I couldn't place her.

"Good afternoon, Dr. Raven," she said as she approached me, and holy shit, I recognized that tinkling voice. Then her eyes widened and she winced. "I'm so sorry," she whispered, obviously devastated at her inadvertent mistake. We both knew I was no longer a doctor. While a felony conviction didn't always mean someone had to surrender their medical license, doing so had been a condition of my plea agreement. One I didn't fight even though my brother tried to get me to. With anyone else, or if I didn't know this woman, I'd have thought it was intentional, designed to either make me feel small by reminding me of how far I'd fallen or to see if they could make me snap with mental torment. But not Nadine Brentner.

"It's all right, Ms. Brentner. I know it wasn't intentional."

Her jaw dropped. "You remember my name?" Real wonder and a touch of hero worship tinted her expression. She looked more than a little starstruck and for the first time I could ever remember, I wanted to puff my chest out in pride. Because some girl I never knew very well was happily surprised I remembered her fucking name. Maybe Knuckles, the fucker, was rubbing off on me. I'd heard about him and his woman and how disgustingly mushy they could be. Only this wasn't my woman. Also, when I knew her she was still in high school, in the Explorer program, a "class" in which the students volunteered in different hospital departments so they could see what the world of healthcare was like in and outside the classroom.

I couldn't help but smile. Nadine had been a ray of sunshine from the first day I saw her in my OR waiting room. We didn't interact, though I tried to acknowledge her when I saw her. She had been handing out snacks and taking family to their loved ones as they came out of recovery. It seemed like she had a natural ability to empathize with those around her. On more than one occasion, I saw her help calm someone down when no one else could. Administration had been angry with her for stepping in. She was underage and a student, but she'd been there at the time and had already made a connection with the woman. I didn't see her after that, and I'd wondered on more than one occasion if she'd been moved to another department because of that incident or if she was simply finished with her class.

"Of course I remember you." I tried to drop my "Pain" persona and adopt some kind of gruff, long forgotten version of the "Dr. Raven" she might remember. "You were one of the few Healthcare Explorers to come through my area who I thought might make a career in medicine someday."

She seemed startled before she gave me a smile filled with wonder. Her eyes widened and she looked down at the floor. Taking a breath, she met my gaze again. This time, she looked more settled. Apparently, she hadn't thought I'd notice her. Truth was, it was impossible *not* to notice her.

Nadine Brentner, the teenager, had been beautiful, but like a porcelain doll you were afraid to touch for fear of breaking her. I appreciated her outer beauty then, but it was her inner beauty that caused me to remember her. I don't think there was ever a time I saw her without a smile.

"I hope I live up to your expectations then." She smiled as she pulled a computer in front of her and began typing. "Give me just a moment," she mumbled as she continued to peck on the keyboard. "Stupid thing locked me out again." She gave me a sheepish grin. "I took too long and it thought I'd left." She was muttering under her breath now and it was almost too cute for words. Mainly because I could remember her doing much the same thing a few times back when I'd had a life and an identity. Only thing she'd improved upon was that now, she seemed to need to stick the tip of her tongue out while she concentrated.

She sat across the small table from me. I was shackled at the ankles and wrists and secured to a bar bolted in the middle of the steel table. This might be medical, but I wasn't sick or injured and the guards didn't know me. No one was taking any chances. New face, new place.

As she continued her login, I glanced around the room. The big guard who brought me here was gone, but there were two other guards. One of them cleared his throat and frowned in our direction.

Nadine glanced at him before she looked up at me again. This time, her smile was still polite but not as welcoming. I noticed she seemed nervous now when she hadn't before. I made a mental note and waited until Nadine was deep into her questioning about my medical history and such before I snuck a glance at the guard. There were no names on their ID badges, but I'd find out who he was and what beef he had with Nadine. And why the fuck she was scared of him.

As Nadine continued her questioning, I answered on automatic pilot, my mind elsewhere. Mainly I focused on everything and everyone in the room. No one in here was of any particular interest other than the one guard. Even shackled, I was easily the most dangerous man in the room.

The only thing that surprised me about this whole situation was little Nadine. My stomach had actually tied itself in knots. I was never nervous. The shackles around my wrists felt heavier, more constricting than usual. Some of it was because the guards here always made sure to take every precaution with a new inmate. The rest was because I was likely giving off predator vibes to their inner prey. I clenched my fists, nails digging into my palms. Shame I thought I'd rid myself of burned hot in my chest, but I forced my chin up. I wasn't the man I had been, but I was still a man. I'd made my choices. Now I had to live with the consequences. That was the way the world worked. But my experiences also changed me in fundamental ways.

There was a softness to Nadine's demeanor that seemed out of place in this harsh environment. It was as if the prison hadn't had a chance to jade her yet.

As Nadine finished up her exam, I noticed the guy who'd given Nadine the stink eye earlier had backed off and now looked bored where he leaned against the wall. While Nadine's attention turned to her computer screen for a few seconds, I studied the guy again. Yeah. Definitely a bully. Which put him squarely in my crosshairs.

I watched as Nadine closed the laptop and

moved it to the other side of the counter, her honey-colored hair catching the harsh fluorescent light. Something stirred in my chest. A feeling I thought I'd buried long ago. I'd been given a fifteen-year sentence which my lawyer got down to five with a possibility of parole after eighteen months. My brother, Wyatt Raven, was with the Iron Tzars MC in Evansville, Indiana and was not the family fuckup. He was a brilliant attorney. While I hadn't wanted to fight the charges or sentence, Wyatt had gone behind my back and brokered the deal which I'd berated him for. He'd simply shrugged and walked out of the courtroom without a word.

Now, I was nearly done with my eighteen months. It was why I'd ended up back in Terre Haute. But after my life went to shit, I knew I'd never be able to have a relationship again. Not a permanent one anyway. But that Goddamned light of Nadine's was threatening to swallow me whole.

When she started to signal to the guards we were finished, I caught her gaze with my own. "Before I go, Ms. Brentner, may I ask you a question?"

"Of course. I can't promise I'll answer, but you can always ask." She smiled to take the sting out of her words, but I knew what she meant and didn't blame her.

"The last day I saw you, there was a commotion in the OR waiting room when a family member had been taken to the conference room and told her husband had died on the table. Do you remember that?"

Her face softened and the sadness there made my fucking heart ache. I caught myself wanting to rub my chest to ease the pain, but the cuffs prevented it. "Yes. Mrs. Derek. Her husband had a complication on the table and passed away. She was devastated." I watched in fascination as those wide gray eyes glimmered under the fluorescent light with tears before she blinked them back. "I knew, uh, they were going to sedate her and I knew she was terrified of medicine that made her sleepy." She stumbled over the word "they" because I was the one who called for something to calm her down. "She hadn't wanted her husband to have surgery for that very reason. She'd been afraid he wouldn't wake up. But he was getting to where he couldn't walk."

"Wait." I held up a hand to interrupt her. "You stepped in because you heard me tell the nurse to get her a dose of Ativan to help her calm down?" I tried not to sound accusing -- because I wasn't accusing her of anything, I just wanted to be sure I understood her correctly -- but I knew it came out that way when her face fell and she actually looked panicked.

"I --"

"Nadine," I smiled at her, reaching deep inside me for the bedside manner I prided myself on having developed early on in my career. "I'm not mad at you or think you did anything wrong. What I want to know is, did you deliberately ignore the rules because you knew how Mrs. Derek would be even more terrified if we sedated her?"

She looked at me for several seconds before nodding her head several times in a small movement. "Yes." The word was barely above a whisper.

"That was the last day I saw you in my department. I didn't see you in the hospital either."

She tilted her head to the side, confused. "You looked for me?"

"I did. Does that surprise you?"

Again she nodded. This time, though, she was

more confident in her movement. "Yes. It does."

"Tell me why I never saw you again." Because I had a bad feeling I knew what had happened. I might have to add a few names to my list of people I was going to fuck up when I got out.

"I broke the rules and could have gotten myself or someone else hurt. I was supposed to leave everything to the professionals."

"Sound advice."

"Since I couldn't follow the rules, they expelled me from the program. Mainly because the hospital didn't want the liability of a high school student getting hurt. I knew going in it would mean I'd be dropped from the class, and I tried to tell the staff around me. I told at least three of them. But when I heard you tell the nurse next to you to get medication to sedate her, I couldn't let it happen. Even if it hurt me in the process."

I stared at the girl for a moment. She was older and looked like she worked way too fucking hard, but that innate compassion in her still shone through. Fuck, this girl needed protection more than any person I'd ever met. "I'm going to give you some advice, Ms. Brentner," I started. "It's going to sound gruff and I'm going to look mean when I say this, but I want my words to really sink in because you are a singular individual, and the world needs people like you in it. So I'm apologizing in advance, but you need to hear this so you keep yourself safe. Do you understand?" I waited until she nodded her head again. She was back to the small movements, a reflex when she knew she'd disappointed someone. And I knew in my fucking bones she was afraid she'd made me angry for not following the rules. "Just because someone looks harmless or you think you know what they are capable of doesn't mean they are, or you do." I hardened my expression. I didn't want to terrify the girl, but I wanted this to sink in. "Doing something like that in this place will get you fuckin' killed," I snarled my warning at her, knowing it would terrify her but needing her to understand.

She didn't say anything, and her face paled. Sweat broke out over her brow, and I could see the pulse fluttering in fear at her neck. "I'm sorry," she whispered.

I let out my breath and relaxed my features. The need to stay in character, to be Dr. Raven again, overrode my need to frighten little Nadine into submission, but it hurt something inside me to think she was afraid of me. Of all the people in this God forsaken place -- including the staff -- I was the one person who'd never hurt her. "I'm sorry, Nadine. Just don't let your guard down in this place like you did that day in the waiting room." I gave her a small smile, unable to help myself.

She motioned for the guards, and I sat back in my chair. "Thank you, Ms. Brentner." I didn't smile but spoke softly and gave her a courteous nod.

Nadine's gray gaze met mine in surprise. Yeah. I know the warning was a dick move, but I wasn't going to apologize. Then she nodded once before speaking softly. "You're welcome, Mr. Raven."

As I was escorted from the infirmary, the guard I'd been watching earlier moved to Nadine and sat in front of her at the table where I'd been sitting. He spoke to her, but she ignored him. At least, she didn't look up or acknowledge him. Then I was moved down the hall back into my cellblock.

One of the guards locked my cell door before opening the small window for me to put my hands through so he could unlock the cuffs. When I turned around, he pulled a phone from his back pocket.

"From Knuckles. Said to check in with him."

I took the phone with a grunt. After any guards in the hall were safely out of the way and I was on my own, I opened the single text.

Knuckles: *Keep phone on you. I'll call at 1am.*

Great. No sleep tonight. Because I always slept so peacefully my first night in a new cell. Right. I guess Knuckles knew exactly what he was doing.

I tucked the phone beneath my thin mattress, mentally calculating the hours until one in the morning. Knuckles wasn't the type to make social calls, especially not at that hour. As I waited for Knuckles's call, I thought about the guard at the infirmary. Something about him bothered me more than it should. The way her demeanor changed when he cleared his throat, the subtle shift in her posture. I'd seen enough predatory behavior in my time -- both in the hospital hierarchy and in prison -- to recognize the signs.

Dinner came and went. The usual slop I was willing to bet they tried to pass off as food in every prison in America. I ate mechanically, my body needing fuel even if my taste buds objected. The new cellblock was quieter than my last one, which was both a blessing and a curse. Quiet meant less immediate danger, but it also left room for thinking.

I was about to roll out of my bunk and do some pushups to focus my mind on something other than Nadine and the guard when the phone buzzed. One o'clock sharp.

"Yeah." Knuckles didn't care about niceties any more than I did.

"You've got six months unless you tell me you

need out now." Knuckles' statement puzzled me.

"Why the fuck would I not want out now?"

"I hear you and I'm not a complete asshole. If you've reached your limit, I'll pull you out tonight. But if you can make it the last six months, I'd prefer not to have to do an urgent extraction."

"Motherfucker," I grumbled with no real heat. "Honestly, I think staying is the best thing right now. But I need your help with something."

"I'm here, brother. What do you need?"

"There's a nurse here. Name's Nadine Brentner. Have your guys check into her."

"Everything OK?" I could hear the genuine concern in Knuckles' voice. The man was a hardass but he protected everyone in his circle. I was lucky enough to be in that circle.

"Not sure. There's a guard here who feels off to me. He intimidates her and she cowers too easily. I can work this end and can be here if he's a danger to her."

"You'll need to be able to move freely from your cell to her. Your girl a guard?"

"No. She's in the infirmary. A nurse. My block is a straight shot down the hall. And she's not my girl. I knew her on the outside."

"Makes things simpler. You got a name on the guard in question?" Of course Knuckles knew I'd want to look into him, too. He also ignored my denial that Nadine was mine.

"Not yet. I'll have it tomorrow, though."

"Good. Roberts or Johnson will bring your access card and code before their shifts end."

"Any way you can get me a computer?"

"Give me a couple days. Knight will take care of it."

I sighed, tension easing in my chest. I hadn't

been to the Kiss of Death compound before, but I knew the majority of the men who belonged to that MC. We'd all met in prison and had bonded together because of Knuckles. The man had some crazy hard pull with someone high up in the Bureau of Prisons. It's how I got transferred to Terre Haute from San Quentin where I'd done the majority of my time. It was an unusual transfer and the guards grumbled about it the entire flight, but here I was.

All the housing in this block were singles, so we had more room than most. It was originally set up to be a solitary confinement wing, but it got turned into Terre Haute's version of a luxury hotel. Hell, we even had mini fridges for snacks and drinks. Yeah. Knuckles came through big time for me when he got me this transfer. I had to grumble at having to pull the last six months, but honestly, the accommodations here were a vast improvement over San Quentin. I could manage six more months. Which meant I had six months to find out what the fuck was going on with Ms. Nadine Brentner.

Chapter Three

Pain
Three Months Later...

I leaned against the crumbling wall of the courtyard, arms folded across my chest as I eyeballed the powder keg of inmates before me. Tension was a living thing, crackling in the stale air like static before a storm. I'd seen this before, a hundred times over. Body language doesn't lie and today it was very easy to read the aggression in every line of every inmate in the yard. Even those of us who had no intentions of participating knew something was about to happen.

Then, like the spark that ignites the gas, a fist holding a shank sailed through the air, finding its mark with a sickening squish. The inmate's eyes widened in shock before blood bubbled from his lips. Violence was unleashed like water crashing through a busted dam. Shouts erupted, creating a symphony of rage that filled up the space.

Yard fights always looked like a mosh pit at the world's most violent and angry concert. I stayed back against the wall, crouching down and waiting for the guards to get involved. Most of the time mace and tasers were enough, but I wasn't taking a chance on one of them shooting first and asking questions later.

Given the numbers of men in the yard who were armed, I figured this was a planned event. Lovely. Likely had something to do with the influx of a couple different gang members into gen pop. Someone was looking to make a statement and anyone who got caught in the crossfire would just be fuck outta luck.

Right on cue I spotted the scrawny kid with eyes too big for his face, looking like a rabbit caught in the headlights of an eighteen-wheeler. The poor bastard was all flailing limbs and sheer panic, trying to dodge fists that flew at him from every direction.

"Shit," I muttered under my breath, the word slipping out like a prayer to a God I stopped believing in a long time ago.

The kid stumbled, getting shoved between two hulking brutes who were too busy trying to tear each other apart to notice the reed-thin boy bouncing off their muscled forms. It was one of those freeze-frame moments, where everything slowed down and you could see the disaster before it hit. But this wasn't Hollywood.

Seconds later, before the kid could shove his way free of the much bigger men surrounding him, a third man stabbed him in the side. He must have been aiming for one of the other guys because instead of finishing the kid off with another half a dozen stabs, he yanked the shank free but stumbled out of sight.

"Son of a bitch," I growled, the words tearing from my throat as I plowed through the sea of bodies. The kid was on the ground, clutching his side, blood seeping through his fingers like he was trying to hold onto life itself.

"Move!" I barked at the kid. He tried to scramble to his feet but couldn't quite get off his knees. I grabbed one arm and dragged the kid away from the melee to the relative safety of the prison wall. I moved us carefully, making sure I kept us in sight of the yard cameras. Last thing I wanted was to get blamed for the young man's death if he didn't make it.

I whipped off my shirt and shoved it over the wound before helping him cover his head in case the fighting got closer to us. We were out of the way for now, but I didn't want to take chances.

The siren finally went off, though everyone not

directly involved in the fighting was ready to assume the position, only not lying flat on the ground straight away in case they needed to protect themselves.

I could feel the tension ratcheting up. Not just because of the riot, but because here I was, right in the fucking middle of it when I'd spent years keeping my head down. The last thing I wanted was to get a couple years tacked on to my sentence when I was so close to getting out.

"Get your ass down, Pain, or I'll take you out myself!" Mother fuck. If it wasn't that same Goddamned guard I'd been looking into. Fucker would love to shoot me because he knew I was on to him. Nadine was right. The fucker was a predator. He'd been shuffled around the federal system from prison to prison because no one wanted to deal with his skank ass. Everyone knew he had some serious misconduct but, to put it bluntly, no one gave a good Goddamn if he was hurting prisoners or not.

I moved slowly, keeping my hand over the young man's wound, until I was on the ground on my stomach. I still held pressure because I could already feel blood seeping through my balled-up shirt. I needed to actually look at his wound because I could be doing more harm than good if the shank penetrated his lung.

"Get your fuckin' hand away from him, man. Don't be fuckin' stupid."

"You realize he's bleeding out. Right?"

"I don't give a fuck! Get your hands away from him!"

"Stand down, Grayson!" The command sliced through the clamor, sharp and unexpected. It was Guard Roberts, his voice cutting through the mayhem in our vicinity.

Grayson lowered his weapon but not his glare. His lip curled up just enough to let me know he had me in his sights. But for now, he stepped back, letting Roberts take the lead.

"Don't move, Pain. Keep pressure on his wound or whatever you have to do, but lie still until we get things under control." Roberts was standing slightly in front of us, protecting us from anyone who got too close. Roberts was one of the guards in Knuckles' pocket. He would protect me because Knuckles told him to, and Knuckles was the one making sure he got paid. He was also the one who would take any skin I lost in here out of Roberts' hide.

"We're gonna have to get him to medical, Roberts. Fast. He's bleeding, but I think the shank also penetrated his lung."

"He'll be the first to leave when we get the yard locked down." Roberts grabbed Grayson by the vest and jerked him away from me and the kid on the ground next to me. "Go help the guys on the East side of the yard. These two aren't going to be a problem."

"You sure? I don't trust Pain. He's just itchin' to stab someone. You can see it in his fucking eyes."

"Get your ass to the fucking East side, Grayson!" Roberts snapped. "Or I'll see to it you accidentally get locked in the yard on your own."

With a snarl, Grayson did as Roberts said, stomping off like a fucking toddler.

I chanced a glance at the young man beside me. "Hang in there, kid."

"Do you have any idea how clichéd that sounds?" Though his words were strained, I was glad to see the kid had a sense of humor.

"I mean, I grew up watching Clint Eastwood reruns on WGN in Chicago. It was all clichéd. That's a line Eastwood would say."

"Or John Wayne," Roberts offered.

I rolled my eyes. "Ain't you supposed to be helping to get us all under control?"

Roberts shrugged. "I got a hurt prisoner who was just tryin' to get out of the fuckin' way. If you think that gives your sorry ass a little added protection, mention it to Knuckles. See if he'll give me a bonus."

The kid laughed before wincing and clutching his side. I urged his hand underneath mine, so he held my shirt tightly.

"What's your name, kid?" I needed to keep him talking until Roberts got the all-clear for us to go to the infirmary.

"Jermaine." It was easy to see his strength was fading fast, but he looked up at me like he thought I was going to save him.

Another kid about the same age crawled toward us. When he got close, I pinned him with my gaze. "Where do you think you're goin', huh?"

"Jermaine's my cellie." The kid had white hair and eyes that were a curious shade of almost violet. At least, his irises were blue, but there was some red bleeding through where he had no pigment. Poor kid. His coloring almost guaranteed prison was not going to be kind to him.

"Give me your shirt." I didn't phrase it as a question and the kid wiggled out of his white, prison-issue tee and handed it to me. I shoved it over the wound in the Jermaine's chest. "Roberts, let medical know he's got a sucking chest wound."

Roberts keyed his mic, relaying the information. "Sounds bad." He made the comment to me as things calmed down in the yard.

"It is. They're going to have to medevac him

out."

"Great," Jermaine said, his voice getting weaker, sounding slightly drowsy now. "My first time flying and I'm probably gonna die."

"I mean, with that attitude..." I trailed off and Jermaine barked out a small laugh before motioning me to come closer to him.

"Listen, man. I deserve to be here. But Chuck over there, he's just a scared kid."

"And you're not?" Surprisingly, that comment came from Roberts.

"Yeah, I guess I am. But I've been tryin' to look out for Chuck."

"I know." Roberts didn't turn around. "I'll watch him while you're gone. But I don't babysit. You'll get your ass back here and take back over."

OK. I'd tolerated Roberts before. I might have just a tiny bit of respect for him now. I didn't know the guy well, but I knew from watching him he was a man of his word. If he said something definitively, he stood by it. Of course, more often than not, he would give a non-answer or deflect. But if he said something, he meant it. I also had the suspicion he'd phrased himself the way he did so the kid knew he wasn't going to die. Which I hoped gave Jermaine something to fight for, too.

"How'd you two click up?" As I continued to talk with Jermaine, I noticed a medical team was coming with a gurney. Maybe the kid would get a fighting chance.

"We went to school together," Chuck spoke up.

"Yeah. And Chuck knew I didn't have money for breakfast or lunch and would order doubles for himself and give me half."

"Christ," I bit out. "You two got no business in

this fuckin' place."

"Tell me about it." I could practically see Roberts rolling his eyes.

The gurney stopped in front of us. All the prisoners in the yard had been moved back to their cells and it was only me, Chuck, and Jermaine in the yard other than the medical staff and Roberts. Another two guards emerged from the building hurrying to Roberts.

"Go with this one to the infirmary." Roberts indicated Jermaine. "I'll take these two back to their cells."

"I got a gash on my side," I said, turning so Roberts could see the wound. I really wanted to go to make sure Jermaine got the treatment he deserved. I only had about three months left before I finished my sentence, but Knuckles had managed to get me a job in the infirmary for the duration. Which had the added benefit of getting to know Nadine better.

Roberts snorted. "Uh-huh. Go on, then." He grinned with genuine amusement. "Tell Nadine I said hi."

"Fucker." My retort had no heat in it, but it had to be said.

"Yep. I'll look out for Chuck." He grabbed the kid by the upper arm. "Gonna have to lock you in your cell, though. You good with that?"

"He's good with it." Jermaine bit out. "He's perfectly good with it."

The kid's face was ashen now. He was still fighting, but I could see fear creeping into his eyes as he realized he was in pretty bad shape.

They carefully rolled Jermaine onto a backboard before lifting the backboard onto the stretcher and heading for the infirmary. I followed close behind.

Jermaine turned his head so he could see me, clinging to my gaze like I was his lifeline. Fuck. I didn't need anyone looking at me like that. Not here. Because I knew there was no way in hell I could save him beyond the immediate situation.

Roberts must have cleared a path to medical because we rolled with the stretcher straight inside the infirmary without stopping. I had my attention on Jermaine, not paying much attention to anything around me, which hadn't happened since before I went inside. It was disconcerting in some ways because not paying attention in here could get me killed. But also, I was amazed at how easy it was to slip back into my old life. Even if it was only a few minutes.

We burst through the double doors, the chill of the infirmary wrapping around us like a cold embrace.

"Can someone get two lines started please?" I called out as the staff entered. It was the afternoon shift, just before shift change. Which was lucky for Jermaine because the infirmary was fully staffed.

"I'm sure I don't need to remind you I'm in charge, Dr. Raven?" Dr. Martinez always addressed me as Dr. Raven, even though I'd pointed out I wasn't a professional any longer. She responded with, "You earned the right to be called doctor when you graduated medical school. Revoked or not, you still graduated." Having said that, she was still territorial.

"Not at all, Dr. Martinez," I answered. "I was anticipating your needs." I nearly grinned at her. I would have, too, if the situation weren't as bad as it was.

"I see. Well, give it to me, then."

"Jermaine got in the way trying to get out of the way," I started. "Stab wound from a shank. Now he has a sucking chest wound and probably a hemothorax." I removed the shirts I had balled up to control the bleeding and immediately Jermaine started breathing easier, confirming the suspected lung injury.

I snagged a pair of trauma shears that shouldn't be near my reach and started cutting off Jermaine's shirt. I needed to get to the wound.

Nadine moved to Jermaine's side, using sterile water to wash the site carefully so we could see the wound underneath the blood. Once cleaned, I examined the wound as best I could.

Dr. Martinez handed me a pair of gloves. "I called for an air ambulance, but this guy's going to need immediate intervention."

"You got a chest tube kit?" I glanced at Dr. Martinez while Nadine placed an occlusive dressing over the wound to keep air from rushing into Jermaine's chest cavity with every breath he took. Too much air trapped between the lungs and the chest cavity would compress the lungs and be even more deadly than the current situation.

"I do. You realize you can't legally do this. Right?"

"I'm more than happy to assist you, Dr. Martinez."

"And you know very well you're way the fuck more qualified to do this procedure than I am," she snapped. "Just do it. But if you fuck this up, I will totally throw you under the Goddamned bus."

I snorted. "No, you won't."

"Don't test me, Pain."

"Wouldn't dream of it." I stepped back out of the way as Nadine and Dr. Martinez prepped the area while I washed my hands and put on a clean shirt. This was what we did. It felt so much like an ER I could almost make myself believe the last few years had been a bad dream. Except the ER came with its own set of problems I tried to avoid at all costs. The inappropriate humor in that department had kind of offended me at one time. The energy in Emergency Room was vastly different from Surgical Departments. If I ever saw any of my old colleagues again, I'd have to apologize. Or something.

Thirty minutes later, I had the chest tube inserted and Jermaine was visibly looking better. From what I heard, the helicopter was here but still trying to make it through security. Such was life in prison with a medical emergency.

"I can't offer you much, man," Jermaine said, grabbing my hand in his, "but I'll have your back as long as we're in the same facility."

"Just look after Chuck when you get back."

"Yeah. Poor kid don't stand a chance."

I stepped back as the flight team came in and swiftly took over. Dr. Martinez filled them in and took over and I moved back to my little area to change my clothes -- again -- and wash my hands.

"Dr. Raven?"

I turned at the sound of Nadine's soft voice. She sounded hesitant, but the fact that she'd approached me at all told me it was important. "Thanks for your help earlier, Nadine." I smiled at her over my shoulder as I put on an orange top over my white T-shirt. "What can I help you with?"

She blushed and ducked her head. This side of Nadine always made me smile. She was so like the girl I'd observed five years ago. Out there, when she had to interact with anyone on a professional level, she was all business and confidence. I could already tell she was a good nurse, but today had proven to me exactly how competent and capable she was.

"I just wanted to say thank you. Dr. Martinez could have done that procedure, but she didn't want to. She says it's not fair to think we can do procedures on prisoners if we're not a hundred percent confident in our own abilities." She lowered her gaze. "I like that she thinks that way. Not all the staff here do."

Instantly, I was on alert. I knew Grayson was guilty as sin of multiple things -- I was taking care of him -- but if he'd threatened or hurt Nadine, I'd kill the motherfucker in front of God and everyone as a warning not to fuck with my woman...

Fuck.

Fuck!

I was so Goddamned fucked as to not even be fucking believed.

Guess Knuckles was right after all. And I'd have to make sure that fucker, Roberts, knew to warn everyone off.

"What do you mean, Nadine? Has someone threatened or hurt you?"

She immediately shook her head. "No. Not me."

"I know about Grayson," I said without further discussion. "What I want to know is, has he threatened you? I know he intimidates you. Saw it the first day I was here."

"Yeah. He does. But no. He's never threatened me. I feel threatened sometimes, but he's never said or done anything overt. I think it's a warning to keep my mouth shut about his extra *activities* here."

I turned slowly, careful not to get in her personal space, even though I really wanted to. Not to intimidate her or even to drive home a point. I wanted in her personal space because I had a right to be. I wanted her to welcome me, to expect that I'd pull her close when I was near. And, Christ! Now that those thoughts were in my head, I knew I'd never be free of them.

"Listen to me, Nadine." I waited until she met my gaze with hers. "Don't test Grayson. If you see something, go to Roberts or me, but don't confront him in any way. Don't go digging. Leave all that to me."

"I know there are different cliques and groups inside. I know that you sometimes police each other depending on the infraction. But you just got here. Are you sure this is something you can handle on your own?"

I grinned at her. "Are you worried about me, Miss Brentner?" I had to resist the urge to move closer to her. This wasn't the place or the time. And even though I'd worked in her area the last few months, if I got too close to her physically the guards wouldn't hesitate to take me out. Not because they'd be protecting Nadine, though that's the report they'd give. No. They'd kill me because they had an excuse and a very reasonable expectation they'd get away with it.

"Of course! I don't want you hurt. In case you hadn't noticed, not all of the guards are as helpful and humane as Roberts."

"Don't kid yourself, honey. Roberts is as vicious as everyone else. He simply has a decent moral compass and will do what he's paid to do, and part of that, at the moment, is looking out for my interests."

"What?" Nadine's eyes were wide and she looked more than a little confused, but she'd heard what I said and understood it. She just didn't want to believe what she was hearing.

"It's not important. You just need to know he's as dangerous as any of the guards here, but if you find yourself in a situation and Roberts is near, you stick to him like glue. Understand?"

"No. But I'll remember what you said. I've never seen Roberts be intentionally cruel. More than once, he had just cause to shoot an inmate and managed to talk his way out of it."

"You have no business working here, Nadine. Go work in a hospital OR. Or a nursing home. Or anywhere there is at least a chance of a good buffer between you and everyone else. You're too trusting. Roberts has a reason for everything he does. He's not overly aggressive, but you're deluding yourself if you don't think Roberts could kill for even half a reason if he thought it would benefit him."

She gasped, taking a small step back. "That's a hell of a thing to say about someone."

"And when you knew me, I'd never have said it. But you need to hear it because this place will chew you up and spit you out if you're not careful."

"I've worked here for a couple of years now. I know I'm not going to make a career out of this, but the money is good for now. When I get to where I hate coming to work, I'll find something else."

"The problem with that plan is you won't see it coming until it's too late." I kept my voice low, gentle even, but I needed her to understand. "You won't wake up one morning and decide you hate this place. One day, something's gonna happen that changes you forever, and by then the damage will be done."

"You just told me this place changes people. You've been in the system a while now. How do I know you're not trying to scare me away for your own reasons?"

"That's not what I'm talking about, and you know it." I kept my voice low, but I could feel the intensity bleeding through. "I'm talking about your physical safety. Not your job satisfaction."

She crossed her arms, and I could see that stubborn streak I remembered from years ago. "I can take care of myself, Pain." I thought she was using my road name to remind herself I was a different person and not the man she'd known before.

"Can you?" I stepped closer, just barely within the acceptable distance. "Because from where I'm standing, you're walking around here like you're still in some suburban hospital where the worst thing that happens is someone gets snippy about their Jell-O."

Her gray eyes flashed. "Don't patronize me, Dr. Raven. I know exactly where I am."

"Do you? Because Grayson isn't just some asshole guard with an attitude problem. He's dangerous, Nadine. Really fuckin' dangerous. The kind of dangerous that ends lives. And you…" I ran a hand through my hair, frustrated as hell. "You still look at people like you expect them to be good."

"And what's wrong with that?"

"Nothing. Everything. Fuck, I don't know." I glanced around the infirmary, making sure we weren't drawing attention. "Look, just promise me you'll stay as far away from Grayson as you can. Roberts and Johnson are supposed to be making sure he's never in your area unless one of them is with him, but accidents happen. So keep your head on a swivel, girl." I bit out the words, harsh and demanding. I hated the fear on her face. It wasn't like I was going to let anything happen to her. The second I suspected Nadine might possibly be in danger, Knuckles added to the guards he had on me to do whatever I needed. Which I promptly put on Nadine.

"I'll be careful. Some of the guards have started walking the women to their cars."

"As long as you always go with either Roberts or Johnson. Understand?"

She cocked her head, her brows drawing in confusion. "Why are you telling me all this? Why do you care?"

How to fucking answer that? "I don't know, Nadine. Maybe it's because you're a link to my former life, or maybe it's just your innate goodness that draws me in. Whatever makes me care is too strong to ignore."

I really wasn't sure she was going to say anything else, but finally, she nodded her head. "OK. I'll do what you asked me. Roberts or Johnson, and I will not look into Grayson. I'll bring any concerns with him to you."

I couldn't help but beam at her. "That's my good girl."

"Don't push it, Pain." She pointed a finger at me, but I saw her lips twitch as she fought a smile.

"It's what I do best, sweetheart."

Chapter Four

Nadine
Two Months Later...

The bruises on Chuck's ribs weren't from a yard fight like he'd claimed. Or the dislocated shoulder. Or the broken tibia. Or the dislocated jaw. To say nothing of the other, more private injuries listed in his records from the outside hospital. The kid had been left for dead. Had it not been for his buddy, Jermaine, I have no doubt Chuck wouldn't have survived. Normally, I'd have Pain take a look at him. Dr. Martinez wasn't afraid to use his skill and expertise, even though it broke pretty much every rule in several books on many different subjects related to ethics in prison. And in medicine. And God only knew everything else. But Pain had been released a couple months ago and I admitted I missed him. For more than one reason. Especially now, though. This kid was a hot mess.

I'd been working in this hellhole long enough to know the difference between injuries from a brawl and something else entirely. The reddish-purple bruising at his hips had faded to a dark purple turning greenish-yellow over the last few days. Fingerprint bruises. They were on his upper arms and around his neck as well. I suspected there were other injuries. Injuries he likely wouldn't tell me about willingly.

I watched him through the window before entering the room. As always, since he got back from the hospital two days before, he stared blankly at the wall, silent tears tracking down his face. He would interact if spoken to directly, but he never volunteered conversation.

The door creaked open as I stepped inside, the familiar scent of antiseptic hitting my nostrils. My gaze immediately locked onto the young inmate, Chuck. Yeah. Fight, my ass. I'm sure there wasn't much of a "fight" to it.

My stomach clenched as I approached, keeping my expression neutral. "Hello, Mr. Smith," I said softly, offering a small smile. "I'm Nurse Brentner."

"Call me Chuck." His voice was monotone and he didn't look at me, like he was on autopilot, saying something he normally would say but was actually detached from his surroundings.

I'd read his file from the outside hospital, of course. He still hadn't admitted to the rape, saying simply he'd been in a fight and, no, he didn't know who did it. As I moved closer, I noticed his knuckles were unmarked. Odd for someone who supposedly threw punches.

"Can you tell me what happened?" I asked, gently probing the bruise on his cheekbone. He winced, and I muttered a quick apology.

"Just a fight," he mumbled, not meeting my eyes.

I hummed noncommittally. "Well, you've got two more days of IV antibiotics. I've talked to Dr. Martinez and she agrees we should keep you here at least until you've completed the medication. I don't want to have to stick you twice a day when you can keep that IV intact. We can also give your pain meds by that route."

Chuck didn't respond, staring at me blankly. I heard footsteps in the room, turned my head to see who'd joined us, and froze.

"Hey there, Chucky." Grayson leaned against the door, his shoulder braced on the steel frame. "You 'bout ready to go back to your cell? I bet if you talk real sweet-like to Nurse Nadine there, she'll sign you out."

Chuck trembled, breaking out in a sweat. His

gaze darted briefly to the door where Grayson stood, grinning like a maniac. I kept my movements slow and deliberate as I finished hooking up his medicine.

"Oh, Mr. Smith will be in the infirmary for a few more days yet. After the antibiotics, there's still the matter of his shoulder and the leg he had surgery on. He's not going to be able to maneuver well in gen pop. Also, given the jaw dislocation, he's going to have trouble eating." I smiled kindly at Chuck. "I haven't talked with Dr. Martinez yet today about her plans for you in the near future, but I don't anticipate you going back to your cell for at least two more days. Possibly longer."

Chuck kept his gaze down, not looking at me or Grayson, but the kid was sweating now, having a visceral reaction. I didn't have to wonder why. Grayson was a creep on most days, but I knew he could get mean. I'd also linked him to several -- at least eight -- prisoner assault incidents. It's not unusual for inmates to be brought to medical after fights or being ambushed. The strange part was that Grayson was in some way connected to every one of them. What I needed to do was match up the dates and times of each incident with times Grayson was at work.

"Aww. Too bad, kid. I was thinkin' about decorating your cell. Jermaine won't be back for a couple'a days yet. Thought we might have a party or something to celebrate your release from medical." The smile Grayson threw Chuck's way wasn't friendly or pleasant. In fact, I was pretty sure it was a threat.

"If you'll excuse us." I stood and opened the cabinet above the sink and pulled out some dressing supplies. "I need to redress Mr. Smith's wounds and look at his shoulder again. It's not healing the way it should and I'm afraid he might have dislocated it again."

"I think I should stay." Grayson didn't move from his perch, his gaze fixed on Chuck. "Wouldn't want Chucky boy here to decide he wants some primo pussy from naughty Nurse Nadine."

I stiffened. "Excuse me?" My gaze narrowed on him. Since I'd started here two years ago, I'd never truly felt unsafe. Like if there was danger, the guard closest to me would absolutely keep me safe. Right now, the closest guard to me was also the threat.

Every employee with direct inmate contact has a body alarm. Kind of like a panic button. If I was in a bad situation, I could hit my body alarm and it would let everyone know I needed help immediately. I needed to push it, but I was frozen, unbelieving he'd actually called me naughty Nurse Nadine. And right out in the open.

"Now, now, Nadine." The look on Grayson's face was wholly evil. I knew in that moment he was going to hurt me. Likely rape me. Right here. "I didn't mean any harm. I was just makin' sure Chucky here understood what I meant. Don't worry, though. If he makes a move, I'll be your *body*guard." He emphasized the word body.

The crudeness in everything about Grayson was the trigger I needed. Immediately, I hit my body alarm. Several times, just in case someone thought it was on accident. The alarm sounded and a red light flashed in the halls outside the room, much like a fire alarm, as security protocols were triggered by the audiovisual alarm.

"Oh, God." Chuck whimpered his prayer. I had an ingrained need to check on the young man, but I didn't dare take my eyes off Grayson.

"You need to leave," I said, trying not to let my

voice waver and failing miserably.

"Step away from the inmate, Miss Brentner. He's trying to grab you." Grayson's smile was oily and instantly made my skin crawl.

"He's doing no such thing! What are you doing?" This couldn't be happening.

"I'm protecting you from an inmate who is getting violent. Now please step away before you get hurt."

Oh, the implications were crystal clear. Chuck was going to die no matter what. The only question was whether or not I died with him. Chuck understood and whimpered in fear.

"No one's getting hurt!" I snapped, standing solidly between Chuck and Grayson. "Get out of the ward, Grayson. Now!"

The doors to the infirmary burst open and a group of about twenty guards stormed into the room. Chuck gave a startled, fearful yelp but didn't say anything. I recognized Roberts and Johnson at the head of the pack of men and relief swamped me. Maybe everything wouldn't come crashing down on me. Today.

The guards surrounded Chuck, leaving Grayson to pull back and give his account to Roberts before I could. This was going to be tricky, and I had no idea who I could trust. Before he'd been released, Dr. Raven -- Pain -- said to go to Roberts or Johnson if anything happened so maybe I could feel things out from there. I was happy he was out, but I really, really wish he was here right now.

Behind me, Chuck grunted in pain and I couldn't stand by and let the guards beat him up. "Stop! Don't hurt him!"

"Please step back, Miss Brentner," one of them

said in a crisp no-nonsense manor. "We've got to restrain this sack of shit before we take him to solitary."

"He didn't do anything. I hit my body alarm, but not because of anything Chuck did. He's completely innocent and I will sign an affidavit to that effect."

Finally, the guard looked startled and a bit unsure. "Hold up, guys." I thought he called the halt reluctantly, but maybe I was living in the drama. Chuck still whimpered and was shaking like a leaf, but he kept mostly silent. "Grayson! You were here. What the fuck happened?"

"I'll talk to Roberts," I said. "I was here too. In fact, I was the one who pressed the damned alarm in the first Goddamned place." I was fed up with this fucking shit. Judging by the look on Guard Roberts' face, he knew it too. "Now, if someone could please get Dr. Martinez, I need her to check Chuck over to make sure he's not been reinjured." I have no idea where my backbone came from, but I could tell it took more than one of them by surprise. Particularly Grayson, who now looked at me like I was public enemy number one and he was fucking J. Edgar Hoover.

"You heard the lady." Guard Johnson motioned for all the guards but one to leave then spoke into his radio. "Infirmary all clear. Threat contained." Johnson and the person on the other end of the radio traded a few more exchanges which sounded like codes or something. Probably authenticating the all-clear.

"Come with me, Miss Brentner." Roberts waved his hand in the direction of the offices. It was also the way out of the infirmary and to the main part of the prison. Where there were more guards I didn't trust.

"How about we use Dr. Martinez's office. I'm sure she won't mind." I saw the woman in question come up behind Roberts when I spoke and smiled at her.

"Sure. What happened, Nadine? Are you hurt?"

"No. I promise. I'm fine. I'll explain later, but would you mind staying with Mr. Smith until we get done?" I held the other woman's gaze for several seconds while she glanced around the room taking it all in, her eyes narrowing before she

Dr. Martinez gave me a hard look. "What happened, Nadine? Tell me."

I turned to Roberts, giving him a pleading look. "Is there someone you trust to stay with Doc? I mean really trust. Johnson maybe?"

Roberts gave me a hard look before nodding slowly. "Yeah. I'll get Johnson. Livingston, too. He's on the approved list."

I had no clue what an approved list was, but I hoped he knew what he was doing. "Roberts?" He held my gaze. "Make sure Grayson isn't alone with any of the women."

Unsurprisingly, Roberts nodded. "Understood. Now, take me to Doc's office because I think I need to hear this."

Ten minutes later, after telling him everything relevant that I knew, Roberts stormed out of the office and back to the main ward. "Johnson, stay here. No one comes inside the infirmary unless they're on the list. And if you see that fuckin' cunt, Grayson, help him have an accident." Dr. Martinez gasped, but when she looked from Roberts to me, then to Chuck, she didn't say anything. "Nadine?" -- he pointed a finger at me -- "you stay here. Don't leave with anyone other than me or Johnson. Understand?"

"What's going to happen?"

"Do you understand, Nadine?" This time,

Roberts took a step toward me, putting a hard, threatening edge to his words, making my heart race. In fear. This was why we made good money. No matter what part of this place a person worked in, there was always an element of risk. I hadn't been blind to the danger before, but I'd thought myself safe as long as I followed the rules. Now, I was seriously reevaluating my life choices.

"Yes. I understand." I went to Dr. Martinez who looked as wide-eyed as I'm sure I did. "I'm sorry, Rachel." I never called the other woman by her first name. It was a form of respect I tried to honor.

"This isn't your fault, Nadine. But what's going on?"

I pulled her in and whispered softly for her ears alone. "Grayson threatened me. I have no doubt he'd have killed me if everyone hadn't gotten here as quickly as they did."

"What the hell caused this shit?" Dr. Martinez was furious. She was also scared; I could see it in her eyes.

"I'm not sure, but I think it might have something to do with Pain being released."

Dr. Martinez narrowed her gaze, looking off. "That actually makes sense. I thought I caught him looking at the two of you when he worked in here, but I figured it was just him keeping an eye on everyone so nothing went off the rails."

"I've never been inappropriate with Pain, Dr. Martinez." I knew my eyes were wide, but I couldn't help it. Almost every woman who worked the infirmary with Dr. Raven had made no secret she'd fuck him in a heartbeat. If I was being honest, I understood it. The man was sex on a stick, but sexy or not, he was still an inmate. It was more than inappropriate to get involved with a prisoner. I knew not everyone had the same feelings. Some did whatever they wanted, and I knew there were female guards as well as medical staff who disregarded that rule.

"Honey, of all people, you are the last person I'd accuse of fucking an inmate."

"We worked here together. That's all. We kept our conversations professional for the most part. We talked about our pasts, but I didn't bring it up unless he did. Then I mostly listened."

"I know. I think that man spoke to you more than anyone else in this place combined. So the question is, why does Grayson care if you and Dr. Raven have a relationship?"

"I'm not sure. Unless…" I trailed off as a thought occurred to me. "Oh, my God. This is because I've been looking into accidents. The ones I've worked, anyway. Some are really accidents, but there have been several I questioned."

"Let me guess," Dr. Martinez began dryly, "Grayson is the common denominator?"

"You've seen it too then." It wasn't a question.

"Yes. I suspected, I just hadn't had time to put it all together."

"I was going to bring it to you when I had as much information as I could get. But Pain got released, and Grayson has been making more and more inappropriate comments ever since, but nothing overt until all this happened."

"Miss Brentner?" From across the room, Chuck called to me. I glanced at Dr. Martinez before moving quickly to Chuck's side. Johnson was like a silent shadow. Chuck glanced at Johnson and swallowed. "Never mind."

"Son, if it has anything to do with Grayson, tell the lady." Johnson's tone was gentle, but there was still a bite to it. "The more information we have the better. Trust me when I tell you Grayson won't touch you or anyone else again."

Chuck nearly sobbed in relief before looking back at me wide-eyed. "Is he fuckin' with me? Is this a test of some kind?"

"No." I took his hand, which was now handcuffed to the bed. "He's not fucking with you, Chuck. We know Grayson's a bad guy."

"He's not the only one." Chuck's words sent a chill up my spine, but, honestly, it was expected. If something goes on for long enough, there will always be more than one person involved.

"Christ." Dr. Martinez sat heavily in a nearby chair. "What the fuck is going on?"

"Grayson," Chuck started. "He's got a group of buddies, and they like to find a couple of the newer guys to pick on every few months. Me and Jermaine, they pick on both of us because we just came up from juvie. Jermaine got here before me, but we're both young. I guess we were easy targets."

My stomach churned as I listened, but I kept my face as neutral as I could. Inside, though, I was a hurricane of emotions. Horror at what this kid had been through, rage at the guards who'd abused their power, and fear. Bone-deep, ice-cold fear. Because I knew how dangerous this knowledge was. To myself, yes, but more so to Chuck and Jermaine.

I felt the tip of my tongue press against my teeth, a nervous habit I couldn't shake. My mind raced, trying to process it all while maintaining my professional demeanor. "I don't know what's going to happen next, but I promise I'm going to do everything

I can to help you," I said, my voice steadier than I felt.

"Who else is in Grayson's circle, Chuck?" Johnson faced the young man at an angle to make himself appear smaller and less threatening. He spoke softly but there was a note of command I knew Chuck would respond to.

I didn't recognize the names of the guards he mentioned, but judging by Johnson's face, he did. "Is there anyone else?"

"Not that ever came to me. Jermaine never mentioned anyone else either."

"OK. I'm going to take care of this. Is there anyone other than you and Jermaine who are at immediate risk?"

Chuck shrugged. "I keep my head down, man. Jermaine might be able to tell you more, but we both keep to ourselves."

The fluorescent lights hummed overhead, suddenly feeling oppressive. I glanced at the security camera in the corner, wondering if anyone was watching. The thought sent a chill down my spine. This situation with Grayson had really shaken my belief in the idea I was safe here. Maybe Dr. Raven was right. Maybe I should work in a hospital.

I couldn't ignore this. But reporting it through official channels? That could make things worse for him. The prison hierarchy was a tangled web, and I didn't know who was involved or how deep it went.

"Nadine," Johnson's deep voice cut through my musings, and I sucked in a breath. "Don't even think about taking this on yourself. Me and Roberts have it now. We'll take care of this."

"I don't know what to do!"

Johnson stared at me for a long time, holding my gaze with a hard one of his own. "I'm going to give it to you straight, Nadine. Grayson's a raging lunatic. He got this job because of who he knows, not because he's actually qualified or even suited to work here. It's going to take us a while to clean all of this up. So, my advice to you is to leave. Now. Once Roberts comes back, he and I will walk you out."

"What? But I need this job!"

"Do you want to die?"

I gasped, stepping back away from Johnson, all too aware I was ill-equipped to take on a man his size. Grayson was just as big. I was sure Johnson was hoping I'd come to that realization when he stepped back and softened his expression.

"Go home. Pack anything you need with you. Go to Nashville. I'll give you a number to contact Pain, and he can make sure you're set there for as long as you need."

Everything in me stilled. "Pain?"

"He didn't want to give you his phone number before he left because he knew you wouldn't take it. But he knew something like this might happen before we could take care of it, and he left me and Roberts instructions. Part of that was to send you to Nashville with his number and some cash."

I didn't know what to say. Didn't know how to feel. I was certainly terrified, but I knew in my gut Johnson was giving me sound advice. I had just thought to myself how I didn't know who I could trust. Well, that was a lie. I knew I could trust Dr. Raven. Pain. And he said to trust Roberts and Johnson, so that's what I was going to do. "All right. I'll do what you tell me to do."

Chapter Five

Nadine

The fluorescent lights flickered overhead as I hurried through the dingy corridors, my shoes squeaking softly against the scuffed linoleum. Grayson's threats echoed in my mind, his leering face burned into my memory. My heart pounded and my palms were slick with sweat.

I hurried through the security checkpoint for employees leaving the building and out the doors into the muggy Indiana night, sucking in a gulp of fresh air. Hands shaking, I fumbled for my keys as I approached my beat-up Ford Fiesta in the parking lot. I left early, so even though there were several cars in the area, the grounds were pretty empty. "Come on, come on," I muttered, nearly dropping the keys before finally jamming them into the lock. I slid behind the wheel, making sure to hit the lock. Paranoid didn't begin to describe how I felt.

I started the vehicle and sped off, needing to get my shit together and out of town as quickly as I could. I might not know Roberts on a personal level, but Pain trusted him. I'd seen how those two and Johnson had interacted in the past, and knew they had a relationship of mutual respect, even if the mitigating factor was money. I wasn't naive enough to believe Roberts and Johnson weren't getting a kickback. I also knew the only reason either of them was helping me now was because Pain told them to.

Ten minutes later, I hurried up the stairs to the front porch of the little house I rented, looking over my shoulder the whole way. I'd never been so relieved to see that faded green door. I let myself in and locked the door and engaged the deadbolt, slumping back against the door. Slowly, I let out the breath I didn't realize I was holding and the sound broke into a sob. Then another.

I bent at the waist, bracing my hands on my knees. I wasn't going to make a sound. I could swallow this fear and get a grip on myself, use my head, and get the fuck out of here as quickly as possible.

Packing didn't take long. I basically tossed what little I owned into one suitcase, snagged my backpack, and headed down the stairs to my car. The house had come furnished with everything, having been a bed and breakfast before the owner rented it to me. I kept the place neat so I was out of there in twenty minutes, tops. I'd never needed much to make me happy, preferring to save as much money as I could so I could buy a place on my own. I was glad I'd decided to live so frugally now.

As I hurried through the house to the door leading to the carport, the sound of heavy footsteps nearing me sent a jolt of fear through my body. My heart pounded wildly as I realized with sickening certainty I wasn't alone.

A baseball bat was propped in the corner of the living room. Had been since I started renting the place. I snagged it now, curling my fingers tightly around the handle. How many times had I thought about donating that thing to one of the local sports parks? How ironic was it that procrastination was what might give me a fighting chance against whatever was stalking me?

The footsteps grew louder, closer, until they stopped just outside my door. For a moment, everything was eerily silent. I held my breath, straining to hear over the frantic pounding of my own heart.

Then, with a sudden, violent crash, the door flew open. The force of it sent me stumbling back, the bat raised defensively in front of me.

There, framed in the splintered doorway, was the hulking figure of Guard Grayson. His eyes were wild, his face twisted into a grotesque sneer.

"Well, well, well," he drawled, his voice dripping with malice. "Look what we have here. A pretty little nurse, all alone."

I tightened my grip on the bat, trying to keep my voice steady. "Get out of my home. Now."

Grayson laughed, a cold, cruel sound that sent shivers down my spine. He took a step forward, his bulk filling the doorway. "I don't think so, sweetheart. You and I have some unfinished business."

He lunged for me, his meaty hands grasping at my arms. I swung the bat wildly, feeling a surge of satisfaction as it connected with his shoulder. He grunted in pain but didn't loosen his grip.

I screamed as we struggled, my smaller frame no match for his brute strength. Finally, he wrapped one arm around my waist and wrenched the bat from my hand with the other, tossing it aside with a mocking, evil smile. The bat clattered across the hardwood floor before handing hard against the baseboard.

"Let go of me!" I screamed, kicking and thrashing in his grasp. But I felt like a butterfly trying to fight off a bull. He slammed me up against the wall, his face inches from mine. I could smell stale coffee on his breath, see the crazed glint in his eye reflecting back all the pain he intended to cause me.

"You should have kept your mouth shut, Nadine," he hissed. "Now you're going to pay for sticking your nose where it doesn't belong."

Terror clawed at my throat, threatening to choke me. I absolutely did not want to die, but if I was going to, I didn't want this man's hate-filled face to be the last thing I saw. I found I had a flicker of defiance still left in me, though. Mainly because I didn't want to give this fucking bastard the satisfaction of seeing me cower or hearing me beg for my life.

With a burst of adrenaline-fueled strength, I brought my knee up hard between Grayson's legs. He howled in pain, his grip loosening just enough for me to wrench free. I dove for the bat, my fingers scrabbling against the smooth wood.

But before I could reach it, Grayson was on me again, his weight crushing me to the floor. I clawed at his face, feeling a savage thrill as my nails left bloody furrows on his cheek.

Grayson howled, snarling like a rabid wolf as his hand shot out to close around my throat. Black spots danced in my vision as I struggled weakly beneath him. My lungs burned for air as his hold grew tighter, squeezing the life out of me in a very literal sense.

There was a vicious, animalistic roar from the doorway. Through my darkening vision, I saw a blurry figure charge into the room.

"Get the fuck off her, you piece of shit!" Was that... Dr. Raven?

No. No way. I had to be hallucinating. Wishful thinking.

The voice was a guttural roar. His eyes blazed with a protective rage I've never seen before. And, yeah. He was Dr. Raven. Or, rather, it was Pain. This was the difference. Even though he'd shown me a glimpse of a man I didn't recognize when he'd given me the warning in the infirmary that day, I could fully realize and appreciate the complete transformation Dr. Raven had taken in his life. Anyone who knew the man before he became Pain would never believe this was the same person. But I saw him. I saw both sides and recognized them as two halves of the whole.

Grayson's head snapped up, his grip on my throat loosening just enough for me to suck in a desperate gasp of air. Before he could fully react to defend himself, Pain was on Grayson, pulling him from me with terrifying ease.

The room spun as I struggled to take in some more much-needed air and to sit up. My head pounded and my throat ached, but even through my dazed state, I could feel a shift in the energy around us, the crackle of barely restrained violence that emanated from Pain's every move.

He slammed Grayson against the wall, the impact rattling it. The guard's eyes were wide with fear now, the sadistic gleam replaced by a primal terror as he stared up at the man who held his life in his hands.

"You fucking bastard," Pain growled, his voice low and deadly. "You think you can put your filthy hands on her and get away with it?"

Grayson opened his mouth, but before he could speak, Pain's fist connected with his face with a sickening crunch. The guard's head snapped back, blood spurting from his nose and his lip.

I watched with a mix of horror and fascination as Pain unleashed his fury, his movements precise and brutal. That's when I realized there was every possibility Pain was going to kill Grayson. If anyone deserved to die, it was that creep. Grayson was a predator.

I did my best to assess the situation and, though he looked on the verge of out of control, I could tell by the intent, calculating look in Pain's eyes, everything he said or did was done for a specific purpose. That didn't mean he wasn't angry. His features might have been controlled, but his voice shook with rage. Yes, Pain was still in control. He wasn't mindlessly lashing out like a beast.

As Grayson's struggles grew weaker, his face a bloody mess, Pain finally relented. He let the guard slump to the floor. Grayson groaned but didn't move other than to breathe. Pain's chest heaved with exertion and what I thought looked like barely contained emotion.

Slowly, he turned to me, his gaze softening as he met mine. There was a wealth of emotion shining in his eyes. He looked almost… scared? Relieved? Definitely angry. My heart seemed to stutter when I finally recognized a stark possession as he looked at me from head to toe in an assessing inspection.

He reached out a hand, his touch gentle as he helped me to my feet. "Are you okay, Nadine?" His voice was rough but laced with a tenderness that threatened to undo me.

I nodded, not trusting myself to speak. Because in that moment, I wasn't sure what I might say, or if Pain could see the instant lust trying to turn my brain to mush.

Pain's gaze lingered on mine for a moment longer. I thought he was going to reach for me. He raised his hand but stopped short of touching me. The moment was broken by the sound of Grayson's pained groan from the floor. Pain's eyes hardened as he glanced down at the guard, his jaw clenching with barely suppressed anger. Shaking his head slightly, Pain put his mask of anger firmly in place before turning back to Grayson.

"Who else is in your little rape gang, you motherfucker?" Pain snarled the words, getting down in Grayson's face. "Who else am I killin' tonight?"

"You ain't killin' nobody, you fuckin' cunt." Grayson chuckled, like he thought he was going to come out on the right end of this. "You just got out of prison. You kill me, you'll go right back in."

The slow smile Pain pulled was nothing short of evil. "Might. Might not. You're still gonna die. How hard depends on how much you tell me."

Finally, Grayson's ballsiness faltered. Then he... glanced over at me?

"The fuck, Grayson? Don't you fucking look at me! You tried to fucking kill me, you son of a bitch! If Pain kills you, I'll swear he was across town with me in a bar. I'll even find witnesses who'll swear they spoke with both of us, and we all spent the whole fucking night together barhopping." I stopped to catch my breath. "You're a fucking maniac!"

"And you're a fuckin' bitch, lady! Mind your business and bad shit won't happen to you."

Pain grabbed Grayson's arm and wrenched it upward at an angle. Grayson's scream was shrill and long. And oddly satisfying.

"You're about to find out why they call me Pain, Grayson."

The crunch of bone echoed through my living room as Grayson screamed again, his face contorting in agony. Pain had dislocated his shoulder with terrifying efficiency, like he'd done it a hundred times before.

"That's just the beginning," Pain whispered, his voice eerily calm. "Names. Now."

"Fuck you," Grayson spat through gritted teeth, though his nerve was crumbling fast.

Pain's hand moved to Grayson's fingers, bending one backward until another sickening crack filled the room. I winced despite myself, bile rising in my throat. The sound was like nails on a chalkboard, sending unpleasant shivers over my skin and down my spine.

"Roberts and Johnson know about most of your crew," Pain said conversationally, as if discussing the weather while he systematically broke one finger and then another. Each snapping of bone was accompanied by screams that became more and more shrill each time Pain broke something. "But I want to make sure we get everyone. There are two hundred and six bones in the adult human body. So, this can go on for a long time. Or…" Pain grinned as he let the pause linger. "You can start talking."

Grayson's resolve finally shattered. "Meyers, Donovan, Wilcox," he gasped out between pained breaths. "They're the main ones."

"Didn't ask for the main ones, Grayson." I jumped when another Pain snapped another bone in Grayson's hand. "I want them all."

Three bones and his other shoulder later, Grayson lay slumped on the ground at the corner of my house. Thank God the place I rented was in the middle of nowhere. Otherwise, I was certain the neighbors would have called the cops. It wouldn't surprise me to hear an approaching siren. I'd had to swallow back bile more than once. Each time a bone snapped it set me on edge until Pain dislocated his other shoulder. Then I'd had to stumble around the corner and vomit.

"Is he… dead?" I wasn't sure how I managed to get the question out, but I knew I did because Pain answered.

"No, honey. Not yet, anyway."

"What do we do?" Now that the shock was starting to wear off from one trauma, the adrenaline in preparation for the coming battle was threatening to make me sick again.

"We need to get out of here," he said, his voice low and urgent. "Knuckles has some of the guys from Iron Tzars comin' to help us out. They'll take care of the body and clean out your presence."

I nodded, my mind racing as I tried to process everything. "Where will we go?" I ask, hating the tremor in my voice.

"The Iron Tzars are gonna escort us safely to meet Kiss of Death."

"Motorcycle clubs?"

"You remembered." He looked pleased I'd recalled that. It was nauseating how much I soaked up the implied praise. "Yes. The Tzars are going to bring us into Evansville where we can eat and shower. Knuckles has a crew coming to Evansville to bring us to Nashville."

I took a deep breath. "This is moving so fast. I don't know what to do." I was trembling now, my voice wobbling with every word. I didn't like this feeling at all. I wasn't an indecisive person. In this case, my head was telling me one thing, but my gut another.

"I know, honey. But do you honestly think you're safer staying here?" His voice was kind, gentle even, but I knew he had to be aggravated. I was hesitating when he'd just rescued me.

"Right," I muttered. "Good point. How about we reevaluate when we get to Evansville?"

To my surprise, instead of being irritated or impatient, Pain gave me a lopsided grin any rogue would be proud of and nodded his approval. "I can work with that."

It wasn't long after that when the distant rumble of approaching motorcycles filled the air. Three bikes and one black Ford truck pulled down my driveway.

The night was still hot and muggy, the summer

not showing any sign of relief. A really tall, heavily muscled, bearded man climbed out of the truck, his movements fluid despite his size. He nodded at Pain before his gaze shifted to me, assessing but not threatening.

"Nadine, this is Brick. He's the vice president of the Iron Tzars in Evansville," Pain said, his hand coming to rest lightly on my lower back. That simple touch sent a current of electricity through me that had no business existing in this moment of crisis.

"Ma'am," Brick said with a respectful nod before shifting his gaze to Pain. "We need to move quickly. The boys will clean up the trash and make sure there's nothing left." I had the feeling he actually meant something other than the obvious, but I wasn't about to say anything. Two other men were already heading toward the house, carrying large duffel bags that I desperately did *not* want to know the contents of.

"You ready? Got everything you need?" Pain asked, his voice a steady anchor in the chaos swirling around me.

I nodded, gesturing weakly toward my suitcase and backpack near the door. "That's all I have."

"Good. Less to worry about." He grabbed my suitcase with one hand, his other hand still at my back, guiding me toward the truck.

"What about my car?" I asked, suddenly remembering the beat-up Fiesta. "It's not much, but it's all I've got."

"We'll take care of it," Brick said softly. The big-man energy around Brick was surprisingly low for someone so large. No doubt it was a skill he'd perfected so people underestimated him.

"You ready?" Pain gave me a steady look, like he knew I was freaking out but was holding myself together by a thread. Pain was my thread.

"No," I said honestly. "Not even close." I shook my head. I clung to my backpack like my lifeline. Before I realized what I was doing, I'd backed away a step, looking from Brick to Pain and back again. All of a sudden, the realization crashed over me that I was in an extremely remote location with men who were big and strong enough to break me in half. I was powerless to stop them if they attacked.

"Nadine. Honey." Pain set the suitcase down. One of the other men I hadn't been introduced to picked it up and took it to the truck without a word. Everyone else seemed to have gone into the house. "Hey." He snapped his fingers to get my attention. When I looked back at him, there was a worried expression on his face. "It's all right. Do you trust me?"

"I don't know." My voice was barely above a whisper and even though we were outside in the open, everything seemed to be closing in around me.

"Of course, you don't," Pain said, his voice gentle but firm. "You shouldn't. Not after what you've been through. But right now, staying here isn't an option."

I glanced back at my little rental house. The place I'd called home since I'd started working at the prison was about to become a crime scene. Or worse, it would be wiped clean as if nothing had happened. As if no one had ever existed here at all.

"They're going to kill him, aren't they?" I whispered, not looking at Pain directly.

Pain didn't flinch or look away. "Yes."

The single word hung in the humid night air between us. No excuses, no justification. Just the truth.

"I'm a nurse," I said, my voice cracking. "I help save lives. I don't take them."

Moving closer but still keeping enough distance that I didn't feel cornered, Pain reached in slow, deliberate movements and took my hand in his, caressing it gently. "Sometimes the world isn't black-and-white, Nadine. You know some of what Grayson and his crew have done. Roberts told me."

"Yes. And I'm not sure I even scratched the surface."

"You didn't, honey. And I don't want you to. Some things I never want you to know about." He gave my hand a gentle squeeze. "Look, I realize you don't know me. Not really. Even if we'd been friends elsewhere, I've been through so much since I went to prison you wouldn't recognize me."

"I don't… I don't know what to do." The words were pulled free against my will in a strangled sob. Showing weakness was the worst option imaginable, but Pain only stepped closer, pulling me to him with a growl and holding me tightly against him.

"It's all right." He whispered the words next to my ear. "I swear I'll protect you, Nadine. On my life."

For some stupid reason, my fists seemed to clutch his shirt and my fingers simply to God would not loosen so I could let go. My breath hitched and I held to him even harder.

"You guys need to get going." I wasn't sure who was speaking but I knew he was talking to Pain.

"Give her a minute, Roman. She's not comfortable going yet, and I'm not forcing her."

"Not suggesting you do. It's just better for you to put as much distance between you and Terre Haute as possible. Venus and Piston will lead you to the compound in Evansville, then take you on to Nashville tomorrow. Me and Clutch will get you through until Kiss of Death meets you. Venus and Piston are going all the way."

"Good. Venus will help put Nadine at ease."

"If you want to ride with her in the truck, I can make sure your bike gets back to our compound. Otherwise, Clutch will take good care of her."

"I know. But I want her with me." As he spoke, Pain held me tighter, like he was as reluctant to let me go as I was him. That's when I knew I should trust my gut. Pain wasn't going to let anything happen to me.

"I'm sorry," I whispered. "I'm sorry I doubted you'd keep me safe."

"Honey, you have nothing to be sorry for."

"I can go with Clutch if that's what you want me to do." It was hard to put myself in someone else's hands, but Pain had saved me. If he said I should go with Clutch, then that's what I'd do.

Pain stared at me for a long moment, searching for something in my gaze that gave him whatever answer he was looking for. Finally, he turned away and walked toward the truck. He opened the back door and pulled out a black helmet before stalking back toward me.

He held out the helmet to me. "You ever ride a bike?"

"I'm assuming you don't mean a bicycle." I took the helmet. Pain snagged my hand again, giving it a squeeze.

"You'd assume right." He jerked his head toward one of the bikes and tugged at my hand. I followed without protest. "Get your helmet on. I'll show you where to put your feet."

He mounted the bike, then I climbed on behind him. He reached back and grabbed my ass, pulling me closer to him. "Sorry," he muttered. "I shouldn't have…" He cleared his throat. "Just get as close to me as you can." I did, keeping my hands on his shoulders. "Wrap your arms around me. I don't want you falling off the back."

"It's OK." I said, swallowing nerves. Because, oh my God, I was sitting behind Dr. Ford Raven on a freaking motorcycle!

"What's OK?" He looked at me over his shoulder.

"That you grabbed my ass." I have no idea why I said that, but out it came.

"I see." His lips twitched before puckering slightly. Then he gave up entirely and chuckled. It was the first time I'd ever heard him laugh. At the hospital he was always professional. He might smile, but as a rule when he was in public he showed little emotion other than kind compassion when it was called for.

"That came out wrong," was my lame reply.

"No, it didn't. You were right to call me out. I only meant to pull you closer. It's intimate, but necessary." He still looked amused.

"Just don't tell anyone I said that."

"Wouldn't think of it, sweetheart. Wouldn't think of it."

Chapter Six

Nadine

Holy shit, was I really doing this? My heart raced as we roared down the highway, Pain's body a solid presence in front of me. I never imagined I'd be here, on the back of a motorcycle with a man I barely knew, but there I was.

The wind tugged at my clothes. I almost wished I could take my helmet off just to feel the wind in my hair but, hello... *nurse*. The thought sent a shiver down my spine, but it was laced with more exhilaration than fear. This freedom, this rush of adrenaline that coursed through my veins... it was addictive. It also made me all too aware of the man in front of me.

I took a deep breath, inhaling the scents of the open road. Gasoline, exhaust, and the faintest hint of freedom hit me like a welcome cool breeze on a hot summer night. I tried to imagine this was a teenage rebellion instead of being on the run from God knew who. Working in a high-security prison I'd been in a few dangerous situations, but this... this was on a whole different level.

Pain's muscles bunched under my hands as he took us closer to safety. Why was a guy on a motorcycle so Goddamned sexy? Why was riding behind a man on a motorcycle so Goddamned sexy? And fuck me, but why was Pain on a fucking motorcycle so *God. Damned. Sexy*? I didn't like the vulnerability that came with trusting someone I didn't know to navigate at high speeds on something I wasn't safely buckled into, but I couldn't seem to dwell on it like I should.

I expected the adrenaline crash to hit me hard, but I think the exhilaration of riding the bike let me down easily. It was either that or the warmth of the man whose back I was pressed so intimately against. I wanted to lean my head against him, to take in his scent while I could because I was under no illusion I'd ever be so close to this man again.

Two bikes pulled up on either side of us. I tightened my grip on Pain fractionally, startled by the sudden company. Which was my own fault. I should have been paying attention instead of being in my own little world.

Pain gave them both a two-fingered salute before squeezing my knee reassuringly. We continued on for another hour before we rolled into a gravel parking lot in front of what I assumed was their clubhouse. Several men poured out of the main building while a few more came from the garage.

Pain held out his hand to steady me as I climbed off. He dismounted behind me, careful to keep a hand on me at all times. The older couple who'd met us on the road approached and the man held out his hand, reaching to take Pain's. The two greeted each other with a smile, pulling it in for a quick hug and a clap on the back.

"Glad you made it safe, boy."

"Thanks for the escort, Pops." Pain smiled and swung his gaze to the woman. "Mama." There was genuine warmth in his tone which wasn't something I normally heard from him. Of course, I had never interacted with Pain outside of tightly contained constraints. It was yet another side of the man I found fascinating.

"We're glad to make sure you get home safe, Dr. Raven." Mama spoke to Pain like he was a favorite nephew or something. Definitely a family member. "Venus and Piston should be here soon." She turned her attention to me and her smile softened. "Can I assume you're Nadine Brentner?"

I nodded, "Yes. Thanks for riding with us."

"You're very welcome, dear. And, Pain, just so you know, your grandfather would be so proud of you."

Pain snorted. "I doubt that. I mean, he would have once. But he'd have been appalled at my lack of control getting in that fight."

Mama snorted. "I want it known I'm not speaking ill of the dead, I'm simply stating a fact. Me and Pops had to bail your grandfather out of jail more times for fighting than anyone else in Bones at the time."

"Pretty sure he still holds the record," Pops offered, a huge grin on his weathered face.

Pain had a startled look on his face before he narrowed his gaze. "You're dickin' with me."

"Not in the least." Mama's warm laughter actually made me feel a little lighter. "No, trust me, Dr. Raven. He'd be very proud of the man you are." She turned back to me. "Now. Nadine. Pain tells me you're a nurse."

"I am." I wasn't sure what to say or if small talk was appropriate. Mama projected calm and motherly trust. If I had secrets, I'd have felt safe giving them to her. I didn't miss the hardness in her gaze, though. I'd seen the same look in the eyes of hardened criminals. Actually, no. I'm pretty sure Mama could be even harder than the men I'd met in the prison infirmary. There was no doubt she was dangerous, but she wasn't indiscriminate with her skills.

"Good. You'll understand why I want you to come with me to see Stitches so he can look you over."

Mama's smile didn't falter, but I wasn't under

any illusion I had a choice in the matter. "Who's Stitches?"

"Iron Tzars' doctor. He's expecting both you and Pain." Her gaze flickered to Pain, smiling to take the sting out of the order.

"You know, Mama, I *am* a doctor. You pointed that out yourself."

"Fully aware, young man. I'm also aware that, as a doctor, you are ethically bound not to treat yourself or any close family member."

"Nadine's not a family member."

"Yet."

"Mama…"

"Pain…"

They stared at each other before both of them chuckled.

* * *

Stitches was surprisingly thorough in his exam. Not in a creepy way, but in a way that showed he genuinely cared about my comfort. Once he was satisfied I was good, he sent us on our way with a warm handshake and a smile for both me and Pain.

Mama gave him a warm hug then turned back to us. "Come on. Iris has a room ready for you."

All of a sudden, there was a little cry and a small figure practically flew around the corner from the club house and straight to Pops.

"Uh-oh," Mama said, her smile widening with affection. "Here comes your girl, Pops."

Pops turned and, spotting the child, knelt and held out his arms for her to run and jump into. She wrapped her skinny arms and legs around him in a death grip. The older man hugged her back, patting her back and rocking back and forth with her.

"There's my girl! Guess who's coming later?"

She pulled back, a huge smile on her face and shook her head but didn't say anything. "Venus…" He let the woman's name hang in the air. The child's eyes got wide and her fist bunched in Pops's leather vest as she waited for him to tell her. I could tell whatever name Pops dropped to her better be the person she hoped it was or I might have to punch the older man for the girl. She looked so hopeful. He let the pause draw out for a moment before the girl slapped at his shoulder, her face scrunching up. Still, she didn't say anything. "And she might be bringing Piston with her." The little girl let out another squeal, kissed Pops on the cheek, then wiggled down and took off back around the corner of the clubhouse.

"I'm guessing she likes Piston?" I couldn't stop the question. Watching the little girl so excited and obviously comfortable with the big, scary older man settled something inside me I hadn't realized was upset. While I had no doubt every single adult inside this place was very dangerous, they were obviously kind and nurturing to that child.

"Piston is her favorite person. Probably even more than Iris. And Clover loves Iris with everything in her." Mama looped her arm through mine and led us toward the large building that apparently was the clubhouse.

The interior of the clubhouse surprised me. I'd expected something darker, more intimidating, based on the rough exterior and the dangerous men who called it home. Instead, it felt warm and lived-in, with comfortable furniture arranged in conversational clusters and family photos scattered on tables.

"This is nice," I said, meaning it.

"It is." Mama guided me through the large room toward a wide staircase at the back.

"I confess, I wasn't expecting this." I waved my hand to indicate the homey interior.

Mama chuckled. "Yeah. Not what one typically thinks of as a motorcycle club's clubhouse. This section is for the families. Many of the men here have old ladies now. The families wanted a place free of club girls."

"Club girls?"

Mama gave me a side-eye.

"Right. Stupid question. Please continue."

That got a bark of laughter from Mama. "I like you, girl. You're trying to keep an open mind."

"My whole world got turned on its head today. The people I thought were the good guys are actually the bad guys. And some of the bad guys are *really* bad guys. Having said that, I have no problem giving any group of people a chance when the hardest-looking man of the bunch gets a tacklehug from an overly enthusiastic eight-year-old and he suffers it like a proud grandpa. As far as I'm concerned, you guys are great in my book."

Mama beamed down at me. "We all love the children and would protect them with our lives. It's the main thing we tried to instill in everyone associated with us. And to be quite honest, these men are protective as hell, so they really didn't need much encouraging."

Stitches was surprisingly thorough in his exam. Not in a creepy way, but in a way that showed he genuinely cared about my comfort. Once he was satisfied I was good, he sent us on our way with a warm handshake and a smile for both me and Pain.

As we walked away, I glanced over my shoulder to find Pain close behind us. He lifted one corner of his lips in a half smile as he winked at me. The intimacy of that moment struck me. I sucked in a breath, unable to take my gaze off him. Until I stumbled on the top step. Both Mama and Pain reached for me.

"Careful, dear. You'll have plenty of time to ogle your young man once we get you settled."

"Oh, Christ. You called me out!" I couldn't help the laughter bubbling up inside me. "I can't believe you actually called me out."

"Believe it. But then, all the women in all the clubs I'm affiliated with have eyes for their men. No one expects you to be any different. Not in the Iron Tzars. Not in Kiss of Death."

Again, I glanced over my shoulder as we walked down the hallway. Pain simply raised an eyebrow at me. "Um, you know I'm not with Pain. Right? I worked at the... uh, the facility where he was housed. He saved me, but we're not, like, *together* together."

Mama stopped at a closed door, taking a card and swiping a mechanized lock panel. She opened the door and held it open until we were both inside with her.

"How about you give it a month. If you still insist you're not his woman then, I'll take it back." She handed me and Pain each a key card. "Sofa unfolds into a bed. Get me a list of anything you need for the next few days -- both of you." Her gaze flickered from me to Pain and back. "Tape it to your door before you go to bed and I'll make sure it gets taken care of."

"I'll take care of it, Mama." Pain set down my suitcase and stepped closer to me. I felt his hand at the small of my back and wasn't sure how I felt about the touch.

At first I wanted to melt against him, to let him pull me into his arms and keep out all the bad shit that had happened to me only a few hours ago. Right on top of that was the knowledge that I was being pushed toward Pain in a not-so-subtle fashion. Immediately following that thought was, would it really be so bad? I seriously doubted he would want something more than a few pleasant days and nights. The man hadn't been out of prison long. I was certain he wouldn't want to be tied down. I knew I'd take what he offered for the experience, but I wasn't sure I was ready to give in just yet.

And wasn't that a sobering thought? I'd never been a one-night-stand kind of woman. Even in nursing school when everyone was hooking up after exams, I'd always needed more than physical attraction. But Pain... he was different. Everything about today was different.

"You're deep in thought," Pain murmured close to my ear as Mama left us alone, the door clicking shut behind her.

I jumped slightly, not realizing how close he was standing. "Just processing everything."

His eyes, dark and knowing, studied my face. "You want to talk about it?"

"Not really," I admitted, running a hand through my wind-tangled hair. "I feel like if I start talking about everything that happened today, I might not stop. And then I'll probably cry, and honestly, I'm too exhausted for that right now."

Pain nodded, understanding without pushing. "Fair enough. Why don't you take the bathroom first? Hot shower might help."

The thought of washing away the day's events sounded heavenly. I grabbed my suitcase and headed for the bathroom, grateful for the moment alone. Under the hot spray of water, I let my muscles finally release their tension. The reality of my situation hit me in waves. I'd fled my home, my job, my entire life. I was now in a motorcycle club compound with a man I barely knew but somehow trusted with my life. I thought I should have some internal alarm going off, telling me how fucking stupid I was, but the only thing my gut was telling me was that I was exactly where I was supposed to be.

When I emerged in a large T-shirt and yoga pants, Pain was sitting on the edge of the couch, his forearms resting on his knees. He stood as he looked up, his gaze perusing me from head to toe before he turned his head.

"You okay?" He didn't look at me and for some reason, it felt like a rejection.

"Honestly? I have no idea." I sank onto the other side of the couch, suddenly exhausted. "This morning, I was a prison nurse. Now I'm... what? A fugitive? A witness? I don't even know what to call myself. 'Collateral damage' sounds pretty appropriate." I muttered the last part mostly to myself.

Instantly, Pain's attention was squarely on me. "You're alive. That's what matters."

"Because of you." The words came out with heartfelt emotion that simply refused to be contained any longer. To my complete and utter horror, I completely broke down and started sobbing.

Chapter Seven

Pain

Her tears hit me like a fucking sledgehammer to the chest. I couldn't stand it. Couldn't stand seeing this strong, beautiful woman broken down because of what that piece of shit did to her. My hands clenched into fists as I watched her shoulders shake with sobs, and all I could think about was how I should have made Grayson's death slower. More painful. The bastard got off easy with a quick snap of the neck.

"Nadine." I moved closer, my voice rough. "Hey, baby. Look at me."

She shook her head, burying her face in her hands before scrubbing at her eyes with her fingers and wiping her wrist under her nose. "I'm sorry. I'm being ridiculous. I should be stronger than this."

"The fuck you should." The words came out harsher than I intended, and she flinched. I forced myself to soften my tone. "You almost died tonight, Nadine. You're allowed to fall apart."

I reached for her, slowly, giving her time to pull away if she wanted. When she didn't, I put my arm around her slim shoulders and pulled her closer to me until she turned into my chest. Her small frame fit perfectly against me. She smelled like the discount soap the club kept for surprise guests, and something uniquely her. A scent I'd dreamt about for far too fucking many nights. There was something clean and sweet about her that made my chest tight.

"I keep thinking about what would have happened if you hadn't shown up," she said.

I took a deep breath, forcing down the rage. It wouldn't help her right now. What Nadine needed was comfort, not more violence.

I tightened my hold on her and she shifted, pressing more firmly against me. I'm not really sure how it started, but somehow, Nadine ended up straddling my lap with her knees on either side of my hips, her arms wrapped around my neck, crying like her heart was breaking.

"You're safe now, honey. I'm not gonna let anything happen to you."

Her muffled sobs were like a knife to my heart. This vibrant, kind woman reduced to this because of that monster. Nadine wasn't a woman who should ever be exposed to that kind of violence. No woman should. But Nadine was so gentle, so kind and good. In my eyes this was an abomination.

I nuzzled her temple, wanting only to comfort. "Nadine?" I kept my voice low and gentle as I spoke to her.

She looked up, her gray eyes red-rimmed and filled with pain. For a moment, we just stared at each other. I saw a flicker of relief in her gaze, quickly followed by shame. She tried to wipe away her tears, but fresh ones kept falling.

"I'm sorry," she whispered, her voice hoarse as she visibly tried to pull herself together.

"You have nothing to be sorry for. Nothing at all."

She gave a shaky laugh that was more of a sob. "I should be stronger than this. I'm a nurse, for God's sake."

"You're the strongest person I know. You had to be, to work in that place. But you're still here, still fighting."

Nadine looked at me, her chin quivering. "Am I? Sometimes I feel like I'm just going through the motions."

"Honey, you forget I worked in hospitals with nurses on the outside. You have more compassion for the people you treat than any nurse I've ever met. I told you to work in a nursing home or a hospital, but I was wrong."

That statement startled her. She stilled, then pulled back to look at me in confusion. "I don't understand."

"A place with truly sick people would slowly take every ounce of compassion you had. Those places would drain you of life, then discard you like surgical instruments no one wants to clean." I grinned. She might not have been allowed in the actual patient care areas, but everyone heard managers talking about the tossing of equipment when more had to be ordered. Especially the fucking gold-handled needle drivers. Which... didn't matter now. "I never wanted you to be attacked and scared out of your mind, but I'm glad you're here. With me." I added the last part without even considering what I was about to say. But the fact was, I *was* glad she was with me. I wanted her with me. I wanted to watch her flourish in a positive environment.

She nodded. I really thought the whole moment would change, that she'd climb off my lap and we might talk for a while until she got tired enough to sleep. She surprised me by leaning forward, resting her forehead against my shoulder. I froze for a second, then carefully wrapped my arms back around her.

"I've got you," I murmured, feeling her relax slightly against me. "You're safe now. I'll make fuckin' sure of it."

"I volunteer on my nights off with a program that gives rides to people too drunk to drive." She sniffed as she made her confession. "One woman I took to a hotel saw my name badge in the console of my car and flipped out." She sniffed and clung to me tighter. "I thought she was just drunk, but she mentioned Grayson by name. That was back when I first moved here. I thought Grayson was an asshole, but I never saw the side of him she described." She took in a shuddering breath. "Until today."

"There's so much to unpack in that confession…" I couldn't help but mutter even as I found myself kissing the top of her head reassuringly.

She snorted delicately. "You could be right. Can we unpack most of it later?"

"So you volunteer to help drunk idiots get home safe." I wanted to scold her for willingly letting drunk men she didn't know in her car, but I couldn't. Not now.

"It's not like you think. They had a dash cam on us at all times, and I only transported women. They were actually glad to have a female driver because they felt it was safer for everyone."

"OK. I can buy that." I really couldn't, but it didn't matter because she was never doing that again. Sure, someone had to do it, but if this was something she had to do, I'd be doing it with her.

We sat there for a long time. I actually thought Nadine had dozed off, but she hadn't.

"Pain? What's going to happen to Chuck and Jermaine?"

That startled me. I hadn't expected her to even think about those two, let alone wonder about them. "You're too compassionate for your own Goddamned good, Nadine." When she stiffened and would have pulled away, I tightened my hold on her. "Don't move, honey. I'm not criticizing you." I chuckled. "After everything you've been through, you're worried about those two clowns."

"Pain! They're just kids! Chuck's got it rough. And Jermaine can only protect him for so long."

"I know, honey. I've already taken care of it. I've got someone on them, watching over them. They might still get in trouble, but anything not of their own making, my guys will take care of it."

"I just don't think that's a good place for them."

"Christ, woman." I wasn't sure if I wanted to laugh or cry. "You're killing me."

"Look, I know what they both did. Jermaine was playing with a loaded gun and shot another teen. Because of the political climate in the area, he was charged as an adult and painted as a monster, but it was an accident. Irresponsible and stupid, but an accident. Chuck killed his mother and stepfather after the mother let the stepfather rape him. Repeatedly. His stepbrother was the district attorney, so even though he recused himself you know he had sway over the process."

"I know, honey. It's why I've got them being looked after."

She sighed, slumping back against me. "Oh." She sounded deflated. Almost despondent. "Sorry."

"Nadine, honey. Look at me. Please." I traced my finger over her jaw, urging her to tip her head back to meet my gaze. "Everything is going to be OK. Chuck and Jermaine have to do their time. I can't fix that. But Kiss of Death has strong ties with Terre Haute. We have some pull and some people on the payroll, so we can look out for men inside we want to protect. We can't prevent every bad thing that happens, but we can provide a strong deterrent to anyone causing problems for the ones we're protecting. So, yeah. We've got their backs as much as we've got anyone's in that place. And you're a remarkable woman for recognizing those two for what they are. You and Dr. Martinez are the only ones who try at all."

"Dr. Martinez is a wonderful person, and she's going to make a great mother."

"She's being protected too. Though she doesn't know it."

Then the sun came out and a warm ray of golden light fell on me like a blessing... Which is to say, Nadine smiled at me. A genuine, happy, almost worshipful smile. And that was it. I was done. I would forever be a slave to this woman's will because there was absolutely nothing in this world I wouldn't do to put that smile on her face and fucking keep it there.

"God, you're beautiful." The admission was raw and spontaneous. I couldn't take it back if I'd wanted to, and when her gaze snapped to mine, her eyes wide with shock, there was no way I would ever want to take it back.

"What?"

"You heard me, Nadine. You're fuckin' beautiful."

I leaned in slowly, my heart pounding like I was some damn teenager again. My lips brushed her forehead, lingering just because I couldn't get enough of the feel of her skin on my lips. I meant the gesture only to comfort, but the moment I made contact, it was like a live wire sparked between us. I think I actually grunted, the impact was so sharp.

Nadine let out this tiny sigh, and I swear it was the sweetest sound I've ever heard. She tilted her head back to meet my gaze, those gray eyes locking onto mine, and suddenly I couldn't breathe.

I saw the trust in her features, the vulnerability, but there was something else too. A flicker of desire?

Was I projecting my own interest and hoping she felt some of what I did?

"Pain?" My name was a sweet breath on her lips. She said it like a prayer and a question all at once.

I cupped her face gently, my thumb tracing the curve of her cheekbone. The tears were still glistening but were no longer falling. Instead, she gazed up at me with something like wonder. It made my chest tight in a way I never thought I could.

"I'll never hurt you, Nadine. I'll protect you with my life."

She nodded. "Yeah."

"You with me, sweetheart?" I asked, my voice rough with need. Not really a sexual need, though there was plenty of that inside me. It was so much more than simple lust. I needed this woman with me. I needed her beauty. I needed her compassion. Most of all, I needed her to always look at me like I was her hero and could make all her demons flee in terror.

She nodded, the tip of her tongue darting out to wet her lips. It was a quirk of hers I'd noticed. But now? Now, that simple moistening of her lips was driving me crazy. I wanted to kiss her like I wanted my next breath.

"I'm with you," she whispered, and it was like a punch to the gut, how much I wanted to believe her. The problem was, she might think she was with me, but she didn't know me. Not really. She also didn't know I meant she was with me *forever*.

I leaned in slowly, giving her every chance to pull away. Nadine met me halfway, her lips soft against mine. Her touch was tentative at first, barely more than a graze. I wanted to deepen the kiss, to pleasure her until she was stupid with lust and only wanted... *me*. My body. My cock.

But I couldn't. She needed to make the choice. Consciously. She might be OK with me pleasuring her a little, but she wasn't ready for sex. If I were honest with myself, I wasn't ready for sex either. Not because I didn't want to fuck Nadine. The woman had fueled my dirtiest fantasies since the first day I met her as an adult. Before I made her mine, I needed her to believe in me. That I would always be with her to protect her. She wasn't ready for that. And I wasn't sure I could survive the rejection.

"This okay?" I murmured against her mouth.

She nodded, pressing closer. "Yes," she breathed. "More."

I brushed away the last traces of her tears with my thumbs as I deepened the kiss. Nadine sighed into it, and I felt the exact moment something… shifted. Her initial hesitance melted away, replaced by a hunger as ravenous as my own.

She fisted her hands in my shirt, tugging me closer. I knew that, if I took us there, if I tried to have sex with her, she'd willingly follow me. I also knew she'd regret it later. That doesn't mean I wasn't torn between wanting to slow down, to savor every second, and the need to consume her entirely.

"Nadine." I whispered her name like a fucking prayer, pulling back just enough to look at her. Her cheeks were flushed, eyes bright with a mix of desire and something deeper that I was afraid to name.

She looked up at me, a small furrow between her brows. She tugged on my shirt, pulling me closer to her "Don't you dare stop now, Ford Raven."

I couldn't help but chuckle. "Wouldn't dream of it, sweetheart. Not until I've tasted you." Nadine's eyes widened, her mouth parting as she sucked in a breath. "Oh, you like that idea. Don't you."

Her skin was soft and tempting as I slid my hand under her shirt to spread my fingers across her back. Her bra seemed to mock me as the clasp dug into my palm. I loved that her breath hitched and she was passive in my arms, letting me kiss her. Touch her.

She arched into my touch, her breath coming faster as her hips shifted restlessly against mine. I could feel the heat of her through our clothes, and it was driving me insane.

"Need you," she whispered.

"I know exactly what you need," I murmured, capturing her mouth again as my fingers traced the clasp of her bra. With practiced ease, I unhooked it, feeling her soft gasp against my lips as the tension released. My hand slid around to cup her breast, thumb brushing over her nipple through the thin material of her shirt.

She shuddered against me, her head falling back with a soft moan that shot straight to my cock. I trailed kisses down her throat, savoring the way her pulse jumped beneath my lips. When I reached the curve of her breast I rubbed my chin over the sensitive skin.

"God, yes," she breathed, fingers tangling in my hair as if she couldn't decide whether to push me away or hold me close.

When I moved back to her mouth, she darted her tongue between my lips first with a little moan. Nadine pressed her body against me, moving her hands to the waistband of my pants and tugged my T-shirt out, sliding her hands up over my abdomen to my chest. Her nails dug into my skin in the most delicious kind of pain.

I stood, taking her with me. Her legs wrapped around my waist instinctively, and I carried her to the bedroom. I might not be able to actually have sex with her tonight, but I was going to give her so much pleasure she'd never forget it. Hopefully, I could make her come to crave it.

When I set her on the bed, Nadine whipped her shirt off, dropping her bra from her arms and putting her shoulders back. It was like she was daring me to judge her and find her anything but perfect. Well. That would take a stronger man than me.

"I'm gonna eat you up, baby." I reached for the band of her pants, cupped her sides at her waist, and let my hands span as much of her as I could. "Stop me if you don't want my mouth on your pussy, Nadine. Stop me now."

"Are you fucking kidding me? Don't you dare stop!"

Her words were like gasoline on a fire. I groaned, my control hanging by a thread as I tugged her yoga pants down her hips. She lifted herself to help, and I pulled them off completely, leaving her in nothing but a tiny pair of panties that made my mouth water.

"Christ, Nadine. You're perfect." I traced my fingers along the edge of the lace, watching her breath hitch. "So fucking perfect."

She reached for me, trying to pull me down to her, but I caught her hands and pinned them gently above her head. "No, sweetheart. This is about you. Let me take care of you."

I kissed my way down her body, taking my time at her breasts, drawing each nipple into my mouth until she was writhing beneath me. Every soft moan, every gasp, was like music. I wanted to memorize every sound, every reaction.

When I reached the waistband of her panties, I looked up at her. Her eyes were dark with need, her chest rising and falling rapidly. "Still with me?"

"God, yes. Please, Pain."

I hooked my fingers in the lace and slowly dragged them down her hips and thighs to slip the rest of the way down her legs until I tugged them free and tossed them to the floor.

I settled between her thighs, my hands gripping her hips as I lowered my mouth to her. The first taste of her pussy made me groan against her sensitive flesh. She was sweet and warm, and I knew I'd never get enough.

"Pain!" Her voice broke on my name as I worked her with my tongue, finding the rhythm that made her thighs tremble against my shoulders and her skin slicken with sweat. She tasted like heaven and sin all wrapped up together, and I couldn't fucking get enough.

Her hips bucked against my mouth as I sucked gently on her clit before flicking it several times with my tongue. She fisted her hands in the sheets, hanging on with a white-knuckled grip. "Oh God, oh God!"

"Let go for me, baby. I've got you."

I slid two fingers inside her, curling them just right as my tongue continued its relentless assault. She was so tight, so wet, and the way she clenched around my fingers told me she was close.

"Please," she gasped, her back arching off the bed. "Pain! Please! Oh, God!"

I increased the pressure, the pace, watching her face as she climbed higher. Her cheeks were flushed, lips parted as she panted, and she was the most beautiful thing I'd ever seen.

Finally, she rounded her shoulders off the bed so she looked down into my face where I was latched on to her pussy. With one shuddering breath, Nadine finally shattered with a cry that went straight to my cock.

I kept licking and kissing her wet sex, praising her, bringing her down slowly. When she finally relaxed on the bed, her legs still splayed wide, I moved from the bed. Nadine lay there, cheeks glowing in post orgasmic bliss, sweat making her skin shimmer under the last rays of sunlight filtering through the window. Her eyes were closed and she wore the most satisfied smile I'd ever seen on a woman.

I leaned down to press a gentle kiss to her lips before dipping once more to her pussy for a tender lingering kiss right over her clit.

Much as I needed to release some pressure, I didn't have time. I wanted every possible second with Nadine in that bed, even if I didn't fuck her. I needed her close. Needed her in my arms.

I grabbed a washcloth from the bathroom and wetted it under warm water. Nadine hadn't moved a muscle other than to suck in a breath and shudder when I'd kissed her clit. I washed her sensitive flesh gently so she'd be comfortable in the bed, because I had no intention of putting her panties back on.

Nadine didn't protest when I urged her under the covers and followed her into the bed, pulling her snugly against me. She simply turned into me, resting her head on my shoulder, and was out like a light.

As her breathing grew deep and steady in sleep, I got lost in my thoughts. The weight of her against me was everything, grounding me in a way I didn't think I'd ever felt. It was both exhilarating and utterly terrifying. I was probably at least fifteen years her senior, and she was the glue holding the tattered pieces of my soul together.

I hadn't put the list of things I thought we needed on the door yet for Mama and I wasn't certain I was going to be able to bring myself to get up and do it. Not now anyway. I finally had this woman in my arms and there was no fucking way I was willingly leaving this bed.

Mama would forgive me. She probably hadn't expected me to follow her instructions anyway. Not really. I had no doubt she would take care of us. Not for me. For Nadine. Mama knew I could take care of myself, but Nadine needed a strong protector. Mama would know that.

Right now, though, none of that was important. What mattered was the woman in my arms. If I had my way, this was absolutely where she was going to stay.

Chapter Eight

Pain
The Next Day...

The rumble of our Harleys echoed off the warehouses as we rolled through the gates of the Kiss of Death compound. I felt Nadine's grip tighten around my waist and knew likely she was scared to death. Much as I loved the place, it had to be intimidating to her. Part of me wanted to turn around and take her somewhere else, somewhere normal. The other part, the much, much bigger part, knew there was nowhere safer for her than right here with me. Surrounded by my brothers inside this compound.

I guided my bike through the maze of camo netting that covered the pathways between buildings, acutely aware of how this place must look to Nadine. The compound sprawled out in a perfect square, massive warehouses forming the outer perimeter with smaller warehouses and various structures nestled inside like a castle fortress. It was impressive as hell, but also intimidating. Exactly what we wanted outsiders to think.

But Nadine wasn't an outsider. Not now. She was mine to protect.

Venus pulled up beside us on her pink Harley, with Piston's bike flanking our other side. Mama and Pops pulled up alongside with Tiny and Griffin to complete our little convoy, their engines rumbling to a stop as we parked near the main entrance. The sound of our arrival brought several prospects jogging out to handle the bikes.

I held out my hand for Nadine. When she took it, I placed her hand on my shoulder. "Hold onto me to brace yourself, baby, and be careful of the pipes."

"OK." Her voice trembled, as did her hand on my shoulder.

Once she was off, I took her hand again, this time, lacing my fingers through hers as I got off my bike. She looked up at me, meeting my gaze. I could see her nervousness. And Goddamn if she didn't stick the tip of her tongue out to moisten her lower lip.

I groaned, leaning in to capture her mouth with mine because I absolutely had to taste that intriguing lower lip myself. "You're killin' me, woman."

Her eyes were now glazed, half lidded as she lost herself in my kiss. Which, I wasn't too proud to admit, made me want to puff out my chest, give my brothers a big thumbs up, and shout, "I've still got it!" at the top of my lungs.

When she finally let herself drift out of the moment and back to reality, she frowned at me, narrowing her eyes. "Are you managing me?"

I almost barked out a laugh. "No. But if kissing you is the way to get your attention, I'll gladly do it all the damn time."

Her gaze softened and she reached up to stroke my beard with her hand. "I should be careful around you. You'll take me over if I let you."

"No. I don't want to control you or anything, Nadine. I want you happy. Right now, you're nervous."

"That's putting it mildly," she muttered.

"You'd be crazy not to be. I trust these men with my life, but you barely know me, let alone them."

"I know you." Her smile was soft and almost reverent. "You'd never put me in danger intentionally."

"I'm not the same person I was before prison, Nadine. You realize that, right?"

"Yes. But you're still protective. Not just of your family and friends. Everyone around you."

"I think you're seeing more than is really there, honey. I'm an asshole on the best of days. Especially when men get hurt doing something stupid."

"Oh, yes. I know. But pointing out someone's stupidity doesn't mean you still don't try to take care of them."

I started to refute what she said, but I stopped and really reflected on her words. Was she right? I mean, she was definitely right about me pointing out people's stupidity. I'd had enough of holding back my opinions working at the hospital. Instead of arguing, I turned it back to her. "What makes you say that?"

"Chuck and Jermaine."

I blinked at her. "What do you mean?"

"I have no doubt you have men inside the prison. It was hinted at, and I overheard things some of the guards said. I also know that you're not operating a prison babysitting service. Assuming you told me the truth and you had someone keeping an eye on them, you've taken that person from a task they would normally be doing. Because, while multitasking is a thing, I imagine it's much, much harder to do that kind of multitasking while in prison. Guard or prisoner." When I gave her what must have been a blank look, she lifted her chin. "Tell me I'm wrong."

I shook my head slightly, then stopped. Was she right? "I mean, you saw their files. They didn't need to be there. The system failed them both."

"So you made it your responsibility to protect them?"

"Not in so many words, no. I just felt sorry for them."

"Uh-huh."

I frowned at her, taking a step back, but retaining hold on her hand. I pointed at her. "You're trouble."

"Remember that when you try to manage me again." Nadine took a breath and looked around her, taking in everything in the immediate area. "Looks like something out of *Mad Max*," she muttered under her breath.

I chuckled. "Come on." I tugged her after me. "Let's get inside. You can shower or take a soak in the bath if you want. It wasn't a long ride, but if you're not used to it, you can be a bit sore."

"You call two and a half hours not a long ride?" I just grinned at her. Which made her scowl at me. "Fine. But please, let me work my way up to rides that long next time, huh?"

I leaned in and kissed her cheek. "I'll look forward to it."

"I'm hearing a double entendre there."

"Not denying it."

I couldn't help the grin that spread across my face as I led her through the compound and toward the inner warehouse that housed most of the living quarters. Venus and Piston had said their goodbyes outside the gate while Mama and Pops had stayed to see Gunnar for a while, which left us alone when we reached the apartment Knuckles' wife, Hannah, assigned us.

"It's got two bedrooms and two bathrooms, so you'll have as much privacy as you want." I opened the door and let her go in ahead of me. "If you're not comfortable with me staying with you, I've still got my old quarters. I didn't let Knuckles order anyone to move my shit."

"No! I want you here!" She slid her hands up my chest to circle my neck and pull me down for a kiss.

"I'm nervous, but I trust you and I'll feel better with you here."

"I know this is a lot for you to adjust to in not a lot of time. But you saw how everyone worked at the Iron Tzars while we were there. Right?" When she nodded, I continued. "It's the same here. We support each other no matter what. Probably more so here because of our shared experiences in prison and our respect for Knuckles."

"Yeah. I could see that. I only saw part of how things were for you, but I saw enough. While there were some inmates I thought deserved everything they were getting, the whole process just seemed a bit dehumanizing. Treat someone like an animal long enough and they become one."

"Knuckles helped all of us at some point while we were inside. So, yeah. I guess what you said is true, but it's also paying it forward."

Nadine smiled at me before turning to take in the room which ended up into an airy living space with floor to ceiling windows along two sides. There was a couch that had seen better days, but was clean. A sturdy coffee table sat in front of the couch and a flat screen was mounted on the wall. The kitchen was small but functional with dark wood cabinets and stainless-steel appliances that gleamed under the overhead lights. Two doors led off the main room, one to the bathroom, the other to the second bedroom.

"Two-bedroom suite," I told her as she walked around, opening a closet door. I shoved my hands in my pockets. "There's a bathroom through there." I gestured toward the hallway. "And the main bedroom is at the other end with its own bathroom. You can have that room."

"Aren't you sharing it with me?" She turned

back to me, meeting my gaze from across the small distance.

"If you want me to. But I want you to know that's your space. I'll be there if you want me, but only by your invitation."

Her expression relaxed. We'd only had the one interlude together before we'd slept, and then we'd left to come here. I knew she was still unsure about me, but I thought it was in the sense that she was afraid I was playing with her somehow. It might be easier on me if I was, because I could see her unease with my club. The difference in her body language at the Iron Tzars compound and here at Kiss of Death told me a lot. I was sure she was trying to reconcile the fact that everyone here had served time in prison for one reason or another and that none of us were truly bad men. We defended those we loved to the death, but we had our own code and we stuck to it.

"Well, you have an open invitation. If I decide I don't want you there, I'll rescind that invitation."

I leaned down to kiss her, needing to taste her one more time before I left. "I've got to meet with Knuckles," I said. "Club business. Won't be long."

"Are you sure about this, Pain?" Her voice was steady and there was still a sweet smile on her face, but there was an edge to it. Maybe a hint of fear.

"Yeah," I said with complete confidence. "I've never been more sure of anything. I'll be back soon. Soak in the bath. Then get some rest."

"Thank you, Pain." She rested her forehead against my chest briefly before looking back up at me. "Thanks for coming for me. I can't even think about what would have happened if you hadn't."

"Honey, I'll always come for you. Always. No matter what, I'll always find a way to get to you."

After I left our apartment, I went back to the main clubhouse in the compound. I pushed open the heavy door to Knuckles' office.

The room smelled faintly of motor oil and sweat, a mix that helped settle me by surrounding me with all the familiar things I'd left behind. Knuckles was already there, leaning back in his chair with a half-empty bottle of Jack on the desk. His thick arms were crossed over his chest, and that permanent scowl carved into his face like someone chiseled it out of stone was firmly in place.

"Pain," he grunted as I stepped in, shutting the door behind me. "Took your sweet fuckin' time."

"Had shit to do," I said, dropping into the chair across from him with a grin. We both knew I wasn't coming to see him before I got Nadine settled.

Knuckles grinned back, warm and inviting. It wasn't a look I'd have associated with Knuckles before, but things were different now. "Good to have you back, Pain."

"Good to be back."

"I still think your brother could have gotten you off."

I shrugged. "I didn't deserve it. I did the crime; I did the time. Besides, if you've talked to Wyatt about this, he'd agree with me. Otherwise, he *would* have gotten me off. I'd still be working at the hospital, and I'd never have met Nadine." I took a breath before meeting Knuckles' gaze. "She's mine, Knuckles. I'm sure I can convince her to stay with me. She wants to, though she's being cautious."

"Given she worked in a prison, that's not unexpected. She's just been thrust into what could be her worst nightmare if we were like some clubs." Knuckles picked up a pen and twirled it absently between his fingers. "How's she holdin' up?"

I shrugged. "Not bad. She had a rough time processing everything that happened at her home, but she's trying. I think with some time, and getting to know the other old ladies, she'll fit in here perfectly."

There was silence and I knew there was another reason Knuckles wanted to meet with me. "We might have a situation. We're trying to take care of it, but this was something that hit us out of the blue. I'm telling you privately because this literally just happened. While you were on your way here from Iron Tzars last night."

OK, that didn't sound good. "What's going on?"

"The city just hired a new police chief. He's coming in from Memphis. Bringin' his core officers in the department, who also happen to be his muscle on the inside."

"I don't understand."

"His name's Benjamin Roscoe. He's as corrupt as they come and hell-bent on cleanin' us out of the area."

That surprised me. "Seems pretty sudden."

"Yeah. Even your brother got taken by surprise on this one." Knuckles scrubbed a hand over his face before slamming the pen back on the table in frustration. My brother, Wyatt Raven, was my lawyer. He was affiliated with Iron Tzars, but he was my older brother. Which meant anything and everything going on around me, Raven -- his road name in the Tzars -- knew about and had at least a modicum of control over. Why? Because he was a bastard control freak who constantly had to have his nose in other people's business... because he had a fear of losing more people close to him. Like he had our parents, our younger sister, and then me. "Not to mention, Tonio is furious." He was talking about Antonio Miles, a major player in the family who controlled the Nashville underground. Nashville was his city. Kiss of Death was the muscle. I didn't think Antonio was the head of the family dynasty, but he was definitely in the upper echelon.

I sat up straighter. "*He* didn't know?"

"Nope."

"Sounds serious."

"It could be. Roscoe has his men watching our every move. His excuse is that we're a bunch of ex-cons gathered in one place. He has no evidence to back up claims we demand protection money from the dock workers, or that we basically have our pick of shit we want coming into Nashville, but that's not stopping him."

"So he's just throwing shit out there?"

"Yep. The media picked it up because why not, and ran with it."

"And given the city's current political environment, it was easy to get everyone to believe we're causing a problem."

"Yep. Which means this Roscoe is making a concerted effort to take out the Miles family's muscle."

"The fact is, he's not wrong about us being a menace. We're just not a menace in the way he's painting."

Knuckles sat back in his chair and shrugged. "True. But I'm pretty sure he's making this move on someone else's payroll. Little cunt's not smart enough to do it on his own, though it's obvious he thinks he is."

"Which means there's someone new making a move." I crossed one ankle over the opposite knee. "Great. This isn't the calm, carefree environment I'd hoped to show Nadine."

"Yeah, we're gonna scare the poor girl to death.

Keep her in the center buildings as much as you can. The other women are gathering there. They're making use of Oasis One a lot. Given the heat -- both literally and figuratively -- the officers all agreed it's better to keep the women and kids inside the inner protection of the compound."

"Not gonna get a disagreement from me, Prez."

"Not you I'm worried about. It's your girl." Yeah. Knuckles might be a hard ass, but he wasn't a monster. We all loved women, but Knuckles had extended his protective streak to all the women in the club. Old ladies or club whores, it didn't matter. Our women were treasures, and we did our best to treat them as such, so this expression of concern didn't surprise me now like it might have when I'd first come here awaiting my trial.

"If anyone can put her at ease, it's the old ladies. Nadine's in her apartment cleaning up and getting some rest. I'll explain things to her. With the help of the other girls, I'm pretty sure I can get her to do what we tell her to."

The smug grin on Knuckles' face said he knew everything to be already under control.

"I wouldn't count on it." I chuckled, thinking about Nadine's stubborn streak. "She's got a mind of her own."

Knuckles laughed, a sound almost like gravel in a blender. "All the good ones do. That's what makes 'em worth all the shit they put us through. All the women in this club have a mind of their own, in case you've forgotten."

I rubbed my beard, thinking about how to handle this. "I'll talk to her tonight. Let her know what's going on but ease her into it."

"Good. Now, you got her property cut in the

works?"

"Nope." I grinned. "Already done. I'm giving it to her tonight when we --"

A sharp knock interrupted us. The door swung open and Diesel, a prospect Knuckles had brought in sometime while I was in prison, filled the doorframe.

"Sorry to interrupt," he said, not looking sorry at all. I didn't know the guy, but I'd been hearing from the others he was a quiet, solid guy. Figuratively as well as literally. "We've got movement on the east side wall. Unmarked car, two men taking photos. If they're not police, I'll eat his shorts." He nodded at me, and I barked out a laugh.

Knuckles didn't acknowledge the byplay. "Make sure we got good eyes on them but don't engage. I expect this is just the beginning."

Diesel gave Knuckles a curt nod. "Already on it. Knight has a good view of the car all the way around. Probably has an ID on the occupants already."

"Good." Knuckles stood. "Tell him to have the information ready for me. I'll be there in five."

"On it, Prez."

After Diesel left, Knuckles stood and came around his desk and I followed suit. He stuck his hand out to me. "Good to have you back, man."

I gave him a lopsided grin, the pressure in my chest finally easing. I was all too aware I'd let the club down by getting my ass busted on the biggest night of my life. "Knuckles…" I reached out and took the hand he offered. "I'm sorry."

"Nothin' to be sorry for. Yeah, the timing could have been better, but, whether you wanted him to or not, your brother came through with flying colors."

"Yeah. I berated him for that."

"'Cause you felt guilty."

"I am guilty! I didn't mean to kill the bastard, but he grabbed my date's ass. I had to do something."

"You don't have to justify yourself to me, Pain. As far as I'm concerned, you don't have to justify yourself to anyone. Any man who won't defend a woman when she's touched against her will ain't much of a man, in my opinion. In some ways, I'd classify that person as worse than the one doin' the touchin'."

That statement threw me. Yeah, it had been my first date with Sondra -- Shonda? Sonda! -- but she'd still been with me. I'd shoved the guy, then punched him when he'd laughed and tried to make a grab for her again. He was too drunk to keep his balance and fell, his head landing on the corner of a brick step inside the bar. The impact of the landing caved in his skull at the temple and he later died. At the same hospital I'd just been hired on as a full-time surgical attending.

"You ever hear from your date again?" Knuckles' question caught me off guard.

"No." And that had hurt more than I'd expected. I hadn't been in love with the woman. It was our first date! But I'd defended her. She had barely made a police statement before she'd hightailed it out of the bar. "But I learned better than to date from the nursing pool."

"Shoulda known that from the start."

"I did. But I thought I was the shit." I shrugged. "Thought I could handle myself on one date. I'd already decided we weren't going to fit anywhere. Not even in bed. The woman had a voice that simply to God grated on my last nerve."

"Then why the fuck did you ask her out to begin with?"

"Heard she had good pussy. If that makes me an

asshole, so be it. I told her what I wanted up front. Probably why I never saw her again."

"Sounds about right. Tell me you're not glad she split."

"Nope. I don't lie. By her giving me the kiss-off -- and probably rightfully so -- she saved me the trouble of dumping her after I met Nadine. Because no one is keeping me from Nadine but Nadine. And only if I can't sweet talk her into keeping me."

"She'll stay. She's a little reserved now, but you're right. The women will bring her around."

"Speaking of which, I need to go check on her. I don't want to leave her alone too long. She'll start questioning her decision to come with me and I'm not fighting a battle I've already fumbled my way through."

"Good plan. Church will be at eight tonight. I think Hannah and Pippa are getting together a barbeque for afterward."

"That a good idea? You know, with eyes on us?"

"They're setting up in the center warehouse by the pool. I'll make sure there are lookouts all around the perimeter and a couple up on the roofs at each corner. We'll have a good warning if they decide to breach the place. We've all prepared the women, and they know what to do. Best get Nadine filled in. Hannah will make sure she's taken care of if we get hit."

"Ain't likin' this." I scrubbed the back of my neck.

"Me neither." Knuckles clapped me on the shoulder. "Go see to your woman. Get her firmly on your side so you can protect her. She's got to trust you to keep her safe before she'll let you."

"On it, Prez. On it good and proper."

Chapter Nine

Nadine

It's funny how quickly a place built like a fortress could start to feel like home. I'd been at Kiss of Death for three weeks with Pain. Sometimes I could see flashes of Dr. Raven, but most of the time, he was Pain. I thought I might be more comfortable with Pain than I was Dr. Raven. It didn't take long to establish a routine that felt almost normal. I mean, if you ignored the camo netting.

The whole place had seemed on edge from the beginning, but given what Pain had told me, I guessed I could understand. I'd seen the traffic around the compound, and even I could tell it wasn't usual. It was disconcerting. It also made me hyperaware the men housed in this place weren't safe. Not in any way. Having said that, I'd never felt more like I was part of a family than I had since coming to this place in Nashville.

"Hey, Nurse Hottie!" Tillie called as she sauntered into the clinic, her heavily pregnant belly leading the way. "Got time to check my blood pressure? Baby's kicking like he's auditioning for the damn UFC."

I smiled warmly at the other woman. Tillie was with Xavier. Apparently, she'd gotten pregnant soon after becoming Xavier's old lady, and now she was about eight weeks from delivery. And the kid was going to be a hellion if the way it kicked its mother was any indication.

"Come in. And I've told you to stop calling me Nurse Hottie."

"Not gonna happen." She laughed. Tillie was a stunning woman with the most beautiful silvery green eyes. Mid laugh, she winced before settling herself in the chair next to my desk with a grunt. "The guys have already caught on. I heard Diesel call you that yesterday."

"Where Pain could hear?" I raised an eyebrow.

"Yes! That was the whole problem. Diesel had no idea you were Pain's woman. He was the one telling Pain what a hottie you were." She laughed merrily before wincing once more. "This kid's a little shit already."

"Great," I muttered, wrapping the cuff around her arm. "Just what I need."

But the truth was, I didn't mind it much. The nicknames, the teasing, that's how they showed acceptance and affection. No one was malicious about it. It was more like siblings. I found I'd come to crave the interaction.

These people were nothing like I'd been afraid of when I'd first come here with Pain. These were good people. Did they do some shady shit? Yep. Pain had explained some of it to me because he said he didn't want secrets between us.

"How are you and Pain getting along? Everything good?" Tillie's question was genuine. She rubbed her belly absently, but I could see she was genuinely interested. All the old ladies were.

"Great, actually." I smiled nervously. I still wasn't used to being able to have an open relationship with the doctor of the clinic but nothing about any of this was formal and no one fucking cared. "I mean, we're getting to know each other."

"So you've not had sex yet."

In my old life, I'd probably have been embarrassed at the direct question, but now I laughed. "No. It just hasn't seemed like the right time."

"If it helps, I can tell you that every single one of us had sex with our men within the first few days of meeting them. A couple within the first few hours. They all seem to have some seriously powerful mojo."

"OK, I believe that." I finished taking her blood pressure. "You're a little higher than usual, but still in the normal range. Are you having any contractions?"

"No. I don't have any pain at all except when the little fucker kicks my ribs."

Laughter bubbled up inside me and I realized I'd laughed more in the last three weeks than I had in the last few years. Maybe since I'd finished nursing school.

"You have the prettiest laugh," Tillie said with a soft smile. "I'm glad you came here, Nadine. You're good for all of us. Especially Pain. We were worried about him when he first came back. But since he brought you back with him, he's much better. Calmer."

That startled me. "What do you mean? You were worried about him?"

"Hannah said Pain usually kept to himself. Was a little withdrawn, but then, that was when she first got to Kiss of Death, and I don't think Pain had been here too long before she got here." She rubbed her belly again. "When he first came back, he was almost manic. More than once I heard Xavier threaten to knock his ass out if he didn't settle the fuck down and let them work the problem."

"Wow. That doesn't sound like Pain at all."

"Exactly. Now he's better. You are the common denominator."

Heat flooded my cheeks at her words. "I don't know about that. He seems pretty steady to me."

"Nadine." Tillie's voice was gentle but firm. "Trust me on this one. That man was wound tighter than a spring when he got back. We all saw it. And now? Well, he looks at you like you hung the moon."

That statement sent a warm flutter through my chest. I'd seen glimpses of a protective streak in Pain, especially with the continued police presence at the wall around the compound. He always insisted on going with me if I went outside, even from one building to the next.

"I really like him," I confessed. "I'm not sure why he hasn't made a move again. To be fair, I'm not sure I was ready."

"Are you now?"

I didn't even have to think about it before a big smile split my face. "Oh yeah. I think I was ready the first time we fooled around, but he knew better." I propped my elbow on the table then rested my chin in my hand. "I've never been around a man like Pain. He's literally always looking out for me. In everything. Even down to knowing my favorite food and that I have to have someone remind me to stop and take a break when I'm working."

"I think most of the guys are like that. Some of them have been in prison most of their lives. Some for some pretty long stretches. When they got out, none of them had any intention of going without women like they had to do in prison." Tillie laughed, obviously loving what she was about to tell me. "They talked about it and decided the best way to keep women around was to treat them like princesses. They play as hard as the time they did, and that's to say they play a fucking lot."

"Yeah. I've noticed by the injuries coming in on football nights." We both laughed.

Before I could respond, the sharp wail of sirens pierced the afternoon quiet. My blood ran cold as the sound grew closer, and I heard Pain yelling for me before he opened the door to his clinic.

"What the hell?" Tillie glanced out the window, her brow furrowed in concern. "Oh, God…"

I was on my feet, rushing toward the window to look outside. The sirens grew louder, a discordant symphony that set my teeth on edge as I tried to make sense of the unfolding chaos.

Flashing red and blue lights illuminated the late afternoon overcast, casting eerie shadows across the front of the compound. Police vehicles screeched to a halt, doors slamming open as officers exited the vehicles, their weapons drawn and voices raised in urgent commands.

"Everybody stay where you are! Hands where we can see them!"

"What the shit?" Tillie moved beside me, her hands balled into fists as she took in the group of police officers with weapons ordering the men in the compound into passive positions.

"I said, on your knees!" One big, burly man in a bulletproof vest shouted over the megaphone in the cruiser he was hiding behind.

One of the men shoved a cooperating Xavier so he stumbled. Another officer moved his foot into Xavier's path so Xavier had no hope of keeping his footing.

"Oh, *hell* no." Tillie shoved away from the window and ran across the room to the door that led to the lift.

"Tillie, wait!" I hurried after the pregnant woman, acutely aware she didn't need the stress or the physical activity. I barely got inside before she shut the gate and hit the button to go down.

"He wasn't doing anything wrong!" she snapped.

"Tillie, you can't run out there like this. What if you get hurt?"

"I'm not letting them take Xavier away, Nadine."

"Stay in the doorway, then." I needed to compromise my way out of her charging into the middle of a police raid. "If not for yourself, for your baby. If you got hurt, you'd never forgive yourself."

"Nadine." She clutched at my arm, tears now spilling down her cheeks. "Please, don't let them take Xavier. I need him here." My new friend looked at me like I was the only one who could fix this situation. Why me, that was anyone's guess. Probably because I was *here*. I understood her fear because I felt the same fear for Pain. Her hormones were likely running rampant inside her and she was terrified. Hell, *I* was terrified! Tillie was a strong woman. Seeing her clutch her belly, tears sliding down her cheeks, stirred my protective nursing instincts and made me determined to fix this for her.

I hurried out into the yard, still under the camo netting but not out of sight of the greater area. A couple of the officers roughly shoved several of the guys to the ground, forcing them to their knees with their hands behind their head. With each passing second, the police grew more aggressive. I could see a couple of the guys in Kiss of Death losing their patience.

"Hey!" I called out with more aggression than I probably should have. But Goddamnit, they were making the pregnant woman cry! "They're not resisting! What's wrong with you?!"

An officer turned toward me, his eyes narrowing. "Step back, miss," he warned, his tone leaving no room for argument.

But I couldn't step back. Not when I saw Pain

being forced to his knees by two officers, his jaw clenched tight as they zip-tied his hands behind his back. Not when I could see the barely controlled rage in his eyes the second he caught sight of me standing there.

"Get back inside, Nadine!" Pain's voice cut through the chaos, sharp with command and fear. "Now!"

This was exactly what Pain had warned me about. The new police chief was targeting them, using any excuse to harass the club. My heart hammered against my ribs as I took in the aggressive posturing of the officers, the way they were treating these men like animals instead of human beings.

"If you're trying to get a reaction from them, you won't get it," I said as I moved toward the group of men in the yard. "You should also know we've put in a call to their lawyer." Not exactly a lie, because I knew Knight, or Hannah or Pippa would be all over that the second these guys breached the gate. It had been part of the protocol handed down to us by Knuckles.

A tall, imposing man in a crisp uniform standing apart from the other officers watched the scene unfold with cold satisfaction. His dark hair was slicked back, and there was something cruel in his smile as he surveyed the result of the controlled chaos he'd orchestrated. I had no doubt this was the new police chief.

"I seriously doubt this lot has a lawyer on retainer." He chuckled lightly as he reached for something from the officer beside him. The next thing I knew, he pointed the orange-handled Taser at me. Then pulled the trigger.

Chapter Ten

Pain

The second I saw Nadine crumple, her face contorted in pain, a cold, sickening dread settled in my gut. Along with white-hot, burning rage. I was on my knees, hands zip-tied behind my back. I hadn't felt this helpless since my first day in prison. Now, in my home, surrounded by my family, with my woman -- who I'd given my property patch to but hadn't properly claimed yet -- the feeling of helplessness and being completely out of control was so much fucking worse than it had ever been.

"You fucking bastard!" The words ripped from my throat as I watched Nadine convulse on the ground, her body rigid from the electrical current. "She's not even part of this!"

The police chief -- Roscoe, had to be -- stood over her with that same cruel smile, like he was enjoying every second of her pain. "Interfering with a police investigation. Resisting arrest."

"She wasn't resisting shit!" I roared, straining against his restraints.

I struggled against the zip ties, feeling the plastic bite into my wrists as I tried to get free. Nadine stopped convulsing but was still on the ground gasping for breath. Every instinct I had screamed at me to protect her, to get between her and all these fucking bastards, but I was completely fucking useless.

"Pain!" Knuckles' voice cut through the chaos. "Stay down!" I bared my teeth at my president but did what he said.

"You son of a bitch!" Xavier's voice joined mine, his own fury matching the rage burning through my veins. His jumping to Nadine's defense wasn't unexpected. His woman, Tillie, was pregnant and Nadine was the best mother hen, making her comfortable and always being there to help calm her fears. While all the old ladies in the club seemed to have formed their own club within the club, Nadine and Tillie were exceptionally tight.

Roscoe turned his attention to us with obvious amusement. "Failure to comply with lawful orders. I could go on." He shrugged like it was nothing. "Sometimes civilians get caught in the crossfire when gangs are involved." He stared down at Nadine, a cruel smirk on his face. Then he squeezed the trigger on his Taser with its second, and last, discharge.

Her body stiffened where she lay on the pavement in the fetal position. The image would be one that would forever be seared into my mind. I heard an animal roar off in the distance, only to realize I was the one making the noise. The raw brutality in that roar was bloodcurdling. Someone was about to die, and I hoped to bloody Christ on the fucking cross it was that motherfucker, Roscoe.

The next thing I knew, there were men on top of me, dragging me through the gravel while in front of me, Nadine's body had gone limp. Her eyes were open and her hair was in her face and over one eye, but the other eye was open, staring at me.

Weakly, she reached her hand out to me. "Pain..." My name was whispered, and her hand shook with the effort she was using to hold it out to me. "Don't..."

"Hold it together for a couple more minutes, Pain. Cavalry's on the way." Was that Knuckles? I looked to my left where someone gripped my shoulder. I have no idea why I focused on that touch rather than the two or three men holding me to the gravel, but it was Knuckles who commanded my attention. It was why he was president of the Goddamned club.

My breath came in deep, heavy gasps and I realized I was fighting for air because of the heavy weight on top of me. I went limp, my gaze locked on Knuckles. I wanted to look back at Nadine, but my president commanded my attention. The second I surrendered all the pain in my body came surging forward.

"Fuck," I muttered.

"You're back with us." Knuckles sounded almost like a proud father, but his gaze shifted to the front gate and a black SUV pulling up. "Almost done."

"What's happening?" I was still on the ground, but the pressure pinning had eased significantly.

"You gonna lose your Goddamned mind again, or can I get you up and cut those fuckin' zips off you?"

"Nope. I'm good."

"Uh-huh." Knuckles knew better but got someone to help him get me on my feet before cutting my hands free.

The SUV stopped in the middle of our little party. The driver stepped out of the vehicle but stayed close. The passenger buttoned his suit jacket before stepping away from the vehicle and toward the police chief. They exchanged quiet words, Chief Roscoe getting angrier by the second if his body language was anything to go by. He was tense, his shoulders back, and he wouldn't meet the gaze of the man speaking to him.

It kind of looked like Chief Roscoe told the suit to go fuck himself, but what did I know? The suit shrugged as if to say, "Suit yourself" before striding back to the SUV and opening the back door.

Even though I'd never met the man, I knew I was looking at Antonio Miles. And he was *not* happy.

Antonio Miles had the kind of presence that made even hardened men straighten their spines. His tailored suit couldn't hide the power in his frame, and his dark eyes took in everything with calculated precision. The moment he stepped fully out of the SUV, the entire atmosphere shifted.

My gaze darted back to Nadine. She was trying to sit up now, her movements shaky and uncoordinated. Tillie had made it to her side, followed closely by Hannah and Violet, with Caleb hovering like a guard dog. Violet and Hannah helped Nadine sit, murmuring something I couldn't hear. Relief flooded through me when Nadine's gaze found mine again, though her eyes were still glazed with pain.

"Benjamin." Antonio's voice was deceptively calm. "I don't believe this is a place you really want to be."

Roscoe's face flushed an ugly red. "This is a police matter, Miles. You have no authority here. This ain't your property."

Antonio smiled, the expression never reaching his eyes. "Authority? No. Influence? That's another matter entirely." He casually adjusted his cufflinks. "The mayor would be disappointed to learn about this unauthorized raid. Especially since I just left his office." He half turned before adding, "And you're wrong. This *is* my property. These men are here at my insistence. They work for me. In the future, I'd appreciate it if you directed any questions regarding this property or the people in it to my office."

I took advantage of the distraction to move toward Nadine, but one of the remaining officers stepped into my path, his hand moving to his weapon.

I froze, every muscle in my body coiled tight, ready to tear this fucker apart if he so much as breathed wrong.

"Not a good choice, officer." Antonio didn't so much as glance in the officer's direction. "Getting between a male and his injured mate? It tends not to work out so well."

The officer looked between Antonio and Roscoe, uncertainty flickering across his face. Roscoe's jaw worked furiously, but he gave a sharp nod. The officer stepped aside, and I immediately went to Nadine, dropping to my knees beside her.

"Baby, look at me." I cupped her face gently, my thumb tracing the line of her cheekbone. Her skin was still pale from the trauma of the electrical shock, and I could see the fear lingering in her gray eyes. "You're OK. I've got you. I'll make sure you're OK."

She leaned into my touch, her hand coming up to cover mine. "I'm sorry," she whispered. "I couldn't just stand there and watch them --"

"Don't you dare apologize." My voice came out rougher than I intended. "This ain't your fault and I won't have you thinking it is."

Antonio's voice carried across the compound as he continued his conversation with Roscoe. "I think we understand each other now. Any further issues you have with my associates will come through my assistant, and I'll deal with them. On any charges."

Roscoe's face was a mask of barely controlled fury, but he knew he was beaten. The political weight Antonio carried in this city was undeniable, because Antonio and his family *owned* Nashville. This was their city, and they controlled business done within it with an iron fist. "This isn't over," Roscoe snarled, but he was already signaling his men to pack up.

"Oh, but it is." Antonio's smile was razor-sharp.

"At least for today. And Benjamin? The woman you assaulted? She's under the Miles family's protection along with everyone else inside this place. I'd suggest you remember that."

The threat hung in the air like smoke. Roscoe's eyes flicked to Nadine, then back to Antonio, and I saw the exact moment he realized he'd made a serious fucking mistake.

As the police vehicles pulled away, leaving tire marks on our gravel and the acrid smell of their exhaust, I helped Nadine to her feet. She swayed slightly, and I immediately wrapped my arm around her waist to steady her. "Easy, honey. Take your time."

"I'm okay," she said, but her voice shook and she was trembling in my arms.

"No, you're not." I kept my voice gentle but firm as I lifted her into my arms, cradling her against my chest. "You've been tased. Twice. Your muscles are going to be spasming for hours."

She didn't argue, which told me just how bad she was feeling. Instead, she looped her arms around my neck and pressed her face against my shoulder.

Antonio approached us, his expression unreadable as he studied Nadine. "Dr. Raven," he acknowledged with a slight nod. "We've not met. I'm Tonio Miles." I thought he'd expect me to shake his hand or some shit when I'd just picked my woman, the woman who'd just been tased twice, probably because that swine, Roscoe, was a fucking bully and he picked who he saw as the weakest link in our group to make an example of. Instead, Tonio proceeded down the path ahead of us and opened the door to the nearest warehouse, where my clinic was. The man wasn't lying when he'd told Roscoe he owned the property. It was in the club's name, but all this was possible because of

Knuckles' connection to this man. Tonio knew where everything in the compound was.

"Thanks," I muttered as I carried Nadine to the gurney in the corner and set her down gently. After looking into Nadine's eyes, seeing for myself she was in pain and scared, but not physically hurt too terribly, I turned back to Tonio and stuck out my hand. "I owe you one."

Tonio took my hand but waved off the debt. "No. Your club works for me. I take care of my own. That includes your families."

"In any event, thanks for the save."

"I wasn't as on top of things as I should have been, and I wasn't aware the situation had escalated so quickly." His gaze shifted to Nadine who lifted her head to look at him. "Miss Brentner. I apologize for your mistreatment."

"Not your fault," she murmured, her voice strained. "Thank you for stopping things from going any further."

Antonio's eyes hardened again. "Be that as it may, Chief Roscoe will understand the error of his ways."

The door opened and Knuckles stormed in, his face a thundercloud of barely contained rage. "This is fucking unacceptable, Tonio," Knuckles growled, pacing the small space. "Tasing a woman who wasn't even resisting is bad enough, but that asshole did it specifically to hurt us. What the fuck?"

"I'll take care of it, Knuckles."

"You fuckin' better. Me and the boys are fair game. I get that. But they will *not* hurt our families. That will cause a war, and right quick."

"I understand, Knuckles. I said I'd take care of it." Tonio's gaze hardened. "Leave it there."

Knuckles took a menacing step toward Tonio, not backing down an inch. "Tell me to fuckin' leave it there when they come after one of your family."

"Are you referring to Miss Brentner or Dr. Raven?"

"Me?" I looked from Knuckles to Tonio and back. "What are they coming after me for?"

"Not you specifically," Tonio said, straightening his cuffs. "I had to do some fast work when Knuckles told me about the danger to Miss Brentner. Since this power grab caught me by surprise, I failed to properly hide my interest in you, Dr. Raven. The wrong people inside the prison got word and informed someone, who informed someone else, who informed Chief Roscoe. In short, our esteemed new police chief thought to use Dr. Raven's parole provisions as an excuse to raid the place and gauge the strength of my muscle." He nodded approvingly at Knuckles. "Pissed at me or not, brother, I approve of the way your men handled themselves. They gave nothing away and complied beautifully with the police so there was no excuse to take anyone in."

"Can't promise it will go that easy again. And I'm not your Goddamned brother, Tonio."

Tonio shrugged. "Half-brother."

"No one threatens our women and lives, Tonio. Take care of him, or by Christ, I will."

Chapter Eleven

Nadine

When everyone left, Pain shut and locked the door to the clinic. He didn't immediately turn back to me, but rested one hand on the frame before thumping his head against the door he'd just closed.

"Pain?"

He took a breath before turning to pin me with his piercing gaze. The fear and anguish I saw in his eyes made my heart stutter. I'd never seen him look so devastated.

"I thought I was going to lose you," he said, his voice raw. "When that bastard tased you a second time…"

I tried to sit up, wincing as my muscles protested. "I'm okay. Really."

"No, you're not." Pain crossed the room in three long strides, his hands gentle as they cupped my face. "You're hurt, and it's because of me. Because I brought you into this life."

"I chose to be here," I whispered, reaching up to stroke his beard. My fingers trembled slightly from the aftereffects of the taser. "You didn't force me."

Pain's jaw tightened, his eyes darkening. "You didn't sign up for this. Being attacked by corrupt cops wasn't part of the deal."

"Neither was being attacked by Grayson, but you saved me then, just like you would have saved me today if you could." I managed a weak smile. "Besides, I think I held my own pretty well."

A choked sound escaped him, something between a laugh and a sob. "Jesus Christ, woman. You're going to be the fuckin' death of me."

We shared a quiet moment. Pain sat on the edge

of the gurney and leaned in to rest his forehead against mine for a long moment. When he was ready, instead of sitting up, he moved down to lay his head on my chest. It wasn't anything sexual. He needed the comfort as much as I did.

"When I saw you on the ground..." Pain clenched his jaw tightly and took another deep breath. "I couldn't get to you. I was right there, and I couldn't --" Again he clenched his jaw. I threaded my fingers through his hair and massaged his scalp, trying to do something -- anything -- to give him some kind of peace. "I've never wanted to kill someone so badly in my fuckin' life. If Knuckles hadn't stopped me, I would have, too. I'd have ripped his Goddamned head off with my fuckin' hands."

I believed him. I'd seen the look in his eyes just before Roscoe tased me the second time. It was a primal, animalistic rage he was still reeling from, the same as I was.

"I saw you," I confessed softly. "I see you now, too."

He didn't move. "What do you see when you look at me, Nadine? Please tell me."

I had to smile. It really was this simple. "I see... a man who loves me." He stiffened in my arms. "So you should know, I'm the woman who loves you."

Pain's head snapped up, his eyes searching mine with an intensity that stole my breath. For a moment, he just stared, like he couldn't believe what I'd said.

"Say that again," he whispered, his voice rough with emotion.

My heart hammered against my ribs, but I held his gaze. "I love you, Ford Raven. I love you... Pain."

He made a sound deep in his throat before capturing my mouth with his. The kiss was desperate, hungry, full of all the fear and relief we'd both been struggling with. His hands framed my face like I was something precious, something he was afraid might break or disappear.

When he ended the kiss, I took a breath. I needed to finish this before I couldn't because I was about to bare my soul.

"I love you, Pain." I had to say them again -- the words felt right, natural and true. "I think I've been falling for you since Terre Haute, but today, seeing you helpless to reach me and seeing how much it tore you apart..." I swallowed hard. "I don't want to waste any more time pretending this isn't exactly where I'm meant to be."

"You caught my attention when I first met you as a volunteer. Not in a sexual way, but in the way you treated people. I've loved you since the first day you walked into that infirmary," he confessed. "Watching how you were to all the inmates you interacted with, seeing that fierce compassion you showed patients and family at the hospital instead of treating them with disrespect... Christ, Nadine. You're the most caring person I've ever met. You have no idea what you do to me."

He kissed me again, soft and reverent at first, like he was afraid I might break. But when I wrapped my arms around his neck and pulled him closer, the kiss changed. Something snapped in him, and suddenly his mouth was devouring mine with a hunger that matched the ache building inside me.

"I need you," I whispered against his lips. "Take me home, Pain."

He pulled back just enough to search my face. "You sure you're up for that? You're hurt."

I smiled up at him. "I'm sore, Pain, not broken." I

ran my fingers through his salt-and-pepper hair. The silky strands were a gentle reminder of our age difference. It also reminded me he'd have vastly more experience than me in every aspect of life. Maybe it should bother me, but I found it oddly comforting to know he could take care of everything. "And right now, I need to feel alive. I need to feel you touching me."

A low growl rumbled in his chest as he carefully lifted me into his arms. "Hang onto me, baby."

The journey back to our apartment was a blur. Pain carried me the entire way, ignoring anyone we passed. His face was set in determination, and I could feel the tension in his muscles, the controlled power as he held me against his chest.

Once inside our apartment, he kicked the door shut behind us and carried me straight to the bedroom. He laid me down on the bed with a gentleness that made my heart ache, his hands hovering over me like he was afraid to touch me.

"Let me see where he got you," he murmured, his fingers hovering over the hem of my shirt.

I nodded, lifting my arms so he could pull off my top. His breath hissed between his teeth when he saw the round, red burn marks on my shoulder and side. He looked like it almost pained him too.

He grunted before going to the bathroom. When he returned, he had a kit that held more medical stuff than any first-aid kit I'd ever seen.

"What's that?" I didn't really care; I was trying to get him talking to me. He was hurting in a way I didn't understand, and I needed him to tell me what to do to make him better.

"First-aid kit on steroids."

"I'll say. You've got everything in there but the

kitchen sink." It was true. There were various kinds and sizes of bandages as well as medicine, from injectable stuff to pills and creams.

This time, he gave me a small grin. "Yep. It's my jump kit. I've always got something with me for emergencies. This is my backup. I swap them out every few months as things are ready to expire."

"Really good idea." I smiled back at him, hoping this was him getting back to normal via his medical background.

When he focused on my wounds, he winced, using a clean cloth to gently clean the small punctures as well as the burn. He used some kind of cream on the area before he covered it with a non-stick bandage.

After he finished, he closed his jump kit and set it on the floor. Then he sat back on the bed and took one of my hands in his. He brought my palm to his mouth, kissing the center before he put my hand on his chest and held it there with both of his. The tenderness of the gesture made my heart ache.

"I went to prison for killing a guy in a bar fight."

OK, that caught me off guard. "What?"

"I was at a bar with a girl I was seeing," he continued, not answering me but I honestly wasn't sure he was completely with me in that moment. "It was our first date. I didn't love her. Wasn't even sure I liked her. She was a nurse I worked with in the OR and I was letting her think she was playing me." The corner of his lips lifted in a humorless smile.

"Anyway, we were at the bar and a drunk cowboy kept hittin' on her. She'd gone to the bathroom and on her way back he grabbed her, pulled her into his arms to dance." Pain frowned, his thumb rubbing over the back of my hand absently. "She struggled but he wouldn't let her go, so I intervened. I mean, I wasn't gonna try to force her away from the guy if she didn't want me to. But she shoved at him." He looked down, shaking his head slightly. "Anyway, I grabbed his shoulder and pulled him off her. One thing led to another and I got the last punch in. Only he fell, hit his head, and caved in his skull."

"Oh, no. I'm so sorry, Pain," I whispered, my heart going out to him.

"I'd have done the same thing. I don't regret my actions. I regret I killed someone. So I did my time without complaint. But, when I was being held down today, when you were lying there looking at me with so much pain in your eyes..." He took in a shuddering breath, his grip on my hand tightening. "I went to prison defending Sonda." He met my gaze then. I could see darkness swirling there. That's when I realized there was nothing in the world this man wouldn't do to protect me. Nothing. No matter the consequences. "I've never felt more helpless in my life than I did when I looked at the man I'd just killed defending a woman I wasn't even sure I fucking liked. Until today. So make really fuckin' sure I'm the bastard you want. Because I will rule you, Nadine. If it means keeping you safe and with me, I'm afraid there is nothing I wouldn't do."

His words should have scared me, but the truth was I felt the same way about him. I'd run out of the clinic into the yard because I had to help him. Looking back, even knowing I'd get tased -- or worse -- I'd have done the exact same thing.

"I know. I told you before. I see you. *I see you.* I'm right here. Still breathing. Not terribly hurt. I'm still here. I'm still yours."

His eyes darkened. "Mine." That single syllable vibrated with possession.

"Yes. I'm yours, and I need you now, Pain."

That was all it took. Something primal flashed in his eyes before he captured my mouth in a kiss that stole my breath. This wasn't like before. This was raw need, barely controlled. He framed my face with his hands, thumbs stroking my cheekbones as his tongue swept into my mouth.

I arched into him, ignoring the protest of my sore muscles. Nothing mattered except feeling his weight on me, his hands on my skin. I needed this connection more than I needed my next breath.

"Need you," I whispered against his mouth. "Please."

Pain pulled back, his eyes searching mine. "I don't want to hurt you."

"You won't." I reached for the hem of his shirt, tugging it upward. "I need to feel you against me."

He helped me remove his shirt, revealing the muscled expanse of his chest. I ran my hands over his skin, feeling the strength beneath my fingertips. The scars that mapped his history. Each one told a story of survival, and I wanted to know them all.

When my fingers brushed an oddly jagged scar just below his ribs, he caught my wrist.

"Prison fight," he explained quietly. Then he grinned. "Got stabbed with a spork."

I blinked. "Wait. That was you?"

"I wish I could say otherwise, but yeah. That was me. And believe me when I tell you no one laughed harder than me. Hurt like a bitch, but I got stabbed with a spork. There is nothing about that statement that's not funny."

"I'd disagree, but as long as he didn't get anything vital, I can't."

"The prongs weren't deep enough to get through

the muscle. Also, it was wooden and not very strong."

I chuckled lightly but leaned up and pressed my lips to the scar, feeling him shudder beneath my touch. "I'm glad. I never want you to have to go through any of that again. I need you here. With me."

"Honey, I will do whatever I have to if it means I get to stay with you."

"Good. Now. Make love to me, Pain. I don't want to wait any longer."

Pain's hands slid down my sides, careful to avoid my injuries as he tugged at the button of my jeans. I lifted my hips to help him, gasping when he dragged the denim down my legs. His gaze traveled over my body, taking in every inch of exposed skin with hungry appreciation.

"Christ, you're beautiful," he breathed, his voice rough with need.

I reached for the button of his jeans. "Too many clothes…"

A ghost of a smile flickered across his face as he helped me push his jeans down his hips. He moved from the bed to stand and remove his boots before kicking his jeans off.

I raised an eyebrow, my breath catching as he revealed himself to me. "Commando? Really, Pain?"

His grin was positively wicked. "One less barrier between us, honey."

The punch of lust was so hard, I nearly grunted. "No barriers?" My voice was husky and I had to swallow several times.

He paused, and I knew he hadn't been thinking the same thing I'd been thinking. Until he caught my meaning. His face flushed and his cock, which was already hard, distended even farther, pulsing angrily. Before my gaze, the tip grew dark purple and precum beaded on the head.

"Oh, now you've done it, baby." There was so much intent in his expression. "You on any kind of birth control?"

I nodded my head. "I get a shot."

"Good. I'm clean. But no. Not this time, much as I want to." He reached for his pants and snagged his wallet, pulling out a condom. He tossed it beside me before climbing back in the bed with me. He covered my body with his and kissed me again.

I arched into him, ignoring the protest of my sore muscles. Nothing mattered except feeling his weight on me, his hands on my skin. I needed this connection more than I needed my next breath.

"Please," I whispered against his mouth.

Pain pulled back, his eyes searching mine. "I don't want to hurt you."

"You won't. I want this, Pain. I need it."

He kissed me again, deep and thorough, his hands roaming my body with reverent touches. When he reached behind me to unclasp my bra, I arched into him, helping him slide it off my shoulders. The cool air hit my skin, making me shiver, but then his mouth was on me, trailing hot kisses down my throat to my collarbone.

"So fucking perfect," he murmured against my skin, his beard scratching deliciously as he worked his way lower. When his mouth closed over my nipple, I gasped, my back arching off the bed. The sensation shot straight through me, making me ache with need.

He seemed to map every curve, every sensitive spot with his hands, then his lips. I swear, the man was determined to make me gasp and writhe beneath him until I was mindless. When he hooked his fingers in the waistband of my panties, I lifted my hips eagerly, helping him slide them down my legs.

"Look at you," he breathed, his gaze drinking me in. "So beautiful. So mine."

"Yes," I whispered, reaching for him. "Yours."

"Open the condom." The dark command in his voice was at once intimidating and sexy as fuck. I reached for the little packet blindly until I snagged it from the quilt where we lay. I opened it, tossing the package over the side of the bed, and looked up at Pain for instructions. That must have been the right thing to do because the look of satisfaction on his face was unmistakable. Probably because he'd had so few choices in prison, he needed someone to let him make all the decisions or at least give him choices. I was good with that. "Roll it on me, Nadine."

With trembling fingers, I did. I loved how hot he was. I loved the way the muscles of his abdomen bunched and contracted when I touched him. As he moved to settle himself between my legs, I slid my palms up his chest to mold his shoulders. Again, muscles played under his skin where my hands touched him.

When he lowered himself fully on top of me, resting his forearms beside my head so his fingers tangled in my hair, it felt like coming home.

"Tell me if I hurt you," he murmured, slowly pushing forward.

I gasped as he entered me, stretching me in the most exquisite way. The slight burn gave way to pleasure as he eased himself in, inch by delicious inch, until he was fully seated inside me.

"Fuck," he groaned, his forehead dropping to rest against mine. "You feel so Goddamn perfect."

He held still for a moment, giving me time to adjust. I could feel him trembling with the effort of his restraint, his muscles taut beneath my fingertips. Sweat beaded his brow, and his breathing was almost heavy.

"Move," I urged, rocking my hips. "Feels good…"

He did move then. Slowly at first, giving me time to adjust to his size, but each thrust was measured, controlled.

I wrapped my legs around his waist, pulling him deeper, needing more of him. The careful restraint he'd been showing started to crack as I moved with him, meeting each thrust with my own need.

"Christ, Nadine," he growled against my neck, his pace increasing. "You're gonna drive me fuckin' crazy."

Tension coiled inside me with each movement. I tilted my hips to get the friction I needed on my clit. When I found it, I gasped out a soft cry.

"That's it, baby," he murmured, his voice rough with need. "Come on my cock."

The combination of his words and his touches and kisses sent me over the edge. I shattered around him, screaming as waves of pleasure crashed over me. He followed me over, his own release tearing through him as he buried his face against my neck, my name on his lips like a prayer.

I still held him weakly with my arms and legs, not wanting him to move his weight from me. I needed it to ground me. I needed him.

Afterward, once he'd finally rolled off me, we lay tangled together, his body a warm anchor to the present. My muscles ached in the most satisfying way, the pain from the taser almost forgotten in the wake of our lovemaking.

"You okay?" Pain murmured against my hair, his breath warm on my temple.

"Mmm," I hummed, too blissed out to form actual words. When his arms tightened around me, I added, "More than okay."

"No regrets?"

"Not a single one." I reached up to stroke his beard, loving the way it felt scratchy on my palm. "Though I might regret not doing this sooner."

That earned me a low chuckle. "We got here, that's what matters."

"Yeah. I couldn't agree more."

Chapter Twelve

Nadine

This was nuts. It had been two weeks since the raid, and the constant police presence was suffocating. Going outside, beyond the camo netting, now felt almost like venturing into the prison yard. I'd never been in the yard at Terre Haute, but I was starting to have nightmares about being trapped in ours. Except instead of being terrified of the prisoners, it was the guards who had me on edge.

I stared out the window at the camo-netted paths between warehouses. The compound felt more like a cage with each passing day, though the women tried their best to distract their men. The only problem was, the police weren't even letting in the delivery people, so there were a few supplies we were starting to need. Including food. Which, likely, was what Chief Roscoe had in mind.

"Why is your big boss man not putting a stop to this?" I grumbled, though I wasn't really in a snit over that. I was just upset they were basically laying siege to the compound. Just not violently. Yet.

"Knuckles said he's working on it. Apparently, Roscoe has an agenda outside the official narrative."

"Of course, he does," I snapped. "In the meantime, we've got a pregnant woman who is six weeks and two days away from her due date but is already having the occasional contraction and is twenty percent effaced. We can't keep going like this, Pain. The stress alone isn't good for Tillie."

"I know, honey." Pain and I were in an apartment on the third floor of this particular warehouse. There was one floor above us and an area on the roof to hang out and sun or grill or just relax away from the rest of the club. The other attached women, the old ladies, had managed to get the guys to put an above-ground pool and a hot tub on the roof for us. We also had a prime viewing spot for the immediate perimeter around the compound. Where we'd watch Roscoe's boys repeatedly turn away delivery drivers with anything we'd ordered. Not that anyone had expected it to work, but it had been worth a try.

More than anything, I was worried about the lack of a birthing kit in case of an emergency. Pain hadn't been here to take care of that until recently and, honestly, a siege wasn't something anyone had prepared for.

I couldn't just sit there twiddling my thumbs while that bastard, Roscoe, effectively held us captive. There had to be some way to get out of this compound without them knowing.

"We've got to get ready for this baby, Pain." We'd danced around this a couple times, and I got the sense Pain didn't want to let himself think about having to deliver the baby here.

"Yeah," was his mumbled response.

Silence.

"And?" I crossed my arms over my chest.

More silence.

"Pain. Are you listening to me?"

"I'm listening, Nadine. I just don't want to think about it, OK?"

I was about to lay into him because, what the fuck, when it hit me. "You're afraid of delivering that baby."

"Look, Nadine. I did my OB rotation on L & D and Postpartum. I delivered exactly two babies. Why? Go on. Ask me why." OK, he was getting a little defensive, but it was still funny as shit because I, having done my own OB rotation, knew exactly what he was going to say.

"How about I ask you a different question?"

"Yeah?" He crossed his arms over his chest, looking as disgruntled as a man could be. "What's that?"

"How many times did you puke?"

He didn't miss a beat. "Four times at the first birth, seven at the second. The poor mother was asking me if I was all right. After that, they let me do everything but deliver babies. They passed me because I got everything else right. That was when it was suggested to me surgery might be the way to go if I planned on working in a hospital. I was also advised to avoid small rural hospitals because they didn't want me to be the only doctor in the building. Just in case."

Yeah. No way I wasn't laughing. "Oh, my God, Pain! You're a fucking *surgeon*! Surely to God a surgeon can deliver a baby."

"Yes. I am. There is a reason I'm a surgeon."

I thought for a minute, narrowing my eyes. "Because... in the event of an unexpected birth, the Emergency Department takes care of it." I chuckled. "In fact, the only doctor in the OR who'd ever get called to help with a delivery would be an OB surgeon or an anesthesiologist." I knew my eyes were growing wider and wider as realization hit me. "You became a surgeon to avoid anything to do with delivering babies!"

"Exactly. L & D has a staffed, dedicated OR of their own. I'm pretty much the very last doctor who would be in the hospital after seven in the evening on the list to call for an emergent delivery. The *very* last. Meaning, if I got called to deliver a baby, there were more things to worry about than just the mother and baby."

"Oh, Pain!" I laughed so hard tears were rolling down my cheeks, and I clutched my sides. "I n-never r-realized you w-were such a p-pussy!"

"It's not that Goddamned funny," he grumbled. But I could tell the endorphin release of laughter did him as much good as it had done me even if he did look disgruntled. The humor was there in his eyes when he tried to glare at me.

"It is, and you know it." I leaned up and pulled him in for a lingering kiss. "But we still need to make plans. Multiple plans."

He sighed, pulling me closer and kissing me more deeply. He swept his tongue in to tangle with mine and I wanted nothing more than to lose myself in the sensations.

I pushed him away gently, kissing his lips several times as I cupped his face in one hand. "Much as I want to, I can't let you distract me from this. And I don't think you really want to forget about it. So tell me what's going on."

"How the fuck do you know me so well already?"

"I pay attention. Now. Spill."

He sighed. "Knuckles said Tonio asked for one more week. Apparently, there's a power struggle going on in the underground and Tonio has to deal with that first. He's also sure Roscoe is making a play for the game. Either for himself or in conjunction with someone else. Which is what he's trying to figure out. I'm keeping an eye on Tillie. And yes, she's effacing, but she's still well within acceptable parameters for her third trimester. Obviously, you're right. With the heightened stress, we need to keep a close eye on her.

But I don't think she's at increased risk otherwise."

"I still don't like it. I'd feel better if we at least had a labor pack."

"I'll see what I can do. For now, try not to worry so much."

"Really? You realize it's been two weeks since anyone went out for toilet paper. Unless you want to start rationing it out one square at a time, you might want to look into getting some supplies sooner rather than later. When you make the TP run, see if you can find a labor pack."

"Smartass."

"Better a smartass than a dumbass."

"I don't remember you being this sassy when you were younger."

"I wasn't." I smiled sweetly. "Then I became a nurse."

"Point taken."

We spent the next couple of hours making love. Because we could. Then Pain had to go to Church. Apparently, that was what they called their club meetings.

I went to the roof and looked out over what I could see of the property. I'd been watching for the last few days. Trying to see patterns in the patrols around the compound as well as where the unmarked cars were parked and what they looked like. They used the same cars every day, so it wasn't hard.

Considering I hadn't been exaggerating too much about the toilet paper, I decided I was making an executive decision. Besides, I really needed to get a birthing kit just in case. I could totally understand Pain balking. It's why doctors needed nurses. So here I was.

Just as I'd been noticing every day since about day two of this quiet siege, there was a hole in their net, so to speak. One of the warehouses outside of Kiss of Death territory had several large dogs. The cops didn't want to keep them stirred up and cause more of a problem than they said the guys in the club were responsible for, so they gave that area a wide berth. I, on the other hand, happened to have some of the dogs' favorite treats.

The big German Shepherds must have been trained not to bark unless there was a threat because they'd long stopped barking at me. And yes. I might have been planning an escape, but in my defense, it was for Tillie. If I needed to get her out of here and to the hospital, then I wanted to know for sure I could get us out safely.

With any guys outside the main clubhouse focusing on the police presence and anyone not on guard in Church, making it to my escape point was easier than I expected.

The split in the fence wasn't obvious or big. In fact, if I'd had to sneak Tillie out this way, it wouldn't have been easy for her to get through. Bushes lined the area which hid my exit point.

I crouched behind the foliage for long minutes. This little adventure was turning out to be more nerve-racking than I'd thought. It was warm but not overly so. And I was sweating like it was the middle of summer.

I heard a dog whine softly but that was the only sound they made. Carefully, trying not to draw attention to myself, I leaned away from the shrub to get a better look at the immediate area.

When I was certain there was no one around, I slipped the dogs their treats through their fence, then headed out of the warehouse area on foot. Yeah. When Pain realized I was gone he was going to be beside himself, but this had to be done. He was also probably going to spank me when I got back. Which... I could totally get behind that. So to speak.

I walked between the warehouses, always doing my best to keep to the outskirts and away from the main road in and out. Once I was a couple blocks away from the compound, though, there was really no need to worry. I didn't see another car or person anywhere.

There was a little diner about half a mile away and I thought that was the perfect place to settle in for ten or fifteen minutes, maybe drink a sweet tea or something, and wait to see if anyone followed me. Then I called an Uber.

I didn't want to take too long on this excursion. I figured if I could get what I needed and get back in another hour or so, I should be fine. I'll feel better and no one will be the wiser I snuck out. No problem!

The first place I went was a women's reproductive health clinic. It was a local, privately funded clinic. I might not be familiar with the area, but bigger cities always had a place that operated on the down low. Not performing illegal or dangerous services, but providing birth control in all kinds of various forms, as well as the home birthing kits for emergencies.

As I'd hoped, I was able to get everything I needed for a home birth with no trouble once I assured the nurse in charge there would be a qualified medical professional with my friend when she gave birth. But honestly, once I explained the situation, the lady -- and every other person working in the place -- was ready to give me anything I wanted. I'd have to make sure to have Knuckles tell Mr. Miles to make a donation to the place. Like either man would listen to me. Then again, I'd been only half joking with Pain when I told him I'd gained my sass when I became a nurse. Working at that prison only strengthened my backbone. So maybe I could make that donation happen.

I made my way back to the compound. My phone hadn't buzzed since I'd left so I hoped that meant Pain was still in his meeting. I rounded the corner to the beginning of the vast area filled with warehouses, of which the entire Kiss of Death compound was only a small part, and ran straight into Chief Benjamin Roscoe.

"If it ain't little Miss Nadine Brentner. Fancy meetin' you here."

Chapter Thirteen

Pain

Some motherfuckers just didn't know when to quit.

The rage that had been building in my chest for the past two weeks finally reached its breaking point when I saw Roscoe's smug face on the security feed, standing over Nadine like some kind of predator who'd just caught his prey. Fuck waiting for Tonio to handle this. Fuck protocol. Fuck everything except getting to that bastard before he hurt my woman again.

"Go," Knight urged. "I'll send some guys to get rid of the garbage."

He'd called me to his office when he'd noticed Nadine leaving the premises. An hour after she'd left. Not only had she slipped past the police, she'd made it past Knight's security. Which was whole 'nother problem. Knight called me to his office the second he'd realized what had happened, but Nadine had already been gone over an hour. I'd been looking over his shoulder while he moved through city camera feeds trying to find her.

I tore out of the main clubhouse and jumped on my bike. I'd normally never disrespect my bike or anyone else's by peeling out in the gravel, but I was past caring. Nadine was the only thing that mattered.

I knew exactly where the break in the fence was, and that it was the perfect place to slip out of the compound. Or into it. I'd been watching it since I got out of prison. Because I strongly suspected the rat in the club who'd let Riot's woman's ex-husband inside the compound had been the one to cut the fucking hole in the fence, but that was something I'd deal with later. And confront Knuckles. I revered the man, but we had a traitor in the club, one with an unknown agenda who was willing to sell out our women, and Knuckles had let the guy live among them for months. But I couldn't think about that right now. Getting to Nadine was my only priority at the moment.

The break in the fence was the only way to get out with any hope of not being stopped immediately by the police. That being said, I wasn't going to be subtle about this.

Once I was free of the tightest gathering of warehouses, I opened up my Hog and sped toward the fence where I knew the break was. I had to duck and grit my teeth. The first to avoid was the horizontal aluminum bar running through the middle of the fifteen foot fence from taking my fucking head off. The second because the break in the fence wasn't a hole. It was just what it sounded like. A vertical break in the fence from the middle bar to the ground. So both sides of my body got gouged and torn by the edges of the cut metal.

Once free, I raced to where we'd seen Nadine on the camera. She was on the very back end of the property, where she should have been safe. Yeah. There was no way Benjamin Roscoe found that hole in the fencing accidentally.

I rounded two corners in time to see Roscoe and Nadine facing each other just on the inside of the gate. The second I processed I'd found her, Roscoe backhanded her with a brutal, full-bodied swing. Nadine staggered backward and my world narrowed to the two figures ahead of me.

I. Saw. *Red.*

My vision tunneled, everything beyond Nadine and Roscoe fading to black. The world slowed down as I watched her stumble, her hand flying to her face, a plastic bag tumbling from her grip. Something inside me snapped. That final thread of restraint I'd been clinging to since prison fucking let go.

I gunned the throttle, the Harley's engine screaming as I closed the distance. Roscoe's head whipped around at the sound, his eyes widening as he registered me bearing down on him. Smart enough to recognize danger, he shoved Nadine hard and reached for his weapon.

Had we not been on the edge of a motorcycle club compound, with dozens of motorcycles moving around inside the place at any given time, I doubt I'd have had enough time between him recognizing me as an immediate threat instead of a distant bystander to reach him before he shot me.

Roscoe managed to get off a shot, but a fraction of a second after I hit him with my bike. Fortunately for me, his shot went wide. Unfortunately for him, I hit him dead center.

Roscoe's body flew through the air over my head. I braked, cutting back to swing around to face Roscoe again. This time, I ran over him. Probably wasn't enough to kill him, but he wasn't going to be able to crawl to his gun where it landed on the ground when he was hit, and he wasn't going to be able to get to Nadine.

Again, I whipped around. This time, I shut my bike down, barely managing to get the kickstand set before I stalked over to him.

Roscoe was sprawled on the asphalt, his left leg bent at an unnatural angle, blood seeping from a gash on his forehead. But the bastard was still conscious, still breathing. "You fucking psycho," he wheezed, spitting blood. "You just assaulted a police officer."

"You put your hands on my woman. Again." My

voice was deadly calm, which seemed to scare him more than if I'd been screaming. "That was your second mistake."

"What was the first?" He tried to sound defiant, like he could give a fuck, but I could hear the fear creeping in.

"Thinking you could walk away from it."

"Pain!" Nadine's voice cut through the red haze clouding my vision. "Oh God, you're bleeding!"

I glanced down at my torn shirt, the gouges from the fence weeping blood down my arms and torso. Didn't matter. Nothing mattered except finishing this.

"Stay back, honey," I said, my voice deadly calm as I pulled the suppressed pistol from my jacket. "Don't watch this."

"Please," Roscoe wheezed, rolling onto his back. Blood frothed at the corners of his mouth. "Don't... I was just --"

"Just what?" I stood over him, the gun trained on his chest. "Just hitting my woman? Just terrorizing my family for weeks? Just being a corrupt piece of shit who thinks his badge makes him untouchable?"

"Having that gun is against your parole -- what do they call you? Pain?" When I didn't answer, he pressed on, his eyes hard and defiant even as he lay broken on the ground. "This whole fuckin' club could go down."

"You think I give a fuck about my parole right now?" I stepped closer, pointing the gun at his leg and fired into his knee. The silenced pistol made a small *crack*, but Roscoe's screams echoed throughout the area. Blood and bone fragments splattered across the asphalt.

"What do you want!? What do you want!?" Roscoe screamed as he tried to scoot away from me, dragging his injured leg and holding one arm up to fend me off.

"I want to know who the fuck told you about the break in the fence where you got inside this compound."

His eyes got wide in shock despite the pain before he recovered. "I cut that fuckin' fence myself."

I shot his other knee. Roscoe's screams and shrieks had drawn attention, but from my club, not his officers. I have no idea what those fuckers were doing, but so far I hadn't seen any of them.

"What the fuck!"

"Who told you about the break in the fence?" I repeated my question calmly.

He took several deep breaths but didn't offer an answer.

"You've got several other joints in your body, Roscoe. Your elbows are next."

"All right! All right! Bitch calls herself Silk! OK? Her name's Silk!"

"Why would one of our club whores let you inside?" I shot him in the elbow. I was acutely aware of Nadine behind me. She had a hand on my shoulder now, but she wasn't trying to stop me, and she stayed on my weak side and behind me. Behind us, the roar of my brothers' bikes built as they grew closer.

"How would I know!?"

"How did you meet her?"

"She came to me! I swear! She came to me!"

"Why would she do that? Why come to you specifically?"

"Because I offered a reward! She came to me because I offered her money!"

I barely heard him over the roar as five of my brothers pulled into the area. When they shut down their bikes and came to my side, I stepped away from Roscoe.

"Pain?" Knuckles stepped beside me as I backed up.

"Did you ever find the person who let in Violet's ex-husband?"

Knuckles stiffened. "*She* let this bastard in?"

"If you knew who your rat was, why is she still here and still able to attack us from the inside?"

Knuckles' face went stone cold. "Because we didn't know for sure it was her until right fucking now." His voice was deadly quiet. "She's been careful. Real careful."

"Where is she now?" I kept my gun trained on Roscoe, but my attention was split between him and this revelation about Silk.

"Clubhouse. Last I saw her, she was with the other girls by the pool." Knuckles pulled out his phone. "Xavier, I need you to find Silk. Now. Don't let her know you're looking for her, just locate her and keep eyes on her until I get back."

Roscoe tried to push himself up on his good arm, blood still pouring from his wounds. "You can't just execute me in broad daylight, you psycho fucks."

"Watch me." I aimed the gun at his head.

"Pain." Nadine's voice was soft but firm. "Let Knuckles handle Silk first. This piece of shit isn't going anywhere."

She was right. Roscoe was done, but Silk was still a threat to everyone back at the compound. Still, every instinct inside me wanted to end him. Now. I lowered the weapon slightly, my jaw clenched tightly.

"I need answers first," Knuckles cut in, his voice deadly calm as he crouched beside Roscoe. "Why are you so interested in us? This ain't just about busting a motorcycle club."

Roscoe laughed, a wet, gurgling sound that ended in a cough. Blood sprayed from his lips. "You think you're so fucking smart. You think your Miles family protection means shit. I control the police presence in this fuckin' town! I can make your life very unpleasant."

"What do you want?" Knuckles crossed his massive arms over his chest. I was muscular, but Knuckles was on a different level. And, as much as I hated to admit it, he was much more intimidating than me.

Roscoe's gaze darted between us before he smirked. "Your precious president has been paying me off for months. Cutting me in on whatever you're running through those docks."

I glanced at Knuckles, who just looked amused. "That true?"

"Partially," Knuckles didn't look concerned in the least. "I followed Tonio's instructions because we thought he was the muscle for a rival wanting to cut in on Miles' family business."

"OK. I'll buy that." I nodded. Knuckles always had shit going on I wasn't privy to and had no desire to know about. "I assume this is all related to why you were holding off on doing anything to those assholes outside the gate?"

"Yep." Knuckles' grin didn't quite reach his eyes. Except in a malevolent kind of way.

"Look." Roscoe sat up a little more, braced on his good arm. Blood still oozed from the three times I'd shot him, but fuck the bastard anyway. "Like I said. I am the law in this town. I can guarantee one hundred percent you'll never have to worry about police involvement in your operation at the docks. All I'm asking for is five percent of what comes through."

Gunnar, Knuckles' right hand and his daughter's man, moved beside our president. "In case you missed it, buddy, you're not in much of a position to negotiate. You're really not in a position to demand protection money."

"My boys'll be here soon. Every single man I brought here to starve you guys out is loyal to me."

"They're loyal to the money you pay them," Knuckles said. "Which means they'll be loyal to the money *I* pay them. Then they'll stay loyal to me because if they don't, this whole incident gets out and every one of them will be on the bad end of a public relations nightmare."

"I might have threatened to cut them into little pieces if they didn't take the money and go." Gunnar looked entirely too smug, but it fit the mood.

I pegged the second Roscoe realized he'd written a check his body was going to have to make good on, and that he saw his death in the immediate future. "Was all this about money?" I asked, suddenly curious. "Just… your greed? Why hurt Nadine?"

"Go fuck yourself." Roscoe spat blood in our general direction.

Knuckles and Gunnar exchanged a look. Then Knuckles shrugged. "He targeted your woman, Pain. How long he lives is up to you."

Yeah. I didn't need to know the why of it as long as I knew he was working alone. Which, sounded like he was.

A harsh battle cry caught me by surprise as Roscoe managed one last Hail Mary, likely in an attempt to take at least one of us with him. Gunnar was closest, and that's who he hit as he threw his body in our general direction. I have no idea how he moved as quickly as he did with the injuries he had, but imminent death has a way of turning people into superhumans for brief moments and I suppose this was Roscoe's.

Gunnar hit the ground. Hard. I heard a sharp *pop* and the younger man gave a snarling grunt of pain. Knuckles grabbed Roscoe by the scruff of the neck and hauled him off Gunnar, flinging him back to the ground where he'd previously lay bleeding.

"Fucker," Knuckles muttered, then pulled his own suppressed pistol and shot Roscoe in the head.

"Fuck," Gunnar gasped. "Fuckin' hell."

"Lie still, Gunnar." Nadine was at his side, her nursing instincts kicking in despite the scene she'd just witnessed.

"Hurts worse." He sounded pained, and when he sat up I could see why.

"Your shoulder's dislocated." I knelt beside him next to Nadine and felt the injury. Nadine gave me a wide-eyed look, and I knew she knew what was coming next.

"Tell me something I don't know." Gunnar didn't fight either Nadine or myself as we examined him.

"OK. How about this. Do you know how I got my road name?"

"What's that got to do with anything?"

I still fiddled with his arm and shoulder, probing gently as I adjusted my hold on his arms to get the leverage I needed going in the right direction. "Do you know why they call me Pain?"

Gunnar glanced over her shoulder at me briefly before the pain was too much to hold the position. "No. How-- AHH!"

I gave a sharp tug on his shoulder, popping it

back into place but causing a momentary burst of blinding pain.

"Because I don't believe in giving dumbasses pain medicine when fixing their stupid mistakes." I grinned down at the other man. If looks could kill, no defibrillator in existence would have been able to bring me back.

"That wasn't my fault! How was I a dumbass?"

"After all that," Nadine said, "the most important question you have is 'How was I a dumbass?'" She shook her head. "No offense, but I think that kind of speaks for itself."

That got hoots from the other guys around us. Hawk and Riot helped Gunnar to his feet before clapping him on the shoulder. The other shoulder. Tiny just shook his head and took out a couple of big cadaver bags from the cage. Hawk helped Tiny get shovels as well as topsoil and sodding in big plastic totes ready to tear up and replace the ground where Roscoe had bled.

"That was mean," Nadine said as she wrapped her arms around my waist. She'd picked up the plastic bag she'd dropped when Roscoe had backhanded her and was clutching it tightly between us.

I shrugged. "If he's pussy enough to bitch about it, I'll see if I can get him some good stuff to help him sleep." I might have said that a little louder than strictly necessary.

"Fuck you, Pain." Yeah, I was gonna have fun with this.

"Pain," Nadine scolded. "Stop it."

"What?" I gave her my best innocent look.

"Don't give me that. You know exactly what. Gunnar was the victim there."

"Of course, he was. He still screamed like a girl."

"Because you jerked his shoulder back in place without warning! If you'd told him to take a deep breath, this was gonna hurt, he wouldn't have screamed like that!"

I looked at her for a long moment. "You can still count it." That got more laughs all around.

"What's that?" I asked, fingering the sealed, thick plastic pack she held between us, though I already knew the answer. I just couldn't believe she'd gone out for this.

"Birthing kit."

"Of course, you left to get a precip kit," I muttered. "Because why the fuck not?" I didn't even try to hold back my irritation. "What the fuck, Nadine? I told you I am not, under any circumstances, delivering Tillie's baby. She will *not* have an emergency where I have to deliver the child here. I will take her to the fuckin' hospital myself if I have to. No. Hard fuckin' limit."

"Pain. We've been through this. It's a precaution we need to take."

I shook my head. "Nope. Nuh-uh."

"Pain." Her voice had a warning to it. Which might have been what I was going for, because it was turning me the fuck on.

"What?"

"Shut up. Take me home. Fuck me. In that order, Pain."

I laughed then, feeling lighter than I had in weeks. "Come on, honey. Let them take out the trash. I need to get you home and look you over. I'm not sure how much more my heart can take of this shit."

Nadine smiled up at me. The wicked gleam in her eyes was its own aphrodisiac. "Yeah. Let's go play doctor." She wiggled her eyebrows at me.

My new life made going to prison worth it. And I'd be all the more protective because of it. Nadine was the one person in the world who could bring me to my knees. Funny thing was, I went voluntarily. If that meant I worshipped at her feet every fucking day for the rest of my life, nothing would make me happier.

Chapter Fourteen

Pain

I'd ripped men apart with my bare hands and never lost a night's sleep. Seeing Nadine hurt yet again on my watch made me feel like I was drowning in my own rage. I wished that bastard, Roscoe, was still alive so I could kill him again.

"Stop fussing," she murmured as I carried her through the doorway of our apartment, her body cradled against my chest. "I'm not made of glass."

"That piece of shit hit you." My voice came out rougher than I intended, but the image of Roscoe standing over her was burned into my brain. "Let me take care of you."

She sighed, her breath warm against my neck as I kicked the door shut behind us. "I'm a nurse, Pain. I know what I need."

"Yeah? I'm a doctor." I flashed her a grin I was certain looked anything but humorous. "I outrank you, so I win." Even though, technically, I wasn't a doctor anymore, I still had the skills. I just couldn't use them legally.

That earned me a small smile. At least, she lifted one corner of her mouth. There was genuine humor in her smile, but the darkening bruise on her cheek and jaw probably caused her pain when she did. The contusion was a stark contrast against her pale skin. My fingers hovered over it, not quite touching, and I was surprised to find they were trembling.

"It doesn't hurt that much," she said.

"Little liar. It has to hurt. You'll be lucky if it doesn't make the tissue around your eye swell." I stood and turned to go to the kitchen. "Let me get you an ice pack."

Nadine snagged my hand, tugging gently. "It can wait." I turned back, ready to tell her that, no it couldn't wait, but she stood and put her arms around me, pressing her lips gently to mine.

"Pain, I'm fine," she said. "Yes, I'm bruised and sore, and I'll complain and whine and wear you out taking care of me. Later. Right now, I want you to take me to the bathroom, get in the shower with me, and fuck me until we're both too wobbly to stand."

The raw need in her voice hit me like a physical blow. My hands tightened on her hips as I searched her face, looking for any sign she was pushing herself too hard. Once I looked past the battle mark on her face, all I saw was determination and heat that matched the fire building in my chest.

"You sure about this, honey?" My voice was gravelly with want, but I had to ask. "Even if you're ready for this, I don't want to hurt you more. I *never* want to hurt you, Nadine. *Ever.*"

"I've never been more sure about anything in my life."

"All right," I said, my voice rough. "But we're doing this my way. Slow. Gentle."

"Like hell we are." She pulled back, that stubborn chin lifting. "I'm not some delicate flower you need to handle with kid gloves."

"Baby, you've got a bruise the size of Texas on your face --"

"And the rest of me is perfectly fine." She stepped back, pulling her shirt over her head in one fluid motion. The sight of her bare skin made my mouth go dry. "Unless you don't want me?" She didn't sound insecure in the least. In fact, she sounded like a woman who knew what her man wanted and exactly how to drive him so wild he kept coming back for more for the rest of his fucking life. Under any circumstances. So, cocky and sexy as fuck. I loved this woman so much!

"Don't want you?" I let out a harsh laugh. "You're baiting me, woman. Don't think I don't know."

She put her mouth right by my ear. "Is it working?" Her soft whisper was like a siren's call. When she nipped my earlobe for good measure, I threw caution to the wind.

"You better fuckin' tell me to back the fuck off if you feel even the slightest bit of pain." This was happening. Whether I thought it was a good idea or not. "You don't, once you're well, I'll beat your ass every fuckin' night for a solid week."

The little witch gave me a wicked grin. "Right. I'll just be *all* over that."

"*And* I won't let you orgasm for a month."

Her eyes widened. I grinned.

"Oh, it's on, motherfucker," she said fiercely.

There was no way to keep the belly laugh from bursting free. This woman! This *fucking* woman!

"Don't you ever change, Nadine." I stroked the uninjured side of her face gently, smiling down at her. "Don't be the timid girl who couldn't stop me from making a bad situation worse by sedating my patient's wife when that was the very thing she was terrified of. Be the brash, courageous woman who took charge of the situation and did what needed to be done. You calmed her down when no one else could and when no one else would listen to you. You did the same thing in Terre Haute. Now, you do it with me."

She gave me that cocky grin again. "You're still sore about the birthing kit."

"Again, it's a moot point because it's never going

- 263 -

to happen. Do *not* bring it up again. Get me?"

"You never worked ER, did you?" It wasn't a question.

I narrowed my gaze as her grin grew wider. "No. I told you I avoided the ER because those guys have to deliver babies on occasion."

"Right." Shook her head, giving me a look that said, *sucks to be you, sport.* "You know you're not supposed to say 'never', right? That's the best way to make it happen."

I paused, thinking about her words before I could make my brain comprehend she was teasing. Then I scowled at her. "Not cool, little hellion. Not cool at all."

I wrapped my arms around her and lifted. She squealed but hung on with her arms and legs as I took her to the bathroom. The sound of her laughter after being so terrified of losing her was like a balm to my soul. Nadine was all right. She was safe. I'd killed the bastard who'd hurt her. She was safe.

She was safe.

Once in the bathroom, I started the shower before turning back to her. "Strip off, baby. I want to see everything. I need to know you're OK, then I need to fuck you. To lose myself in your tight little body." The words felt like they were ripped out of me after they'd been dying to be free.

"Those need cleaning," she said, running her fingers gently over the gouges on one arm.

"Later," I growled, stepping closer until she was backed against the counter. "Right now, I need to be inside you."

"Fine. You strip off too, then. Because I want to suck your cock before you fuck me."

"Son of a bitch," I gasped out as my cock shot

impossibly hard, pulsing and reaching for Nadine on its own, the head angry and purple. "How the fuck do you make me lose my Goddamned mind so easily, woman?"

Nadine's eyes darkened with lust as she watched my reaction. "I pay attention, Pain. I see you. All of you," she said with a teasing smile, though it faltered slightly when her bruised cheek twinged.

The sight of her discomfort brought me back to my senses, but only just. I reached for her, tugging her close again, my hands sliding down to cup her ass. "Careful, sweetheart. Don't push yourself."

"Shut up and kiss me," she murmured, pulling my head down to hers.

I obliged, keeping my touch gentle on her injured side. The bathroom was filling with steam now, the mirror fogging as I deepened the kiss. Nadine moaned against my mouth, her hands working frantically at my belt.

"Slow down," I whispered against her lips.

"Make me," she replied with a hiss, finally getting my belt undone and shoving my jeans down my hips.

Those words hit me like a punch to the gut. Today had been too close. Way too close. I understood her desperation because I felt it too, that primal need to affirm life after brush with death.

"I can't lose you, Nadine," I bit out harsher than I intended. "I can't fuckin' lose you."

"Pain, I'm here." She gripped my head in her hands, forcing me to look down at her. "Do you understand why I left today? Why I went for that birthing kit?"

I sighed. "Yeah. I do. And I'm more grateful to you than I'll ever admit at any time after this immediate conversation. As far as *anyone* is concerned, I never said it." I glared at her for effect before I had to soften my gaze. "But yes. Which makes me hurt all the more because I should have been the one insisting on that fucking precip kit being here the minute we knew Tillie was pregnant. In fact, I need a couple in case of twins." She blinked up at me, her eyebrows raising. "And this marks the end of the immediate conversation."

As I hoped, Nadine burst into giggles. Even with the side of her face hurting she didn't curb her mirth. Son of a bitch that I am, I soaked up her laughter like a flower soaks up the sun. And that was the best way to describe what Nadine meant to me. She was my sunshine. She was my second chance. She was God smiling down on me for some unknown reason and saying, *you're not a bad person. If you were, she wouldn't let her touch her this way. She wouldn't look at you with such affection and emotion in her eyes.* Nadine was my very soul. I would protect her, no matter the cost.

"I love you so fuckin' much, woman."

Her face softened and she stroked my beard tenderly.

"I love you too, Pain. More than I ever thought possible." She leaned up and kissed me softly, her lips gentle against mine. "Now get in that shower with me before the hot water runs out."

I helped her finish undressing, my hands reverent as they traced over her skin, checking for any other injuries I might have missed. When I was satisfied she was okay aside from the bruise on her face, I stripped off my own clothes and followed her into the steamy shower.

The hot water cascaded over us, washing away the blood and grime from today's violence. Nadine pressed herself against me, her wet body sliding against mine as she reached for the soap.

"Let me," I murmured, taking it from her hands. I worked up a lather, my hands gentle as I washed her body, paying special attention to avoid her injured cheek. She sighed contentedly, melting into my touch.

"Your turn," she said when I finished, taking the soap back. Her small hands worked over my chest and arms, cleaning the cuts from the fence with careful precision. "These aren't too deep, but they'll need antibiotic ointment."

"After," I growled. "Need." Great. I was reduced to one-word sentences. But sweet God in heaven, the woman's touch was driving me insane!

Her hands slid lower, soap-slicked and sure as they wrapped around my cock. "What do you need, Pain?" She sounded as on edge as I did, her voice husky with lust.

"You," I managed, my hands bracing against the shower wall as she stroked me. "Just you."

The water sluiced over us as Nadine sank to her knees before me, the sight nearly stopping my heart. Her honey-colored hair was darkened by the water, plastered to her skull and neck as she looked up at me through her lashes, the tip of her tongue darting out to wet her lips.

"Careful of your face," I warned, but the words died in my throat as she took me into her mouth, her lips stretching around me.

"Fuck," I groaned, my head falling back against the tile. Her mouth was hot and wet, her tongue swirling around the head of my cock with just the right pressure. I tangled my fingers in her wet hair, not guiding, just needing the connection as she worked me with her mouth.

"Jesus Christ," I hissed. The sight of her on her knees, water cascading down her perfect body while she took me deeper nearly undid me. Her gray eyes didn't move as she stared up at me.

She hummed around my length, the vibration sending shockwaves through my system. Her tongue slid along the underside of my shaft as she bobbed her head, taking me deeper with each pass. She used one hand to grip the base of my cock while cupping my balls with the other, gently massaging until I almost lost my mind.

I knew I wouldn't last much longer like this. Not with this all-consuming need burning through me like wildfire.

"Up," I growled, gently pulling her up. Her lips were swollen, her eyes glazed with desire as she stood before me. "Turn around."

She complied without hesitation, bracing her hands against the shower wall. I pressed myself against her back, my cock sliding between her thighs as I wrapped one arm around her waist.

"Tell me if I hurt you," I murmured against her ear, nipping at the lobe to let her know I meant business.

"You won't," she breathed, pushing back against me. "Please, Pain. Fuck me."

I slid my hand between her legs, finding her already slick and ready. The hot water continued to pour over us as I teased her entrance, circling her clit with my thumb until she was trembling against me.

"Now," she demanded, her voice breaking. "Goddammit, now!"

I couldn't deny either of us any longer. With one smooth thrust, I buried myself inside her. She was tight and wet, and so silky soft I never wanted to leave her sweet pussy.

"Move," she gasped, pressing back against me. "Please."

I pulled back slowly before thrusting forward again, setting a rhythm that had us both panting. My hands roamed her wet skin, one gripping her hip while the other came around to tease her clit. She arched into my touch, her moans echoing off the shower walls.

"So perfect," I growled against her neck, my teeth grazing her shoulder. "So fucking perfect, Nadine."

Her response was lost in a cry of pleasure as I hit that spot inside her that made her legs tremble. I could feel her getting closer, her body tightening around me with each thrust.

"That's it, baby," I murmured, increasing the pressure on her clit. "Come for me."

She shattered with a scream that would have woken the dead, her body convulsing around me as waves of pleasure crashed over her. The force of her orgasm triggered my own, and I buried myself as deep as I could, resting one forearm on the shower wall, the other arm securely around Nadine's lithe body.

We stayed like that for long moments, both of us breathing hard as the hot water continued to cascade over our bodies. I pressed gentle kisses to her shoulder, tasting the sweet droplets on her skin.

"You okay?" I murmured against her neck, my voice still rough from the intensity of our coupling.

She nodded, leaning back against my chest. "More than okay." Her voice was soft, satisfied. "That was exactly what I needed."

I carefully pulled out of her, turning her in my arms so I could see her face. The bruise on her cheek was darker now, but her eyes were bright with contentment and something deeper -- love, trust, complete surrender to this thing between us.

I turned off the water and snagged a towel I'd tossed over the top of the shower. I dried her, then myself, then tossed the towel to the shower floor before carrying her to our bed.

I laid her gently on the bed, propping pillows behind her. The bruise on her face looked worse in the bedroom light, and I couldn't stop myself from ghosting my fingers over it.

"I'm getting you some ice for that," I said, my tone brooking no argument this time.

She caught my wrist. "Five minutes. Just hold me for five minutes first."

I relented, settling beside her and pulling her against my chest. She fit perfectly, like she was made to be there. Her honey-colored hair was damp against my skin, and I breathed in the clean, fresh scent of her.

"You scared the shit out of me today," I murmured against the top of her head.

"I know." She traced patterns on my chest with her fingertip. "I'm not sorry I went for the birthing kit, but I am sorry I scared you."

"I know you're not sorry." I sighed. "And you shouldn't be. Besides, I didn't really mean it." When she raised an eyebrow, I sighed. "OK, I only partly meant it. I was being stubborn and stupid."

"And squeamish," she added with a hint of laughter in her voice.

"That's not goin' away anytime soon."

She shot me a mischievous smirk. "Nope."

I pulled her closer to me, settling her against my chest so I could catch the scent of her hair with every indrawn breath. "Rest, baby. One hour, then we'll go to the clinic and see what we need to do about the cuts and scrapes."

"Mmm..." Her breathing was already evening out and I had to grin. She lay against me, trusting me completely without hesitation. Her trust was not something I'd ever take for granted.

"I love you, sweet girl," I murmured against her hair. "I love you."

"Love you too." Her reply was slurred in sleep and she didn't move.

I watched her sleep for a while, the steady rise and fall of her chest beneath my hand. Each time I looked at her face, even with that ugly bruise, peace settled over me. She was here. She was safe. She was mine.

When her breathing deepened into true sleep, I carefully extracted myself from beneath her and went to the kitchen. I wrapped some ice in a thin towel and brought it back to the bedroom, gently placing it against her bruised cheek. She stirred slightly but didn't wake.

I settled back beside her, helping her to settle back onto my chest once more.

My phone buzzed on the nightstand. Knuckles.

"Yeah?" I answered quietly, not wanting to wake Nadine.

"Silk's been handled. Permanently. Thought you'd want to know."

I took a breath, closing my eyes and trying to feel bad about the fact we'd had to kill a woman. Even if I hadn't been present, it was still a death in defense of the club. And we were a solid unit. "Thanks, Knuckles. I know Silk betrayed more than just me and Nadine, but I still appreciate it."

"No thanks needed, brother. You've got a good woman. Keep her happy."

"Is there anything you need my help with?"

"We got it all taken care of for the moment. Though…" Knuckles trailed off thoughtfully.

"What do you need?"

"Well, it's not me. It's Tillie."

The hair stood up on the back of my neck and I got a sick feeling in the pit of my stomach. "What about Tillie?" I asked the question slowly. The words felt like they were dragged out of me because I knew without a doubt I did not want to know what he needed me for in regard to Tillie.

"Well, Xavier said she's decided she wants a home birth. She said she tried to get a midwife but she was so late in her pregnancy, none of them wanted to do a home birth. But Xavier says Tillie is freaking out about it. She said the classes she took suggested tomato-based foods to help start her labor or some shit. I kind of stopped listening after a while. But, what he wants to know is, would you be opposed to a spaghetti dinner the night before she's supposed to deliver?"

The second I comprehended what Knuckles had said, I gagged. Twice.

Nadine let loose with peals of laughter while Knuckles practically roared over the phone. I had no doubt the man was bent double with one forearm on his knee while he scrubbed the tears from his eyes.

"Spaghetti? Who the fuck told you? Was it Nadine? Someone's gettin' a beat down!" I hung up on Knuckles, knowing that was the wrong thing to do but doing it anyway. Now he was free to tell the whole of the compound sooner rather than later.

"Pain, it's hospital lore! It's grown every year in the community. I heard five different versions of your OB rotation while I volunteered. It was funny to get your version of it, and I can't decide if you downplayed it or if there really was spaghetti coming out your nose."

I gave her what I hoped was a steely look but was probably disgruntled, sullen. "Yes. There really was spaghetti coming out of my nose. But, by God, I handed that mother her baby. I think there might still be a picture floating around somewhere."

"Oh yes, there is." Nadine nodded eagerly. "I've got it on my phone if you want me to share it with you."

"All right, I give up! You win!" There was no way I could keep a straight face anymore. "That was the funniest moment in my medical career. We all made fun of me. Including myself."

"That's what I was told. It sounded like you got along with all your coworkers."

"I did." I sobered slightly, a smile still on my face at the fond memories. "I honestly never thought I'd ever come close to being as happy as I was during that time in my life." I kissed the top of her head. "But this moment right here? It trumps all of them. My brothers. My woman. Me. All of us sharing a laugh. You made this happen, Nadine. I'd have come home and been fine. But having you with me now is the very best thing to ever happen to me in my whole entire life."

"Wow." She cleared her throat. "That's, um, a *lot* of words."

"And she's still giving me shit."

"Tell me you don't love it and I'll stop. I'll take everything you say seriously and never laugh at you."

I snorted. "No, you won't."

"No," she said with a firm nod. "I really won't."

"Christ, we're gonna have so much fun together."

Nadine looked up at me, love shining bright in

her eyes as she smiled that beautiful smile of hers. "I'm absolutely counting on it, Pain. I'm absolutely counting on it."

Marteeka Karland

International bestselling author Marteeka Karland leads a double life as an action romance writer by evening and a semi-domesticated housewife by day. Known for her down-and-dirty MC romances, Marteeka takes pleasure in spinning tales of tenacious, protective heroes and spirited heroines. She staunchly advocates that every character deserves a blissful ending.

Marteeka finds joy in baking and gardening with her husband. Make sure to visit her website to stay updated with her most recent projects. Don't forget to register for her newsletter which will pepper you with a potpourri of Teeka's beloved recipes, book suggestions, autograph events, and a plethora of interesting tidbits.

Marteeka at Changeling: changelingpress.com/marteeka-karland-a-39

Want more? Meet Teeka's Dark Erotica side -- Wanda Violet O. changelingpress.com/wanda-violet-o-a-226

Bones MC Multiverse

Contemporary MC and Crossovers
- Bones MC
- Shadow Demons
- Salvation's Bane MC
- Black Reign MC
- Iron Tzars MC
- Grim Road MC
- Bones MC Legends
- Kiss of Death MC

Print and Audio
- Bones MC Audio
- Salvation's Bane MC Audio
- Iron Tzars MC Audio
- Bones MC Print Duets
- Grim Road MC Audio

Changeling Press, LLC

ChangelingPress.com